ACKNOV

Alligators are a much beloved tourist attraction in Florida, but they can also be a hazard. I appreciate the professional perspectives of Kimberly Lippman, SNAP Team Member, Florida Fish and Wildlife commission, and Lindsey Hord, Alligator specialist and biologist with Florida Fish and Wildlife Commission.

I must thank the Women of Mystery critique group: Lydia Ponczak, Helen Osterman, and Sherry Scarpaci, for the liberal use of their red pens both to correct my punctuation and to encourage me.

I also greatly appreciate my Beta Readers: Mary Baker, Bev Ferris, Valerie Witt, and Nancy Sorci..

Though *Gator Bait* is purely fictional, a few snippets may have been inspired by my wacky, serious, dedicated, fun-loving tennis friends. Thanks, ladies! Thanks, too, to our Legends tennis professional, Todd Wise, for NOT resembling in any way the tennis pro in *Gator Bait*.

Thanks goes out to Police Chief George Ferris, retired, Sergeant Adam Henkels, veteran of Chicago PD, and Bob Mekeland, electrician for their advice.

As always, I am grateful to my family and friends for their support.

NOTE:
If any mistakes of fact or procedure found in this novel, they are not the fault of the professionals with whom I consulted. I try to get it right, but errors could arise from my own misinterpretation of their excellent information.

A woman is like a tea bag.
You never know how strong she is
until she gets into hot water.

- Eleanor Roosevelt

GATOR
BAIT

1

She came to the slough to breathe—and to remember. This morning Gator Lake, the largest of the preserve's ponds, rippled in the breeze and lapped beneath the deck. Sunlight glared off the surface. Packi tugged her floppy hat lower and scanned the pond for Big Joe. The naturalists all agreed that Joe was old, as estimated by his fourteen-foot length. Younger alligators stayed out of his way.

On the far shore, where slash pines and cypress mirrored themselves on the water, Joe's favorite patch of sand was vacant. Packi pulled binoculars from her shoulder bag and trained them on a raft anchored in the center of the pond where visitors may glimpse Florida's most notorious residents. She spotted only turtles, the size of turkey platters, basking in the sun on the imitation island.

Patience, she reminded herself. Wildlife accepts a human's presence if one is slow and unobtrusive. *If I've learned nothing else in my sixty years, it's how to move through life inconspicuously, making no ripples, no fuss—like that bittern there.* In the reeds to the left of the deck, the camouflaged bird posed as still as a stick, staring upward. The sighting thrilled her. She zoomed her camera lens in on him and composed several photos before adding American Bittern to her notes.

Packi propped her elbows on the railing to steady the heavy binoculars and brought the far western shore into focus. White ibis and egrets stalked the shallows among reeds and fire-flag searching for frogs. No Joe.

She shaded her eyes from the sun's glare and skimmed the open water from north to south and then back. "Ah, there he is." She focused in on a dark object breaking the plane of water three hundred yards away. *Nope. That's a log.* She lowered the glasses and squinted at the bump in the water. Disturbed, she studied the object again.

Unnatural colors confused her. Half blue, half black. Her mouth went dry. "Oh, God, no." *Please let it be a log. Please.* The thing took shape—a human shape, face down and bobbing.

Packi slapped at her vest pockets in search of her phone and almost fumbled the gadget into the pond. *Dang it.* She jabbed at the screen. *911. What's wrong with this thing?* She skimmed back to the home page and started again. On her third try, she aimed at the numbers one by one and a dispatcher answered.

"What is your emergency?"

"I'm at Hammock Preserve."

Suddenly unsure, Packi hesitated and juggled the phone with the binoculars. She refocused the lenses and blinked several times before scanning the pond. The body still bobbed low in the water. She whispered her secret into the phone. "A man is in the pond—floating."

"A man is swimming in a pond?" the voice asked.

Packi bit back an angry response. "He's not swimming. He's…"

Her peripheral vision caught movement off to the right. Big Joe arrived on the scene. His ridged back glided fast along the opposite shore. The natural order of events flashed through her mind.

"No, Joe!"

The gator cruised through the water like a battleship to war. He had the man in his sights.

"Ma'am, what is the emergency?"

"Joe!"

Joe converged on the body. He opened his jaws.

"Ma'am?"

The alligator's teeth snapped shut and the crunch of bone echoed over the water. Joe submerged, dragging the body with him. The man's hands trailed behind, last to disappear into deep water.

2

The door slammed harder than Deputy Teig intended, but he loathed leaving the cool air of the cruiser just because some busybody old lady reported that a damn fool jumped in a pond. *Probably a college student on spring break, still drunk from last night.*

He stopped in the preserve's sandy parking lot to straighten his hat and assume a public-friendly face. Visitors in goofy hats and Hawaiian shirts milled around the entrance pavilion, desperate to entertain grandchildren with a volunteer-led tour of the slough. He marched past with a nod.

"God, I hate this humidity," he said under his breath. *And the old snowbirds that flock here and ruin our state, create traffic nightmares, and have heart attacks.*

What do those people come to the slough for anyway? Bunch of trees, couple of birds. You go into the swamp to hunt pigs, that's what. His stomach growled and he smacked his lips, thinking of last year's barbecue. He walked right into a spiderweb. "Damn it!" He waved his arms to destroy the web, pulled sticky strands from his chin, and spat to remove one from his lip. *Ugh.*

Teig regarded the jungle of cypress and shook his head at the dispatcher's incompetence. *Tanya should've said which pond.* He dreaded choosing the wrong direction and walking the entire two-mile loop. A posted map showed four ponds, so he chose the clockwise route toward the largest pond and trudged into the stinking swamp.

Within ten minutes, his shirt clung to his chest. Sweat stained the armpits. The slow flow of water beneath the boardwalk made his tongue seem drier and thicker. He regretted leaving his ice water in the cruiser.

As he stomped along, he became aware that fat quivered beneath the skin of his belly. *I gotta get in shape.* He remembered flat abs during his academy days. *What? Twelve years ago.* The wooden walkway shook beneath him, and he vowed to lose weight. *No excuses.*

Otter Pond and Duckweed Pond were deserted. He called out, but got no answer. Irritated, he plodded on, deeper into the swamp. He needed a breather, leaned against the railing, and bent to tighten a shoe lace. That was a mistake. He grunted and wheezed as he grasped a post to haul himself up and almost missed a faint sound.

A kitten? The memory of his mother bent over his injured cat flashed through his mind.

The mewling came from further along the boardwalk, but faded. Teig quickened his steps. He studied the brackish water and peered through tangled vines and cabbage palms until a woman appeared. Caucasian, five-two, fifty, thin. She had short blonde hair and wore pink beneath one of those stupid volunteer vests.

"Officer! Officer!" She waved, hopping and jumping as if he was a rock star. He raised his hand above his head in greeting.

"Thank goodness, you're here." She sounded shrill, on edge, not at all like a kitten. She pointed up a narrow boardwalk branching away from the main route. "He was over there, in the middle of the pond."

A hint of crow's feet at the corner of her eyes and a softness to her skin put her nearer to sixty than fifty. Probably a great looking woman in her time.

She grabbed his arm and tried to drag him toward the pier.

"Hold on there, ma'am." He patted the little lady's hand, still on his arm, and stood his ground. *She needs to calm herself.* "I'm Deputy Billy Teig. Tell me your name."

She closed her eyes and lowered her voice an octave. "Nice to meet you. I'm Patricia Walsh. Friends call me Packi."

"Okay, Mizz Walsh, what happened?"

"My phone fell into the water, and I couldn't tell the dispatcher." Her hands flitted like nervous sparrows.

"What's the emergency, Mizz Walsh?"

"I'm sorry." She took a long breath and blew air from her cheeks. "I saw a man in the water—through my binoculars." She held up the oversized lenses suspended from her neck. Her brows scrunched together.

"Swimming?"

She jerked her head a quick no. "Dead, I think."

Hot adrenaline rushed to the surface of his skin. "Show me where." He hurried in the direction she pointed.

On the viewing deck, the deputy shaded his eyes from the blinding sun and scanned the surface of the large pond. Nothing but the usual birds. "Where is he?"

She spread her arms open over the water in a helpless gesture. "He's gone."

"Mizz Walsh, if he was dead, how could he be gone? Are you sure it was a body?"

The woman's lip quivered. Trying not to cry, he suspected. She ran her hands through her hair, dislodging her hat.

"Big Joe took him," she whispered.

"You mean the gator?" Deputy Teig's hand went to his gun.

3

"No guns, young man." Irritated with herself for tearing up, Packi's voice sounded sharper than intended. *What an idiot, crying like that.* She wrapped her arms around her ribs to get a grip. *Big Joe needs a woman of action on his side, not an emotional twit.* "You can't shoot him, deputy. He's gone."

The officer holstered his weapon. "Sorry to scare you, Mizz Walsh. Where was the man? Can you describe anything about him?"

Packi took a deep breath and pointed to the last spot she'd seen the body. "In line with that osprey nest, about half way across the pond." Her hand trembled as she offered the binoculars to Deputy Teig. "He seemed big." She tried to recall. "Black pants and blue shirt, short sleeves—I think."

The officer scanned the water's surface, but soon returned the lenses to her. "There's nothing there, ma'am. Sure you didn't see a log or something?"

She snipped at him. "Do *you* see a log?" Patricia Marie Walsh had been raised to obey the police, but her nerves were frayed. "I told you, Big Joe took the body."

Deputy Teig clenched his jaw and removed a notepad from his pocket. "So why are you out here, Mizz Walsh?"

"I lead nature tours twice a week." Her fluttering hands rested for a moment on the brim of her hat as she pulled it down to shade her face. "Before the visitors arrive, I walk through the slough to spot new flowers or animal activity to point out on the tour. I'm quite observant."

The young man caught the tone in her voice and looked up from his notes. Condescension hid below the surface of his Southern courtesy. He looked down from behind dark, mirrored sunglasses. "You're certain an alligator attacked a man and pulled him under the water?"

"No."

"No?" He raised his eyebrows above the frames of his glasses. "You're not certain?"

"Yes, I am certain." Her words were crisp and firm, though his questions flustered her. "Big Joe attacked no one. The man was floating, already dead." She wanted to slap the smug courtesy off his face, but the notion of a Florida jail cell reined in her anger. "If you don't wait too long, you might recover the body."

Billy Teig pursed his lips and drew himself to full height. He was big. Six-three? Packi spotted her miniature self in a belligerent stance reflected in the deputy's sunglasses. He clicked his pen and seemed to consider his next action.

"Excuse me, Mizz Walsh." He stepped to the side and spoke into his radio. "Teig here. We have a possible fatality at Hammock Preserve. Request a hunt team and divers."

A hunt team? He didn't intend to kill Big Joe? He couldn't. Packi waved her hands at Deputy Teig, while he gave directions to the dispatcher.

"No." She tugged at his arm. "No. Don't send hunters." She'd seen enough reality TV to know about swamp hunters—giant hooks baited with chicken, nooses, rifles.

Teig turned his back to give his report.

Packi grasped the railing of the deck and watched the water for Big Joe. She wanted to warn the alligator, tell him to hide in his cave and let them recover the body. The ugly world had invaded her peaceful sanctuary at Hammock Preserve. *What can I do?*

"Mizz Walsh."

She flinched as if caught daydreaming in math class.

"Let's walk back to the exit," he said. "I'll take your statement on the way."

Irked by her anxiety, Packi tried to see the deputy as human beneath the arsenal of police paraphernalia. "Deputy Teig. Billy, is it?" Her friendly ruse sounded pathetic, even to her own ears, but she plunged ahead. "You don't have to shoot Big Joe. He didn't kill the man."

"We don't know that, Mizz Walsh." Teig said with more patience than she had given him credit for. "Did you *witness* the event?"

"No, I didn't, but Joe's shy. He wouldn't kill a human."

Billy Teig removed his wide-brimmed hat and mopped his forehead with a red bandana. "It's an alligator, a dangerous wild animal."

"I know, I know, but he wouldn't," Packi argued. "The man was already dead. Joe investigated the strange thing in his pond. That's all."

"If a gator gets to thinking humans are food, it's gotta be destroyed." The deputy returned the hat to his head and scowled at the distant shore. "We can't have gators scaring away the tourists."

Deputy Teig put his meaty hand under her elbow and guided her away from Joe's pond. As they walked the half-mile to the visitor's center, he asked questions. Packi answered by rote, worried over the impending hunt. The deputy's lack of concern for Joe's life disheartened her.

Of course, human life is worth more than an alligator's. I'm sad for the victim, for his family, but Big Joe didn't stalk the man, didn't kill him. She wished she hadn't seen the body and was angry with herself for her part in giving the hunters their target. She needed to stop the hunt and wracked her brains for a plan.

Packi noted Deputy Teig's single-mindedness—how he wrote and walked at the same time. He maneuvered through the zigs and zags of the boardwalk without banging his head on sabal palms that leaned low against the railings. The walkway narrowed, and the officer stepped back to herd her along from behind.

"You going back north for the summer, Mizz Walsh?"

"No, we bought full time seven years ago."

"So, you're married?"

Packi shot a glare at the impudent young man and then turned to focus on the ferns sprouting throughout the wetland to their right. "We've been married thirty-seven years." *I'll be darned if I tell him that Ron left me four years ago.* A well of swallowed tears threatened to gag her.

"Where do you live, Mizz Walsh?"

Packi didn't trust herself to speak. She stroked the smooth plastic body of the camera which hung from a strap around her neck. Ron had bought the professional Nikon, hoping she'd start a hobby. They'd been snowbirds, migrating between Illinois and Florida. Together, they'd waded through the warm waters of Sanibel and strolled among the beer parties and sunbathers on Fort Myers Beach.

A cluck of her tongue banished the memories. At least he'd left her well-off, financially anyway. She sighed. Sixty-three was too young to die. She approached that age now and wondered when she'd join him.

A pileated woodpecker drummed on a tree trunk nearby and brought her back into the present. Out of habit, she readied the camera, but remembered her mission, snapped the lens cap back into place, and marched on.

"So do you live in one of those golf course communities?" Deputy Teig continued to pry into what was left of her life.

"Why do you need information about *me*?" She threw the question over her shoulder, guessing that the interrogation made him feel official and important.

"Standard procedure, Mizz Walsh. The medical examiner may need to contact you."

His patient monotone irritated her. "You don't think I had a hand in that man's death, do you?"

He paused a moment too long. "We cover all bases."

Packi turned to confront Billy Teig and his hulking authority. "Or do you think I'm a crazy old bat with bad eyesight or one who invents stories for attention?"

He stopped short to avoid a collision with her and looked down through those dang mirrored sunglasses. "How *is* your eyesight, Mizz Walsh?"

"I saw a body, deputy." She shook the binoculars at him. "High-powered lenses."

"No need to get riled, ma'am. It's my duty to figure out what happened."

Packi clenched a bony, little fist at her side and glared up at Teig. "And it's my duty to stop you from killing an innocent creature."

* * *

A dozen folks lingered around the pavilion adjacent to the nature center's parking lot, waiting for Packi to begin the 9:30 guided tour. Her supervisor, Fran, stood among them, making small talk with a visitor. She frowned as Packi approached with the uniformed officer.

Deputy Teig's bulk parted the crowd with Packi in his wake. Fran intercepted them before he reached his squad car.

"What's going on?" Fran asked her.

Many ears listened for the answer. Packi turned her back to the retirees, grandchildren, and amateur bird-watchers to whisper, "There's a man at…"

"Police business," the deputy interrupted. "No need to advertise the incident. Are you in charge here?"

Fran halted in the face of the deputy's abrupt manner and toyed with the pins on her volunteer vest. "No," she stammered. "I mean, yes, I'm the head volunteer today."

Notebook in hand, Billy Teig took Fran aside. Packi turned to greet the visitors and diverted their attention by telling them about the

11

otters, the green heron, and the bittern, all the while keeping her eye on the officer.

Deputy Teig approached with a roll of yellow police tape in his hand. "Time to leave, folks. Gator Lake is closed until further notice."

"Ladies and gentlemen!" Fran forced a smile and used her teacher-voice to draw the group's attention away from the gruff deputy. "Please walk with me through the preserve's eastern section where we'll encounter lovely bromeliads in bloom and, if we're lucky, a ghost orchid." She waved her hand toward a secondary dirt trail that led behind the building. In an aside to Packi, she said, "He wants me to disperse them. What happened at Gator Lake?"

Packi glanced at the deputy at the entrance to the slough. His belt buckle hid beneath a stomach roll as he bent to stretch yellow tape across the boardwalk. "He thinks Big Joe killed a man," she whispered to Fran. "Lend me your phone."

Fran seemed torn between her obligation to the waiting people and her shock at hearing the news. She handed over her phone, blinked twice, and ushered the visitors away.

Fran's charges got as far as the information center when two squad cars sped into the parking lot, kicking up a whirlwind of dust. The nature-lovers rooted themselves at the side of the lot to watch the action; no doubt forgetting all about the ghost orchid.

While Deputy Teig conferred with the new arrivals, Packi found a shaded spot near the restrooms to call for help. *But who?* She regretted not having a go-to friend. She had made no real friends since they'd arrived in Florida years ago.

Packi tried to force a memory to the front of her brain. One of the tennis players had given her a business card at team practice. She recalled a tennis racquet logo. *The captain, Beth. What was her last name? Where was that card?* Packi rummaged in her fanny pack for Audubon's Field Guide to Florida. Beth Hogan's card marked the osprey page.

"Come on, answer your phone." Packi glanced at her watch. "Dang." She remembered that Beth had invited her to a lesson with the pro at ten o'clock. The call went straight to voice mail.

"If I don't answer, I'm out serving aces," said Beth's recording. "Leave a message."

"Sorry to bother you, Beth. It's Packi. From tennis?" She reminded herself to enunciate. "I'm at the slough and don't have anyone else to call." *Please pick up.* She glanced at the growing crowd of uniforms. "They plan to kill Big Joe. Call me."

Packi groaned. *I'll handle Deputy Teig and the alligator hunters myself.* She watched the blank screen for several seconds before sliding the phone into her pocket.

4

The hunt team, armed with nets, slings, and a rifle, dispersed and tromped along the boardwalk toward Gator Lake. A pickup truck, trailing a skiff, pulled into the parking lot. Its occupants, dressed in serviceable uniforms, conferred with Teig over a map and then drove back out to the main road.

Perhaps they plan to launch their boat into the lake from the opposite shore, Packi thought. She pictured them beating through the undergrowth where the water was nearest the road. Deputy Teig pointed his index finger at Packi, telling her to stay put. She refused to acknowledge the directive and watched him follow the hunt team into the slough.

Packi considered ducking under the police tape, but instead stood in the shade of the kiosk pretending to study the daily accounts of wildlife sightings. She worried about Big Joe and listened for the sound of gunfire. *How long do these things take?*

Fifteen minutes later, Beth's white Lexus convertible roared down the lane in front of the information center. Packi protected her eyes from the dust storm and waved. Beth angled her car across two parking spaces and cut the engine. Before the dust settled on the vehicle, she unfolded her long legs and hauled herself out of the bucket seat, leaving the door open for two other team members to crawl from the back.

Kay and Marilyn, dressed in visors and flippy tennis skirts, rummaged in their purses for singles to feed the parking meter. Beth strode across the lot with a plastic-wrapped plate like a carhop bearing a tray of root beer. Packi met her under the picnic pavilion. Beth flung her arm across Packi's shoulders and planted a sweaty kiss on her cheek.

"Got your message, girlfriend. What's going on?"

Uncomfortable with the familiarity and contact, Packi backed off. "Sorry to bother you. They're out there now, hunting Big Joe." She waved a hand toward Gator Lake and the yellow police tape. "I don't know what to do."

"Why would they do that?" Beth put the wrapped plate on the picnic table and sat, ready to listen to the story. The other women hurried to join them.

"Hi, Packi," Marilyn called before reaching the shade of the pavilion. "What happened?"

Kay's usual bright smile was absent from her nut-brown face. "Are you all right?"

"I think so," Packi said. "Thanks for coming." She welcomed their eagerness and their concern for Big Joe, but stood behind the table to avoid another round of hugs and kisses. She motioned for them to sit and told her teammates what she had seen at Gator Lake.

When she finished her story, she rested her forehead in her hands. "I expect to hear gunshots at any moment."

The teammates reached across the table to give their support, but cocked their ears toward the slough. Packi felt better, but realized they couldn't help Big Joe anymore than she could.

"The poor man," Marilyn said. Kay and Beth nodded as people do at funerals.

"I can't imagine why he went into the water," Kay said. "Everyone knows that pond is Joe's territory."

"Stupid," Beth said, "and not fair, if they destroy an alligator for being an alligator."

"More people should be here—to protest or something." Packi put the lame idea out there, but let it flutter away on the hot breeze.

Kay absently offered Packi a water bottle. "The kids from the charter school built that raft for Joe. They'll be upset."

Packi waved away Kay's water and pulled her own bottle from her fanny pack. She sighed over the futility of trying to save a man-eating alligator. "I'm sorry you drove out here for nothing. How was your practice with the pro?"

The ladies chatted about their lesson, and Packi half listened. Her thoughts wandered to Big Joe's situation and struggled to come up with a solution. She fixed a stare on the plate Beth had placed on the table.

"Chocolate chip cookies," Beth explained. "Emergency goodies." She lifted a corner of the plastic wrap. "I baked these to welcome a new couple to our building, but figured you needed them more."

"Wow." Packi hadn't realized her phone message sounded so desperate. "Thanks." The kindness touched her and gave her an idea. She put her hand over Beth's to stop the unwrapping. "A certain deputy appears to have a sweet tooth."

"What are you cooking up, girlfriend?" Beth's lean, tan face broke into a grin.

"Let's take half those cookies to share with the deputy and his team out at the pond," Packi said. "Perhaps we can stall them long enough to get protesters here."

"How does that help?" Marilyn asked.

"She's right," Kay said. "I'll call the school to tell them what's going on, then the kids…"

"Can what?" Beth frowned. "Watch them drag the gator's body away? We need somebody with clout."

"Yes," Packi said, remembering her husband as a precinct worker in Chicago where clout got things done. Hope brought color back to her cheeks. "Isn't Mary a lawyer? We could call her. Anybody have her number? Maybe there's something legal she can do."

"A last minute reprieve from the governor?" Beth and the others looked skeptical.

"Maybe. Who knows?" Packi said. "Kay and I will go out to the pond and beg the deputy to stall. Beth, you tell the folks up at the nature center what's going on. Marilyn, call that newspaper. Don't you write articles for the Fort Myers Gazette?"

"Well, yes." Marilyn fiddled with the button on her tennis shirt. "Just fundraising stuff for the homeless shelter and food pantry. I can try. For sure, the editor will be interested in the dead man."

"Good," Packi said. "Kay, call that science teacher at Bentley. What's her name?"

"Amanda Simpson." Kay pulled out her phone. "No doubt, she's in class. I'll text her." Her thumbs danced like a teenager's around her phone's keypad.

Her teammates' energy emboldened Packi, built her confidence. For months she had hovered on the edge of their team conversations listening, not yet belonging. Now all three women leaned forward, watching her with expectant eyes.

"Let's go," she said.

"Yes, ma'am." Beth headed up the ramp toward the nature center. "I'll round up everyone I can think of," she called.

Marilyn pulled her cell phone from her purse. "I'll wait here for the reporters. What should I tell the editor?"

"Everything we know," Packi said. "Say it's breaking news—an emergency." She had the sudden urge to get back to Gator Lake and started toward the trail.

Kay hopped from the picnic table and grabbed the plate of cookies. "I'm going with you, boss." She and Packi committed their first act of civil disobedience and ducked under the crime scene tape. As they hurried along the boardwalk, Kay muffled a laugh.

"For someone who never says a word, you sure got everyone fired up."

Embarrassed, Packi stumbled over her words. "I... You don't think... I mean, should we do this?"

"Sure, it'll be fun." Kay laughed louder. "I'm surprised, that's all. Didn't realize you were so feisty. Even when you attack the tennis net, you don't get excited."

"Was I too bossy?"

"Heck, no. Everyone loves a leader, someone to take charge. Give us girls a cause to champion, and we're all over it."

Packi stopped on the boardwalk before entering the stand of the slash pines. That *leader* title didn't sit well with her. *What would Ron think? What if all this fuss turned embarrassing? Wouldn't it be easier to let the police do whatever they do?*

Kay noticed the hesitation and shaded her eyes to look at Packi. "You're doing a good thing, partner. The newspapers—everyone—will worry about the poor dead man. No one thinks of what's right for the alligator—except you."

Kay's assertions boosted Packi's spirit. "We won't look like foolish old women?"

"Foolish maybe, old—never." Kay laughed and nudged her tennis partner forward with her elbow. "Besides, at our ages, we can do whatever we want." Her eyes lit up as if she'd had a lurid thought.

Packi smirked. "Like what—stay awake till midnight?"

"Or ignore police crime-scene tape," Kay said, grinning. "You planned to call Mary, remember?"

Packi had procrastinated, not forgotten. She held up Fran's phone to underscore her commitment to the campaign. "I'll call her right now."

Worry lines appeared around Kay's eyes. "You realize she's a real estate lawyer, right?"

"I know, but she's dating that judge."

Kay raised her eyebrows and laughed. "You go, girl."

* * *

Cabbage palms and ferns, which had dominated the slough, gave way to cypress and strangler fig. Ahead, the boardwalk angled toward strips of sunlight filtering through the understory. Packi motioned to Kay to quiet her footsteps as they approached the lake.

"There," Packi whispered and pointed through tree trunks to activity on the northern shore. "They're searching in the wrong spot."

Kay maneuvered herself to get a glimpse of the gator-hunters' boat. "How do you know?"

"I guess I don't," Packi admitted, "but every morning Joe's in that mass of reeds on the western shore. I think the entrance to his cave is in the bank. Later, he suns himself on that open area on the northern shore." She focused her binoculars on Joe's favorite spots and then offered the lenses to Kay. "I don't see him, but I'll bet he stashed the body at the bottom of the pond in those reeds."

"He saved the body?" Kay's mouth gaped open.

"Most likely. If it's too much to eat in one bite, he'd store it for later."

Kay cringed and returned the binoculars to her tennis partner without using them. "You going to tell the hunters? About the reeds, I mean?"

"Haven't decided." For the hundredth time, the image of the man's disappearing hands replayed in Packi's mind. "If they track down Big Joe, they'll kill him."

"But the man…"

Packi felt like a traitor to her species and struggled to separate the human tragedy from the campaign to rescue the alligator. "I have pity for the victim, but he's dead. Joe's alive." Packi set her jaw and hooked an arm through Kay's to drag her along. "Let's get to Deputy Teig, before another life is lost."

* * *

Like a bear hunched over the railing of the viewing deck, Billy Teig watched the recovery unit do their work. Sweat printed an hourglass stain on the back of his shirt. Packi dreaded his sour, puffed-up face and worried she'd startle him. She summonsed her courage before stepping onto the pier. "Deputy Teig!" she called from fifteen feet back.

"What the hell?" The bear spun around and glared at the women.

"Hello." Packi greeted him with a smile and marched forward. Kay followed with the plate of cookies, but one step behind in her partner's shadow.

"You ladies ain't supposed to be here," the deputy growled. "Mizz Walsh, don't you understand what yellow tape means?"

"Oh, that." Packi waved away the issue. "We had no trouble getting under it. We're very spry, you know." She pulled Kay from behind her. "This is my tennis partner, Kay Chandler."

The deputy touched the brim of his hat. "Pleased to meet you, Mizz Chandler. Now, go home. This is a crime scene."

"Oh, Billy." Packi smiled at his nonsense. "You forget that I discovered the body and called you. I just wanted to remind you to tell those divers not to kill Big Joe. He's a popular attraction here at the slough."

"I didn't forget nothin', Mizz Walsh." He glanced out at the skiff as a diver surfaced, empty-handed. "We're following procedure. Go back to the nature center."

"I noticed you didn't have water. You must be parched in this hot sun." Packi offered her own water to the angry deputy. "We also have chocolate chip cookies for you." She nudged Kay to produce the wrapped plate.

Packi risked a step forward and offered the cookies as if baiting a shark. The deputy's sunglasses mirrored the plate of chocolate chips. He ran his tongue along his dry lips, but waved away the treats.

"My friend, Beth, baked these this morning." Packi lifted the edge of the plastic to release the aroma of warm chocolate.

Deputy Teig exhaled, his nostrils flared, and Packi put three warm cookies in his hand. "You'll stop them from killing Big Joe, won't you?"

"Ain't nothin' I can do, Mizz Walsh." The first cookie disappeared in one bite. "After the divers recover the victim, they'll..." He caught crumbs in his hand and popped them into his mouth. "They'll remove the gator."

Packi winced and prayed Joe hid deep in his cave or, with all the commotion, migrated to another pond.

"Thank you, Billy, for your help. We'll just leave these here. You can share with your friends." Packi put the water bottle and cookie plate on the wooden bench and backed away. "We'll be at the nature center waiting for news."

"I'm not in charge of the hunt." He jerked his chin toward several men searching the shore. "I can't help that gator."

"But you'll try."

The big man blew air from his lips and reached for another cookie.

* * *

Once they were out of the sunshine and into the shadow of pines and cypress, Kay grabbed Packi's arm and pulled her to a stop. "You were fabulous. You had him eating out of your hand."

"Literally." Packi shrugged rather than admit her trepidation. Her heartbeat had not yet returned to normal. "Let's keep moving. We gotta get back to the parking lot to organize the protest."

Kay hurried to catch up. "That cop scared me to death."

"Don't be ridiculous. Deputy Teig can't hurt you," Packi said to reassure herself as much as Kay. "He thinks we're sweet, elderly women." She grinned at her tennis partner, thinking of the two of them on the court, charging the net and chasing lobs. "I suspect he's afraid of *us*. Perhaps we remind him of his grandmother or a great-aunt."

"For God's sake, woman. We're not that old."

"But if Lee County's finest *think* we're doddering do-gooders, they'll tolerate our meddling."

"He said he couldn't help," Kay said. Her frown wrinkled her forehead, aging her.

"He gave us important information." Packi held up three fingers. "Joe is still alive. They haven't found the body yet, and…"

Kay pulled her sunglasses below her eyes, waiting for the third point. "And?"

"And our new friend, Billy Teig, can be bribed with baked goods."

5

The noise of a crowd reached Packi and Kay when they were still among the cypress. They quickened their steps, but came to an abrupt halt at the edge of the parking lot.

"What's happening?" Kay asked.

Packi marveled at the carnival scene that had taken over the quiet sanctuary. "The tennis team came through for us," she said.

Excited children milled outside their school bus while a woman, not more than a head taller than the kids, tried to keep the gaggle together. A van, emblazoned with the WFMK logo, sprouted antennas and satellite equipment. A reporter with a microphone in hand directed a cameraman toward the slough. Light bars atop police cruisers threw out red and blue pulsating beams and gave the chaos a disco theme.

"Grace and Diane are here." Kay waved to the women over the heads of the crowd. She and Packi waded through groups of unfamiliar people to reach the pavilion where the tennis team congregated.

"Thank God, you're here," Beth said. "These volunteers want to know what to do."

The women waited for Packi's response. Her mind went blank as she stared at the crowd and her teammates' expectant faces. "I don't know... protest for Big Joe?" She chewed her lower lip and struggled to put together a plan. Memories of her college days in Chicago brought bittersweet images. *What do protesters do? March. Chant. Get arrested.*

"We need signs," Packi said as her adrenaline kicked in.

"Amanda's ahead of you," said Marilyn. "She has a stack of poster board on that picnic table."

"Who? Oh, the teacher," said Packi. "Good. Good. Fran, can you give them space in the visitor center to create their signs?" Fran agreed, but looked displeased her junior volunteer had taken control and gave out orders.

"Marilyn, ask Amanda to get the kids going so we can get them on TV right away."

Marilyn nodded and disappeared into the crowd. Packi's mind clicked on idea after idea. "Grace. Diane. Can you create some sort of flyer? Beth, how about a line of volunteers at the entrance?"

"Yeah, yeah." Beth bobbed her head. "We'll wave signs at drivers on the main road."

"Did anyone talk to the news media?"

"I did," said Beth. "They want the story on the dead guy. You should tell them what you saw, Packi. That's the reporter over there."

Packi shrank at the prospect of an interview. "I don't want to be on TV. I'd make a fool of myself." She eyed the reporter who stood before an intrusive camera with a club-shaped microphone in his hand. His suit, tie, and gelled hair were out of place in the slough, but he looked young, eager, and professional.

"Go talk to him." Beth nudged Packi. "I told him what I know. He wants to talk to a real witness. He'd be a good ally."

"But I..."

"Come on. I'll go with you." Kay tugged Packi toward the reporter. "You said you wanted to get the word out about Big Joe. Here's your chance."

Packi and Kay made their way through a cluster of people around the television van. The crowd watched the reporter try to get information from the uniformed deputies standing at their cruisers, their arms akimbo. The women waited on the fringe of the confusion for the reporter to end his broadcast.

"This is Kevin Mitchell reporting live from Hammock Preserve." He signaled 'cut' and lowered the microphone. Kevin's shoulders slumped as he glanced across to the slough's entrance. Frustration showed on his fresh, not-yet-ready-for-prime-time face.

Kay pushed Packi forward, but held back herself. Packi intercepted the reporter as he turned toward the WFMK van.

"Excuse me. Please don't leave yet. I'm Patricia Walsh. I'm a volunteer tour guide here at the slough." She ran her sentences together, trying to get his attention, trying to get her thoughts across. "You'd have a good story if you focused on Big Joe, the alligator. Visitors love to see him, and he's a pet project for the kids from Bentley School."

The young reporter indulged her prattling, but his eyes remained dull. *This isn't working,* Packi thought. *He doesn't care.*

"I saw the body," she said before he could turn away.

"Really?" Kevin Mitchell's face lit up as if his lottery number matched. He switched on the microphone and signaled to the camera operator. "Tell our viewers what you saw."

Packi put her hand over the microphone under her chin. "Before I tell you, I want your promise to show Big Joe in a positive light."

"I can't editorialize," Kevin insisted. "I just report facts."

Packi looked askance at the young man. "Any good reporter can spin *facts* pro or con."

A slight frown appeared on the reporter's TV-perfect features. He tugged the mic away from Packi's hand. "So Ms. Walsh, you saw a body in the slough..."

Packi stepped back, crossed her arms, and pursed her lips. Kevin rolled his eyes and put the microphone at his side. "Okay, Ms. Walsh. Tell me about the alligator."

Because she had relayed the facts so many times during her nature tours, Big Joe's story flowed from her mouth. She ended with the children—how the Bentley School kids built the raft years ago and how each new crop of science students studied the alligator as part of the natural world.

"A class from Bentley is protesting today to save Big Joe's life."

As if on cue, several of the children in playground mode marched down the ramp from the visitor center with poster boards held above their heads. Kevin signaled the camera to pan in that direction. "Sean, get a shot of those kids."

"You should interview Amanda Simpson over there," Packi said. "She's the teacher."

"Okay, Ms. Walsh, I promise I'll do a story from the angle of the kids," Kevin said, "but now tell me about the body. I don't want an outside reporter getting the big story before me."

With the camera in her face, Packi dutifully described the floating body and answered Kevin's questions. She tacked on a plea for Big Joe to be saved from the hunters, but suspected it would be cut from the six o'clock news.

"Thank you, Ms. Walsh." Kevin flashed his bleached smile and handed her a business card. "If you hear any more, please give me a call."

"You promise that Big Joe's story gets on the air?" She looked him in the eye, raised her brows, and waited.

"I'll do what I can," Kevin said, "but the producer has the last word."

"Joe's story must be on the air today," Packi insisted. "Don't forget to interview the teacher. Folks love the story of the kids saving their pennies to build the alligator raft."

"Yes, Ms. Walsh." Kevin gathered his notes and approached Amanda Simpson with the photographer in tow.

Packi hated to manipulate the young man's obvious ambition to succeed as a journalist, but he was her only link to a larger audience. She planned to feed him information in tidbits to keep him on the line. Anything to protect the innocent alligator. She cringed at the possibility of Big Joe fighting for life on the end of a hunter's line with a baited hook stuck in his gullet.

Kay grabbed Packi's arm. "You did great. That interview will be seen by a hundred thousand viewers."

Packi blanched at the notion and allowed herself to lean on Kay for support.

6

Back at the pavilion, the tennis team had everyone well organized. Marilyn had whipped up a flyer at the volunteer office and handed copies to newly arrived visitors. Beth directed a line of adults with borrowed poster board and markers out to the road at the entrance gate. Grace got video of the students parading with signs that read, *Save our Gator* and *I Luv Big Joe.* Her eager, Irish face peeked from behind the cell phone camera long enough to yell to Packi. "This is going on You Tube!"

The team's enthusiasm and quick work amazed Packi, but the commotion agitated her. Afraid to be caught up in the hoopla and forget her most important mission, she turned toward the still peaceful slough. She intended to check on Big Joe in spite of Deputy Teig's warnings.

A deputy stood guard at slough entrance with the yellow tape flapping in the hot breeze against his legs. Stone-faced, he watched the antics of the children and the general melee in the parking lot.

While the deputy focused on the crowd, Packi slipped behind the restrooms to a seldom used path. She knew the shortcut intersected with the boardwalk a hundred yards behind the guard. The path left the shadow of the building and Packi's regret crept in. The shortcut had been obliterated during the rainy season. Still, she pushed forward, aimed in the general direction of the boardwalk.

Wet leaves rasped against her bare knees and calves. Her cotton shirt sagged with perspiration, and muck sucked at her shoes. Her skin crawled. She envisioned black racer and cottonmouth snakes lurking in the mud. *What am I doing here?*

Packi bit at her chapped lips and glanced back the way she'd come—toward dry land. The pickerel reeds and fire-flag had closed in behind her, hiding the path. *I gotta get out of here.* Growing panic urged her to flee. Indecision rooted her in place where her feet sank into the mud.

You're a nature guide, for God's sake. Calm yourself. Think of saving Big Joe.

That was the wrong image to plant in her mind. Worse than a dumb tourist, she had walked into the domain of the largest alligator in the county. Her eyes swept the area for gator trails. Finding none, she exhaled the breath trapped in her lungs.

Packi suppressed her paranoia and convinced herself that the boardwalk was only a few yards further. Her shoes made a sucking sound as she pulled each from the mud and moved on. She grabbed a stick and beat the thick foliage ahead of her to scare away the snakes and to pretend she had some control.

Movement within the vegetation ahead stopped her breath. She froze in place. *Big Joe's my friend.* Packi grasped at crazy hope. *Idiot. He's an alligator. Run!*

Which way? Gators run thirty miles an hour. She stood stick-still, camouflaged like the bittern she'd spotted that morning, but remembered the sound of bone cracking in Big Joe's jaws. She prayed.

Packi stared at the slits of open space between the ferns and fire-flag, searching for the horizontal pattern of grey, reptilian ridges. An anomaly, a disruption to the vertical vegetation. She focused low, at mud-level, where a crocodilian, arched high on its stumpy legs, would stomp from pond to pond.

Packi flinched at the sound of sucking mud nearby. Flashes of white and orange. Her terror-struck mind took a moment to register the information.

She gasped in relief. Ibis. Four birds moved into view, poking their long, curved beaks into the damp earth, focused only on insects. The birds spotted her and squawked, flapping up. They settled again, twenty feet away, to resume feeding.

Get a grip! Packi reprimanded herself for a runaway imagination, then calculated the odds of Big Joe roaming nearby—conveniently ignoring the possibility of smaller gators. *His stomach is full. I'm okay.* Packi shivered as if she'd just made a bargain with the gator: *You've got the dead man, you don't need me.* She slogged forward.

A long three minutes later, the boardwalk came into view. Packi pushed toward the elevated walkway and clambered up. She crouched low and peeked in both directions. No police uniform was in view, so she climbed through the railings.

Weak with relief, Packi sat and welcomed the heat of the wooden planks under her butt. She appreciated the solid design, the connection to civilization. *Some naturalist I am.* She clucked her tongue, disappointed in herself. *Why was I so nervous?* She scraped her shoes against a plank and clapped them together. The caked mud fell back into the slough where it belonged.

As she and Kay had done earlier, Packi tiptoed toward Gator Lake and stopped at a break in the trees to spy on the sheriff's men. The dive team's boat floated in a cove on the western shore. Wading birds had abandoned that feeding ground, but stalked their dinners a hundred yards away. An ambulance inched into the bushes. Its emergency lights threw strange colors into the trees and across the water. They must have found the body, she thought in sorrow. The hunt will begin.

Packi's binoculars shook. She propped her elbows on the railing, steadied herself, and focused on a pair of EMTs. They stood near their vehicle in relaxed stances, their hands in their pockets. A diver bobbed to the surface, clung to the side of the skiff, and gave an empty-handed signal.

Thank goodness. I still have time.

From her hidden vantage point, Packi watched the low-profile boat putter fifty yards to the north and another diver jump into the water. Their methodical progress had gotten them six hundred feet. Packi checked her watch. At the rate they were going, the recovery team would reach the alligator's favorite spot in another hour.

Stay out of their way, Big Joe.

Packi's many hours of tracking the alligator's habits came in handy. She spotted his eyes peeking above the waterline off to her left, well away from his cave and far from the divers. They wouldn't find Joe soon—unless he cruised over to investigate them. *No, he's too shy for that.*

Shy, yes, but she pictured Big Joe eating parts of the body. *A hand? A foot?* A pang of guilt hit her. *Should I direct the divers to the cave, let them locate the victim?*

She argued with herself. *Joe wouldn't be safe. We need time to rally his supporters. Besides, I could be wrong about Joe stashing the body near his cave entrance.* Packi released herself from her obligation to the dead man, but the memory of his hands trailing behind and disappearing into the water stuck in her mind. She shoved the image out of her head and snuck away from Gator Lake.

An unfamiliar ring tone sounded from Packi's pocket. She cringed, muffled the noise, and grabbed Fran's phone before the second ring. "Hello?"

Mary wasted no time with conventional greetings. "Got what you need. I'll be there in five minutes." She hung up without good-bye.

Packi gave herself a silent atta-girl, thrilled with her teammate's news and enthusiasm. She pinned her hopes for Joe's reprieve on whatever legal help Mary had secured. Packi trotted the remaining distance to the exit and slipped behind the restroom to return to the parking lot.

Before Packi could join Kay and Marilyn under the pavilion, Kevin Mitchell threaded through the maze of parked cars and caught her. His shadow followed carrying twenty pounds of electronics.

"What did you discover, Ms. Walsh?" the reporter asked.

"Nothing."

"You've been to the pond." Kevin pointed his microphone at her muddied shoes and arched an eyebrow at her. "How did you get past the guard?" He glanced toward the boardwalk as if scheming to sneak to Gator Lake himself. "Did they locate the victim? Has the gator hunt started?"

Packi's neck muscles tightened. She felt bullied under the scrutiny of the young man and his intimidating camera and microphone. She forced a pleasant smile and lifted the toe of her mud-stained shoe. "You caught me, Kevin."

"Did they find the body?"

"Not that I saw." Packi reminded herself that the reporter needed a story, and Big Joe needed the publicity. "Well—I saw an ambulance team amongst the trees on the other side of the pond." She pointed to the northwest, back to the road. "They may take the victim out there."

"Come on, Sean." Kevin whirled around without saying good-bye and trotted toward the WFMK van with the cameraman close behind. Packi sighed in relief and protected her eyes from the dust thrown up by the departing van.

Under the shaded pavilion, Kay squinted into the sunlight as Packi approached. "Where'd you disappear to?" She slid her cell phone into her pocket. "The TV crew was looking for you."

"They found me."

Packi's stomach growled. She surveyed the picnic table, hoping for a late-morning snack. *Should've grabbed one of those cookies.* She spotted bits of chocolate brownie on a grease-stained paper plate, but suppressed the urge to pick at the crumbs. "Who brought brownies?"

Grace waved her fingers from across the table. "Baked them for the grandchildren's visit tomorrow. I'll whip up another batch tonight."

"They went fast," Marilyn said. She licked chocolate from her fingers, and then pointed to Packi's muddy shoes.

Packi shrugged. "I took a shortcut to the pond. What's going on here?"

Before the women could answer, a royal blue SUV wheeled into the parking lot, bounced over the speed bump, and jerked to a stop at the pavilion. Mary jumped from the car and slammed the door. "I'm here!" She waved papers over her head.

"Yea!" The tennis team's friendly sarcasm added to Mary's exuberance.

"What'd you get?" Packi asked. "What do we have to do?"

"Here you go." Mary pinned sheets of paper to the picnic table with her finger to prevent the hot Florida wind from stealing them. "You're suing Lee County," Mary announced with a flourish. "This is a temporary restraining order to stop action against the alligator known as Big Joe."

The force of the law, the weight of her pending action, made Packi step back. She hesitated while the other women looked at the real estate lawyer in amazement.

Mary's red lipstick widened. The grin wiped years off her face as she swept her long black hair over her shoulder. "I know. I know. I'm brilliant!"

Her teammates patted Mary on the back and bumped knuckles with each other. Packi steadied her nerves with deep breath and smoothed the creases from the stiff document.

"This freezes everything," Mary said. "You have three days to present facts to Judge White." The lawyer pointed a red acrylic fingernail at a signature at the bottom of the paper. "Then this order expires."

Packi's hand trembled as she propped her glasses on the bridge of her nose and tried to translate the legalese. Big Joe's salvation was there in clear, black ink on fine, linen stationery. With renewed confidence, she grabbed both copies from the picnic table and waved them toward the slough. "Should I..."

"Yeah, show it to whoever's in charge."

"Great job, Mary," Packi called as she jogged across the parking lot, dodging cars, nature lovers, and school children.

The police officer at the boardwalk entrance stiffened his posture when he spotted Packi racing toward the yellow police tape. "Whoa, miss. You can't go in there."

"I have to get this restraining order to Deputy Teig." Packi held the legal documents up to his eye level. Her finger tapped on Judge White's signature.

The deputy pulled the papers from Packi's hand. She hadn't intended to relinquish Joe's stay of execution and almost snatched them back. Instead, she bit back a complaint and forced herself to stand still. *Oh, please don't read the whole thing.*

The man's earnest expression turned to confusion as he attempted to decipher the wordy paragraphs. He flipped to the second copy. "Looks legitimate," he said. "Deputy Teig needs to see this."

"That's right," Packi said, plucking the documents out of the young man's hand. "Let's go." She ducked under the plastic police tape.

"Hey." The officer stepped in her path, doing his best to loom large. "You can't go back there."

She confronted his posturing with her own and pointed to the patches and awards sewn to her volunteer vest. "I work here," she said, fixing him with a confident look.

The young man grimaced as if trying to reach a decision.

Unable to stop her restless feet, Packi tapped her foot and listened for the sound of gunshots. She didn't trust the silence. "They could have already started the hunt."

The deputy motioned over the heads in the crowd to a skinny kid in a plain blue uniform. "I'll get a cadet to escort you."

"Good," she said. "He can catch up."

Packi ignored the deputy's exasperation and ran. Her footfalls surely startled every poor creature in the slough. She took the zigs and zags at a speed she never would have imagined for herself, grabbing onto posts and whipping her body around the angles. A gazelle, she thought.

Visualizing a fleet-footed antelope didn't improve her breathing. Her lungs ached from pulling in the heavy humid air, and her heart pounded in her ears. *Who am I kidding?* The gazelle image morphed into a pack mule and slowed her to a walk. She worked at controlling her pulse rate until she reached an opening in the trees with a partial view of the lake.

The plane of water reflected the blue sky, doubling the few clouds and the trees ringing the pond. She spotted the recovery team peering into the depths from their skiff. No body yet. The ambulance and the EMTs stood waiting. Big Joe wasn't in sight. She sent a thank you skyward and hurried along.

Deputy Teig must have heard her coming—her footsteps or her gasping breath. As she approached the pier, he turned away from the pond. His scowl confronted her as if he intended to scare her straight. She faltered, but lifted her chin.

"Oh, there you are, Billy!" Packi raised her hand in a friendly greeting and waved the papers toward him. "I have news."

His scowl deepened, but he nodded a curt welcome and took the documents. "Will you tell me what this means, or do I have to read all this?"

She laughed. "I don't understand that legal mumbo-jumbo either, but it means you can send the alligator hunters home."

His fist crumpled the bottom half of the crisp stationery. "You're interfering, Mizz Walsh."

The deputy's temper disconcerted her. His glare shifted from her to the boardwalk behind her.

The young cadet appeared at the entrance to the viewing deck, flustered and out of breath. "Sorry, sir." His sweat-stained uniform sleeves flapped around his broomstick arms. "I went to the wrong pond," he said and shot a look of reproach at Packi. "She wouldn't wait…"

"Forget it, Ryan," Deputy Teig said. "Mizz Walsh and I have met."

A flash of camaraderie passed between the deputy and the cadet. The boy stood up straighter, his shoulders relaxed. "Should I get back to the entrance?" he asked. "It's way crazy with the protesters."

"Protesters?" Teig jerked his head back toward Packi.

She shrugged in innocence and ignored clues to his anger: red face, creased brow, a deep rumble in his throat.

The deputy adopted his citizen-friendly demeanor and addressed the young recruit. "Sure, Ryan, do that."

The cadet trotted off, and Packi offered a smile, while Deputy Teig examined the judge's order. "I'm only trying to protect Big Joe's life," she said. "He didn't kill that man."

He grumbled under his breath and pressed the button on his radio. "Teig here." He turned his back on Packi. "We got a TRO. No gator hunt."

On the far shore, a uniformed figure straightened up and stared across the pond at the deputy and Packi. Teig raised the papers above his head. The man's disbelief came in static bursts over the radio. Billy Teig's head bobbed as he listened.

Packi backed away from the discussion. From a corner of the pier, she watched the recovery boat floating to the northwest. A diver broke the surface of the water and signaled that he had found nothing. At this rate, she thought, they won't retrieve the body for hours.

"Excuse me, Billy." Packi tugged at the deputy's sleeve, while he read a line of the judge's restraining order into the radio. He turned further from her.

"Billy, listen." She maneuvered herself into his sight.

His mirrored sunglasses caught the sunlight and nearly blinded her. "Ten-four." The deputy turned on Packi with his arms across his chest. His leather belt and holster creaked with the movement. "What now, Mizz Walsh? Your alligator is safe."

Packi ducked her head in acknowledgement. "Thank you. I should tell you." She hesitated, but pointed a thin finger toward the western shore. "They should search there."

He loomed over her and didn't follow her point. "Now why is that, ma'am?"

"I want to help, Billy." She ventured a smile, but then thought better of it. "I'm a volunteer here, you know. I've monitored Big Joe's movements for years." Her words came out too fast. "Every morning he emerges from the reeds over there, just to the right of the three cabbage palms. Last February, when the water was low, I saw his cave entrance in that bank."

Deputy Teig didn't move, except to set his mouth in a grim line. Packi's conscience questioned her motive for omitting that information about Joe's hiding spot. She swallowed the guilt and the little saliva she had left, and continued. "Alligators sometimes store their food."

"I know gators, Mizz Walsh." His gruff voice lacked his Southern courtesy. "Why didn't you say so earlier?"

"Because you'd kill..."

He shushed her by turning his back. Packi clamped her mouth shut and stepped away from the big man while he spoke into the police radio. "Teig here."

"Go ahead."

"This lady with me is a naturalist for the slough. Says the gator has a cave five hundred yards south of you. Good place to stash the body."

Across the lake several men looked in their direction and then to the south. The man on shore raised his arm in acknowledgement before signaling the divers toward the cluster of reeds.

Deputy Teig kept his sweat-stained back to her.

If he orders me away, Packi thought, I'm not leaving—not until the hunters are gone. Would they shoot if Big Joe defended his food stash? She pictured the gator thrashing and snapping his jaws. I'll stay as a witness, keep Joe safe. She formed her argument and bulked up her courage, but the deputy maintained a wall of silence.

Packi crept nearer the railing to monitor the hunters through her binoculars. Two of the men gathered equipment: grappling hook, rifle, bait bucket, heavy-duty fishing rod—and disappeared into the trees. *Were they leaving or repositioning?* She scrutinized the opposite shore for several minutes, alert for movement near Joe's cave. Nothing.

Satisfied the hunters had gone, Packi lowered the lenses. She stretched to loosen her spine and noticed the sun glinted off the cookie plate on the bench. She hid a grin. Either Billy had swept the crumbs into the pond, or he licked the plate clean.

"I'll bake more cookies, oatmeal raisin this time. They'll cheer you up."

The deputy glanced at her over the official insignia on his shoulder. "I don't need damn cookies."

Billy licked his lips to find a stray crumb, but then shook his head in disgust, or frustration. She couldn't tell with those dang sunglasses and forgave his rudeness.

The sun beat down. Packi and Teig stood a shoulder's width apart, her a miniature of him: feet planted on the deck, rigid back, arms crossed over the chest, a stern face keeping watch over the pond.

"Thanks for the cookies."

"You're welcome."

Neither of them moved. She listened to him breathing through his nose. Mud hens squawked off to their right.

"That paper keeps your gator alive only another three days," he said.

"I know."

The deputy removed his mirrored glasses, startling Packi with the blueness of his eyes. He peered at her over sunburned cheeks. "They'll want him dead."

"We'll stop them."

7

Ten minutes later a diver broke the surface of the water, waving his arm. The skiff made a quick maneuver to nose into the reeds just about where Packi had guessed Joe dug out his cave. Another diver plunged in. The EMTs on shore grabbed the gurney and muscled their way through the underbrush. The divers surfaced with something blue between them.

Packi turned away. "I don't want to see this."

"Who the hell..."

Packi looked back to see Deputy Teig staring at the ambulance parked in the scrub across the pond. She squinted to see two figures picking their way toward the recovery scene. One of them wore a suit. The other struggled behind, toting equipment on his shoulder.

"Oh, that's Kevin Mitchell, the news reporter."

"We've lost all control," Teig moaned. "How did they...?" He finished his question with a growl.

"I might have told them about the EMTs."

The big man spun toward her, his mouth tight and unhappy. A tic had developed along the deputy's fleshy jaw.

"Kevin promised to do a story on Big Joe," Packi explained, "to help us build public support."

"Leave, Mizz Walsh." The deputy gripped the railing. "Now. Before I forget I'm a gentleman."

"Yes, Billy." She backed toward the boardwalk. "Thank you for help…"

Deputy Teig's leather holster creaked against his utility belt as he moved toward her. Packi watched herself in his mirrored sunglasses, disconcerted by her fragile reflection. A growl from deep within his uniformed chest chased her away from Gator Lake.

* * *

On her way back and out of Deputy Teig's hearing, Packi stopped at a shaded gazebo to phone Beth. She never did master the art of dialing while walking. "Hi, Beth. It's Packi Walsh."

"Hey, Packi! Our gator-awareness campaign is getting attention."

She held the phone four inches away to protect her eardrums. Her team captain's voice jarred the quiet of the slough and sent yellow finches into higher branches.

"Did the legal stuff work?" Beth asked. "Did they recover the body?"

"Yes to both." Packi's tone better suited the natural environment. "I thought you should put away the signs."

"Why? Cars honked. Drivers stopped to ask about the gator."

"Well, that's good news." Packi pictured her team captain out on the roadside either rallying drivers to Big Joe's cause, or ticking them off. "But the ambulance will drive by you in a while. We should show respect."

"Yeah, yeah, of course." Beth's lightheartedness faded. "Hey, Packi, you know you're doing a great job here. You're a natural-born organizer, a leader."

Packi lowered the phone, unsure of the appropriate response. *You hear that, Ron? Me, a leader.* Her husband had been the organizer, the one in control. She sensed his approval. "Thank you, Beth." Contentment warmed Packi from within, even though the team captain handed out compliments like politicians hand out campaign literature. The praise raised her spirits and took away the sting of Deputy Teig's reprimand.

* * *

Beth stood on a picnic table and put her fingers in her mouth. Her shrill whistle got the attention of Big Joe's fans. "Listen up! We have an announcement." She motioned for Packi to mount the table, but Packi declined.

"They'll never hear me. Go ahead. Thank them for helping."

Beth's voice carried across the lot and into the slough. "Good news! The alligator you came to protect is alive and well."

Amanda Simpson's class heard and repeated the announcement with exuberance. Volunteers murmured in satisfaction and a wave of applause spread. People pressed forward to hear.

"Tell them we need to keep going," Packi said as Beth bent to listen. "The judge gave us only three days."

Beth straightened up and raised her arms. "Packi Walsh, here, started this campaign to protect Big Joe. She asks that you stay involved. The hunters will be back again in three days."

Protest and confusion rolled through the crowd. The children's faces paled. Packi needed to comfort them and climbed onto the table. Beth gave her a hand up and signaled for quiet.

"Thank you, everyone, for caring about Big Joe!" Packi's voice reached only the nearest listeners. Others strained to hear. She pushed more volume from her lungs. "We have three days to convince them to leave Big Joe alone," she yelled. "We'll save him because he's innocent! Tell your neighbors. Post it on Facebook. Call the mayor."

The listeners turned to each other to share their anger and their plans. The buzz overwhelmed Packi's words, so she waved flyers above her head while her teammates waded into the crowd to distribute the information. She lowered herself into a seated position and slid off the table and out of the limelight.

By late morning, the excitement subsided as people left the slough to spread the news of Big Joe's temporary reprieve. The children boarded the idling bus and posted their signs inside the windows. Older folks wandered toward the air-conditioned visitor center. The deputies switched off the red and blue strobe lights, and Billy Teig left without even a wave to Packi.

The tennis team begged off, too, claiming errands to do: a hair appointment, mahjong, tae-bo class. "You did good," Beth said. She squeezed Packi's shoulder and climbed into her convertible. "Go home and get some rest. You seem frazzled."

"Thanks, but I'll stick around, do some thinking."

"I'll stay, too," Kay said. "I want to check out this alligator of yours." Her face crinkled into a smile. "If you'll give me a ride home."

"Sure," Packi said, surprised at the suggestion. She and Kay hadn't spent time together other than on the tennis courts. She wondered if the Big Joe campaign was her foot in the door to their tight-knit group. She pictured herself in on the talk of movies, shopping ventures, golf—even parties. Don't assume anything, she warned herself. Still, Kay's offer to stay cheered her.

The sound of Beth's engine faded in the distance, dust settled in the parking lot, and the preserve began to return to normal. Egrets squawked in one of the distant ponds. An osprey flew overhead. The quiet should have calmed her, but instead panic crept in. *Now what? How do I prove Big Joe's innocence?*

"Want to take a walk?" Kay asked, and hooked her arm through Packi's. The small gesture increased Packi's confidence tenfold.

"What's your next move?" Kay asked.

"I've got three days," Packi said, "but to do what? I don't have a plan."

"Something will occur to you." As they marched toward Gator Lake, Kay offered words of encouragement, but ended with a sniff. "I hate to speak ill of the dead, but if that guy hadn't gone for a swim, none of this would have happened."

Packi had to agree. *But was it a voluntarily swim?* She vowed to find out and kept her suspicions to herself. "Joe's on the move again," she said, pointing across the water.

Kay adjusted her visor to shade her eyes and riveted her attention on the ridge of Joe's back gliding through the center of the pond. The alligator hauled himself up the ramp of the raft as turtles dove for safety. Anhingas, with wings spread open to the sun, moved aside. The raft sunk several inches into the water.

"He's a monster," Kay gasped. For several minutes she watched the reptile and the brave—or foolish—anhingas. "Still, he's just an alligator. Why are you so upset over him?"

Are you serious? Packi tensed to defend her position again, but Kay's passive expression seemed sincere, not argumentative. She chose a milder tone.

"I thought you agreed with me," Packi said. "If you don't think he's special, why did you come here today?"

"For you, of course."

Packi sucked in her breath. Unused to such a straightforward expression of friendship, she sidestepped the awkward moment. "Joe usually sleeps at this time of day," she said, "but he's probably agitated by the commotion."

"What will happen to him when his three days are up?" Kay asked.

"I hate to think about it."

But Packi did think about it. Her stomach churned at the thought of hunters baiting Big Joe, hoisting him on a hook, and posing for the camera with their trophy. She massaged her temples and shut her eyes. "I have to stop them."

"Don't worry," Kay said. "The tennis team will help you save your alligator."

8

Packi flipped on her right turn signal at the last second before turning out of Hammock Preserve. She picked up speed on the busy road.

"Where we going?" asked Kay.

"Do you mind a short detour? I want to check out this side of the slough." Packi raised her shoulders as if questioning her own action. "There were no vehicles in the lot when I arrived this morning. How did the man get here?"

"Mmm. Good point." Kay said. "Could've jogged along this bike path."

"I suppose. Watch for the osprey platform. That's about the place I first saw the body." Packi leaned over the steering wheel to scan the roadside.

"There are several platforms along here." Kay scooted forward to peer out the windshield. "Don't see a side road. How'd the ambulance get to the pond?"

Packi checked her rearview mirror and decelerated to look for a break in the shrubbery.

"Further on, I… Yikes!"

A man darted across the road. Packi slammed on the brakes and swerved onto the shoulder of the road. "Idiot!" The Audi smashed through a row of wild shrubs and jolted into the ditch. She had both feet mashed on the brake and a death grip on the steering wheel. Dust swirled around the vehicle while grit and bits of shell spun into the air.

Packi's head jerked forward and then back as the car finally stopped. She waited to breathe, not trusting the chaos to be over. Kay had stiff-armed the dashboard, a frozen scare on her face. They stared with bulging eyes, first at each other, then out the windshield.

"Did we hit him?" Kay whispered.

"I don't think so."

Packi fumbled first to unbuckle her seat belt, and then with the door handle. Kay's nerves fared no better. The shaken women waded through thick weeds to peer beneath the front bumper. No jogger. No blood. They eyed the gap in the bushes, daring each other to search for the man. Packi swallowed hard and pushed herself to retrace the car's route, bending to peer amongst tangled branches. Nothing. She straightened up when she got into the clear. A delivery van sped by leaving a concussion of air in its wake. The bike path continued on the opposite side of the two-lane road, and the jogger was gone.

"We missed him," Packi called as she made her way back into the ditch. The knowledge lightened her steps.

Kay leaned against the fender of the Audi and swiped her fingertips across the screen of her phone. She paused in mid swipe. "He should have stopped to check on us." She frowned toward Packi and then back at her screen. "I'm calling a tow truck to pull us out of here."

"Good idea. I have a card." Packi rummaged through the glove compartment until she found the envelope marked, "In case of an accident," in Ron's handwriting. Kay took the AAA card and dialed.

"We've got wait time," Packi said. "I'll have a look around." She popped open the trunk to grab the bundle of plastic bags she intended to recycle at the grocery store. She also pulled out a five iron. Glad to discover a good use for golf clubs, she slammed the trunk.

"They'll be here in twenty minutes," Kay said, when she caught up to Packi who had walked along the dry gully. "What are you doing?"

"Searching. We might spot something connected to the body in the pond." Packi handed Kay a plastic bag and continued waving the five iron through the dry, knee-high weeds. Kay chose the asphalt bike path and matched her partner's progress.

"I wonder why that jogger was off the path," Packi said, "and didn't use the intersection to cross the road."

"Ticks me off that he didn't stop to help us." Kay spoke louder as Packi moved further along the embankment.

"A normal person would." Packi flicked away a super-sized cup, but on second thought, put the litter into the plastic bag suspended from her wrist. "It's as if he didn't want to be seen or get involved."

"Or interrupt his running routine?"

"Hmm. Probably." The golf club clanked against metal. "Well, what's this?" Packi pushed back the weeds.

"Find something?" Kay picked her way into the ditch. She screwed up her face and stared at a battered bicycle. "Odd. Did the guy who just darted out of here have a flat and run to get a spare?"

Packi bent to examine the tires and the chain. "Seems rideable," she said, wondering why anyone would abandon it. She gasped at a sudden thought. *Could it belong to the man in Gator Lake?* The rusted Schwinn took on ominous importance. *He rode out here to swim? To drown himself?* She questioned her own theories.

"What are you thinking, partner?" Kay asked.

"I don't know yet." Packi stood up straight and glanced around. A clear path marked her own progress through the broken weeds in the gully. Kay's short approach to the bike was obvious, too. Another matted path led to the road.

"Nobody walked to the pond through here." Packi hopped out of the ditch. She aligned herself with the first osprey platform and trotted along the asphalt. "If I'm right, there will be a path through the weeds in line with that post."

Packi hurried along for a hundred yards, well past the point she expected to find the beaten path. *So much for that idea,* she thought.

Disappointed, she questioned her deduction. *I'd better leave the detective stuff to the professionals.*

Deflated, she turned to retrace her steps. She signaled surrender to Kay who had lagged behind, doing her civic duty by spearing wrappers and fast food containers with a stick and dropping them into her plastic bag.

Packi stooped for a granola bar wrapper. Six feet further, she found a cigarette pack caught in a patch of green vegetation. She dropped the litter into her bag and almost walked on, but noted a variation in the color of the reeds. Some were bruised and drooped beneath fresher, newer leaves. She bent for closer study, stomped her feet to scare off any lurking snakes, and separated the vegetation with her hands.

"Hey, Kay. I found something."

A shoe print marked the damp earth. Packi skirted around the impression and followed the point of the toe toward Gator Lake and found several more prints. Half were about a size twelve, the others smaller. Neither were jogging shoes.

"More evidence, Sherlock?" Kay called from the safety of the mowed weeds.

"A trail of footprints." Packi ignored the tease and indicated with the golf club a probable direction. "Two or more men walked through." She waded back toward Kay, giving the prints a wide berth. "I bet that greenery bounced back since then. Could have been last night. What do you think?"

"Haven't a clue." Kay grasped her jaw and frowned. "Could've been weeks ago."

"No, they…"

Whooping sirens startled the women. Packi jumped and dropped the golf club as a Lee County squad car with its light bar flashing stopped behind the disabled Audi.

"Uh, oh." Kay chewed her lip. "Are we breaking a law?"

"We're picking up litter," Packi said. "How can that be wrong?" *But who knows. It's been an odd day.* She retrieved the five iron and twisted her spine around to work out the stiffness, but kept the car in her peripheral vision. The bulkiness of the deputy hoisting himself out of the cruiser seemed familiar. He surveyed the scene and adjusted his hat. *Oh, no,* thought Packi. *He won't be happy.*

"It's Deputy Teig." Kay groaned.

The big man lumbered toward them, jerking his belt up to where his waistline must have once been.

"Billy!" Packi waved as she and Kay worked their way back to her car.

The deputy paused mid stride until recognition sunk in. His shoulders sagged, but he regained himself and tramped through the damaged shrubbery and down the ditch embankment.

"Mizz Walsh. Mizz Chandler. Are you injured?"

He showed no sign of their earlier friendship, but Packi covered her disappointment with a cheery response. "We're fine, Billy. What a coincidence that you're driving by just when we need you."

"What happened here, Mizz Walsh?" Deputy Teig insisted upon an all-business tone.

"A jogger darted into our path and I swerved to miss him." She gestured to the car. "And we're stuck."

"The jogger?"

"I don't know. He ran off."

The deputy bent down to inspect the wheels and undercarriage. He lay his hand on the car's hood to right himself, but snatched his hand back from the heat of the charcoal gray metal. His upper lip flinched.

"We called for roadside assistance fifteen minutes ago," Packi offered as a means to cover up his moment of pain.

He nodded and spoke in code to his radio. He turned back to them, clipboard in hand.

"Why are you ladies here? Paradise Palms is in that direction." The deputy pointed his pen to the south.

Kay and Packi exchanged guilty glances. "I got to wondering, Billy," Packi said, "about the poor man in the pond. We came out here to get a feel for why he was here so early."

Deputy Teig's thick, pink lips pursed and whitened around the edges. Packi wished he'd remove his sunglasses so she could get a full measure of his annoyance.

"Leave the investigating to the sheriff's department, Mizz Walsh. If this *is* part of a crime scene, you're destroying evidence."

"Oh." The thought withered her resolve. She held out the offending plastic bag to him as a peace offering "But most of it is litter." She took a last peek inside and then stared up into his mirrored glasses. "What about that cigarette pack? There are four cigarettes inside. Now, why would someone toss them away?"

Teig's fat fingers closed around the grocery bag.

"And there's a bicycle fifty feet that way." The volume of her voice grew along with the possibilities. "Could the cigarettes or the bike belong to the dead man?"

Deputy Teig paused and glanced in the direction of Packi's point and then into the bag. "I'll take this." As he tied a knot in the grocery bag, he scanned the tree line which concealed Big Joe's territory. "Why here, Mizz Walsh?"

"Sorry, Billy," Packi said. "We'll go home when the tow truck gets here."

The deputy held up his hand as if stopping traffic. "I mean…" He took off his sunglasses and peered at the women. "What led you to this particular spot? Was it something about the deceased?"

Did I hear that right? Her pulse quickened as she considered that the deputy might value her opinion. She glanced at her tennis partner for her impression. Kay's eyes widened, urging Packi to speak.

"Consider the wind, Billy," Packi said. "The breeze blows across the pond from southwest to northeast. An object on the water would float from the shore near the road here, to where I spotted the body before Joe..." She paused as the memory of crunching bone replayed in her ears.

Deputy Teig kneaded his fleshy jaw. "Go on."

Packi cleared her throat and her mind before continuing. "This morning I lined up the position of the victim with the osprey nest down the road there, but the poor man must have floated for hours, even all night. The body could have started its journey anywhere along the shore to the left of the osprey platform and drifted eastward." Packi motioned toward the longest shoreline which lay beyond the trees before them. "The pond is nearest the road at this point," she said. "There were no cars in the lot this morning. So, if it was an accident or suicide, how did the man get here?"

Teig raised his eyebrows above his sunglasses.

Encouraged to speculate, Packi pointed toward the Schwinn hidden in the weeds. "Suppose he rode that bike and walked through here to the pond. Or did he and someone else park a car on the road here and walk in? If he was dead already, two men could have carried him to the pond to dispose of the body. One of them could have dropped the cigarettes along the way."

Kay nudged Packi's elbow. "Tell him about the path."

"Over here, Billy. This is where I found the cigarette pack." Packi crooked her finger at the deputy and high stepped through dry weeds. Teig and Kay followed her to the faint path leading across the patch of moist, green reeds. She spread apart the broken and bruised foliage to expose the footprints she'd spotted earlier. "See? Men came through here recently. I didn't go any further, afraid I'd mess up your evidence."

"You're suddenly worried about contaminating evidence?" Deputy Teig shook his jowls. He squatted to peer at the footprints and followed them with his eyes toward the pond. He paused, still contemplating the bruised vegetation. "Very good, Mizz Walsh. I see it now." He grunted and groaned back to an upright position.

To give the big man privacy during his struggle to rise, Packi plucked and studied a wildflower. "Right about here," she said, "I found that pack of cigarettes and put them in the litter bag before I discovered the path."

Billy Teig stood like the green, vegetable giant with reeds up to his knees and his arms crossed over his uniformed chest. Sweat dripped from his chin. Ridges lined his brow as he scrutinized the field, the path, and the tree line before looking back at the road. He exhaled with a loud huff.

"Thank you, Mizz Walsh, but now you're done." He motioned toward the Audi. "No more crime scenes for you. Go home." Teig mopped his face with a bandana as his long legs took him toward the ditch. He spoke into his cell phone. "Leland, I think we found the point of entry. Send a tech team a quarter-mile south. I'll secure the area."

The women hurried to catch up. "Wait, Billy." Packi called. "Did you say we found a crime scene?"

Teig clipped his phone into its holder and looked to the sky. "No, I didn't. This is police business, Mizz Walsh."

"Yes, yes, of course." Packi hopped over the last of the weeds nearest her car. "But before we leave, at least tell me the victim's name."

"We…" The deputy stopped himself. "No. You don't need that information."

"I do," Packi insisted. "I have to prove Joe didn't kill him, that it was suicide, an accident, or somebody else did it."

"For your own good, Mizz Walsh." Deputy Teig pulled down his sunglasses and fixed a blue-eyed glare on her. "Don't—I repeat—don't poke around in this investigation."

"Yes, Billy." Packi pretended to listen to his lecture. "What about the evidence I found?" Packi indicated the bicycle laying in the gully. "Maybe the killer…"

Teig held up one hand to hush her and with the other waved the tow truck into position. "I'll take care of the evidence, Mizz Walsh. Now, let's haul your car out of here and get you on your way."

9

Packi cringed as she drove the dusty, scratched Audi through the security gates at Paradise Palms. She had decided against a car wash stop. There was no time. The guard waved them through, but disapproval marred his obligatory greeting.

Sorry, Ron. Her husband hated a dirty car, especially in their upscale neighborhood. He had washed their cars twice a week and topped off the gas in her Audi every other day. Since he died, she tried to maintain his standards, but failed.

Kay directed Packi to her street and one of eight condo buildings affectionately known as the super-eights. She opened the passenger door, letting hot wind swirl into the cool car.

"Do you want lunch?" Kay asked as if the thought just occurred to her. She held the Audi's door open with her foot. "I've got the fixings for a salad."

Packi glanced up at the four-story building and shook her head. *Kay's just being polite. I shouldn't intrude.*

"It's okay," Kay said with her toothy smile. "Mike's out giving a tennis lesson. I got vegetables from the farmers' market yesterday. The avocados are to die for."

Packi's stomach gurgled in anticipation. Suddenly, she dreaded roaming around her own house with no one with whom to discuss Big Joe's situation. "Which floor is yours?"

"Top floor," Kay exclaimed. "Great view of the pond and the golf course. Come on."

No one should live so far from the ground. Packi cringed, but accepted the invitation.

Kay hopped out and pointed to a numbered spot under an open carport. Packi parked the car and threw her volunteer vest into the backseat. Kay waited for her at the elevator.

"Mind if we take the stairs?" Packi said, eyeing the interior of the elevator as if it were a coffin.

"Four floors," Kay warned. "I thought you'd had enough exercise after your trips out to the pond."

"I always take the stairs." Packi's insides twisted at the thought of the elevator doors sliding closed. "But if you want to…"

"Heck, no. If my partner wants the exercise, so do I."

Kay led the way to the stairwell and took the first flight of stairs at a trot. The pace slowed at the second floor, and the women stopped at the third floor landing for a breather.

"The elevator's right there," Kay teased.

Packi gripped the handrail and gritted her teeth. "We'll get there. We're tennis players, for cripes sake."

* * *

Kay's condo had the vista she had promised. While Kay changed from her tennis outfit, Packi wandered onto the balcony to watch an osprey land on top of a palm at her eye level. The golf course spread out below. A golfer teed off on the fifth hole, landing his drive in the water hazard behind one of the other super-eights. A small alligator sunned itself at the water's edge, and Packi wondered why anyone would swim in any Florida pond.

She mulled over the improbability of a nighttime swim while helping Kay prepare lunch. Packi sliced an avocado, twisted it open, and smacked a knife edge into the pit. "I don't believe that man jumped into the pond for fun." She knocked the pit off the knife into the garbage.

"Fun?" Kay gave her a sad smile. "Even a college kid would know better."

"Not a kid from the north." Packi shrugged and scooped the avocado pulp out of its shell. The clothing hadn't suggested a kid on vacation. "I don't believe that's it."

"Heart attack? There's scads of old people around here."

"Possible. To beat the heat, he could have ridden his bike in late evening and then stopped to watch the birds coming in to roost. He had a heart attack on the shore and tumbled into the water."

Kay took two matching plates from the cabinet and added paper napkins with a tennis motif. "That would show up in the autopsy, I suppose. What else could have happened? Suicide?"

More likely, Packi thought. She put the spoon in the sink and leaned against the countertop. "I guess a person could shoot himself and hope the alligators would clean up the mess." She shuddered at another painful image lurking in her distant memory—frigid Lake Michigan water, the body caught in the jetty.

Packi saw Kay's brows pull together and regretted letting emotion show on her face. She turned aside to mash the avocado. "I think it's more than a suicide," Packi said as she dumped onions and tomato into the bowl. "Not a medical issue either."

"Some sort of accident?" Kay paused, holding the water pitcher above a glass. "That's hard to imagine."

"No. Deputy Teig slipped and said *crime scene*. He warned us not to put our noses into the investigation," Packi said, "like there's something dangerous going on."

"Teig's just a tough-guy cop, trying to scare you away."

"Mmm. Maybe."

The women left the depressing conversation in the kitchen and carried the salad and guacamole out to the screened balcony and settled into the cushioned chairs with cold drinks. Packi enjoyed the girl-talk. It was like when she had friends, years ago before Ron got sick. She sighed happily and let Kay chatter on about the latest gossip:

tennis opponents, issues with the clubhouse remodeling, and flirtatious neighbors. Anything darker would have ruined their appetites.

Packi cleared the table, rinsed plates, and reveled in the intimacy. "I've decided," she announced, while she loaded the dishwasher. "I'll track down Deputy Teig and dig information out of him to help me in court."

"That deputy refused to even tell you the victim's name."

"True, but he will, if I catch him at a weak moment." Packi eyed the chocolate cupcakes on the counter.

"Mike baked those for his poker buddies tonight," Kay said. "He won't mind." She grinned and reached for a brown paper bag.

"Thanks, Kay. I'll visit our friend, Billy Teig, and bribe him with baked goods."

Kay started the dishwasher and took a deep breath. "I'll go with you, Packi, though I admit—that deputy still scares the heck out of me."

* * *

Packi wheeled into her own driveway and ran inside to grab her backup phone—Ron's old i-phone. In the kitchen, the blinker on the answering machine caught her attention. *Huh. Three messages.*

"Hang on, Kay. I never get messages." Packi pressed *play.*

"Packi, it's Marilyn Scott. I hope you don't mind. I wrote a quick article to meet the deadline for tomorrow's newspaper. It posted on the Gazette's website ten minutes ago. Sorry. I also scheduled you for a radio show. Chris—she's on the 3.0 team—knows the morning show host, Steve Stearns. He'll tape your interview today for tomorrow morning. I'll pick you up at four-thirty this afternoon, and we'll still have time for Buncotini."

Buncotini? Packi's mind whirled, so she pressed *repeat* to listen to the details again. The next message was from Mary Chin urging her to contact a lawyer known for pro bono environmental cases. Packi scribbled his name and number on Ron's personalized notepads.

The last message was from Grace. "Can you e-mail pictures of Big Joe? I'm doing a new flyer, and we'll put it on Facebook."

"Dang." Packi groaned. "What have I started? I don't have time for this."

"The team wants to help." Kay leaned against the door jamb with her arms crossed over her thin chest. "Why don't you let them handle the publicity, and you concentrate on figuring out how the guy died? Delegate."

Packi sighed and pressed *Delete*. "You're right. I'll delegate—but first I have to do what they ask."

She powered up her laptop and scanned through the photo album to find her most artistic composition—Joe laying on the shore, reflected in the water, with a snowy egret perched on his back. Kay pitched in by finding e-mail addresses for Grace and Marilyn and downloading the picture while Packi called the lawyer.

"Yes, of course," the soft-spoken Dave Stanford said when Packi introduced herself. "Mary Chin told me about the alligator, but let me hear *you* tell the story."

Packi started with the routines of the morning and ended with Deputy Teig warning her away from the investigation. The lawyer didn't interrupt. When she had nothing more to say, she listened to silence. *He hung up? He thinks I'm a nut case.* "Mr. Stanford?"

"All right, Ms. Walsh." He breathed out his words, slow and deliberate. She pictured him leaned back in his leather chair, staring at the ceiling and mulling over the circumstances. "I'll try to help you."

Hope filled her with a positive lightness she hadn't felt in years. She gave a thumbs-up to Kay.

"I'll formally notify Lee County of the temporary restraining order," Stanford said, "and I'll go to court with you before the TRO expires. So, by Thursday you must give Judge White a reason to grant a preliminary injunction."

She waited for the lawyer to offer additional guidance, but none came.

"I must warn you, Mrs. Walsh. It's unlikely the judge will overturn long-standing county procedures, and it's typically up to the land owner, in this case, Lee County, to decide if a nuisance alligator is removed. You must persuade the court to give you time by substantiating your belief that the man was dead before the alligator pulled him under the water."

And what are you going to do? The lawyer's lack of a real solution irked her. Packi reminded herself that he'd handle the legal paperwork pro bono, charging only for court fees. *No knight in shining armor,* she thought.

"What's wrong?" Kay asked when Packi hung up the phone. "Isn't the lawyer going to help?"

"I guess I expected more," Packi said. "At least he'll go to court with me. That's huge, but he expects *me* to investigate." She slumped onto a kitchen chair and let the phone fall into her lap.

"Hey." Kay edged her chair closer to her partner's knee. "Remember, you're not in this alone. The tennis team got on board this train of yours, and a whole bus load of kids are ready to battle for Joe's life."

Packi sat back and glanced at Kay's expectant face. "I guess you're right." She nodded in contrition and forced herself to give more. "I have friends like you to help."

Kay grinned as if she'd been granted a gift. "Come on. Let's go bribe a deputy."

10

The Audi had gotten oven-hot sitting in the driveway. Kay and Packi slid onto the black leather seats, careful not to burn their legs. They opened the windows to let in the hot breeze until the air conditioning kicked in.

As Packi's car approached the Paradise Palms guard shack, Kay leaned forward. "Whoa. Something's up." Two police cars with the sheriff department logo on the doors pulled through the entrance gate.

Packi's head whipped around. "I think that's Billy Teig. I wonder what's going on. Keep an eye on him."

Kay swiveled in her seat to watch the vehicles while Packi did a U-turn around the guard shack and back into Paradise Palms. The guard scowled, but waved his usual greeting. Keeping their distance, they followed the two cruisers through the winding, flower-lined roads of the manicured subdivision. Golf carts, en route to the clubhouse, slowed the parade.

"Don't lose them," Kay warned as they waited their turn to pass the puttering carts. She sat forward to keep an eye on the police cruisers. "They're pulling into the super-eights."

The police cars slowed, probably trying to decipher the condominium numbering system, and finally stopped in front of the building next to Kay's. Packi parked at the curb and watched Teig struggle out of his cruiser. A woman in a business suit and sensible shoes emerged from the other vehicle. They disappeared into the elevator.

Packi pulled the Audi forward and watched from ground level until the officials reappeared on the third floor walkway. Kay opened her window to get a better view.

"That's Carla Baker's floor."

"Carla?"

"From the 2.5 team," Kay said, straining to watch Teig's movement along the open railing. "Her husband's the pharmacist at the drug store on Daniels."

"Vern Baker?" Packi asked. "I know him—met him years ago when Ron was sick and talked to him last…"

Kay gasped and grabbed Packi's arm. "The cops are at Carla's door. Come on!"

The women scrambled out of the Audi, slammed the doors, and ran across the parking lot. Packi headed toward the stairwell, but Kay stopped at the elevator to jab at the button. "Skip the exercise. Stairs are too slow." The doors slid open.

Packi took a step toward the elevator and froze.

"Come on." Kay reached out and dragged Packi over the threshold.

The doors closed before Packi could jump back to safety. She backed into a corner and grabbed the handrail. Her knees threatened to buckle.

Kay poked at the number three button several times. "Dang elevator…" She glanced at her partner. "Are you okay?" She grasped Packi's arm to support her. "You're as white as a sheet."

"I… I hate elevators." The elevator jerked, and Packi gripped the inside rail tighter.

Kay took Packi's wrist and felt for her pulse. "Your heart's racing. Take it easy." She poked at the button with her other hand. "You should have said something."

Packi nodded dumbly, her eyes wide, watching the numbers above the door.

"Almost there, partner." Kay patted her arm.

The doors slid open and Packi launched herself into the fresh air. Kay pulled her to the side and leaned her against the wall. "Breathe," Kay commanded. "Take deep breaths."

Packi gulped in air. "I'm okay. Just give me a minute." Her fear turned to embarrassment. Her face went from white to red. "Sorry, Kay. I thought I could do it, but closed in like that…" She straightened up on rubbery knees. "Let's go check on Cathy."

"Carla," Kay corrected. "You're still shaky. Stay here, and I'll go see if she needs us." Kay hurried off before Packi could protest.

Packi moved away from the elevator doors to the balcony to take in the wide open space. *Get control of yourself, Patricia. This is embarrassing.* She tested her steadiness, filled her lungs with air, and headed for Carla's condo.

* * *

Air conditioning flowed through the screen door of the third-floor condo. Like a tomb sentry, Billy Teig stood in the long narrow hallway silhouetted against Florida sunshine streaming through from the balcony. When Packi creaked open the door, Teig's bulk turned toward her. His face in the shadows, she imagined he sent her an amiable welcome. She tiptoed to his side and peered into the living room where Kay sat with her arm around a woman of about fifty. Packi assumed her to be Carla from the 2.5 team and vaguely recognized her freckled arms.

The woman in the serious suit, a Lee County social worker Packi figured, leaned toward Carla from the edge of a wicker chair. The thick cushions in a colorful tropical print were at odds with the severity of the woman's clothes.

"Who is that?" Packi whispered at Deputy Teig's elbow.

He ignored the question as if he didn't notice her tugging at this shirt sleeve.

"Billy?"

He groaned louder than Packi's whisper, but leaned down to her ear level. "That's Detective Leland. Don't interfere." He resumed his sentinel stance, blocking her view of the scene in the living room.

Packi wondered what bad news Detective Leland delivered to poor Carla. *Is there a connection to the body in the pond?* Scenarios flickered through Packi's brain. *Could the dead man be Carla's husband? Vern?* Packi banished the idea from her head. Vern had been a good listener, an ally, as Ron's illness progressed. He'd fill prescriptions and counsel her when her own family and friends were back in Illinois. Packi sidestepped Teig's shadow to listen.

"Now, Mrs. Baker, we don't know that," the detective said. "All we have is a business card, no ID." She patted Carla's hand. "Does your husband have a reason to be gone overnight?"

"He's away… away on a business trip. We have a rental property in Miami." The poor woman's glassy eyes begged the county official to say that her husband would come home. Her fingers moved of their own accord, picking at slubs on the sofa's large floral print.

"When's the last time you spoke to your husband?"

"Yesterday morning. He should have called today." Carla pulled out of Kay's embrace and jumped up from the couch. "I'm calling him now."

Teig stepped out of the frantic woman's way as she rushed to the wall phone in the kitchen. She punched three buttons, and then gripped her forehead in her fingers as if squeezing the number from her memory. She hung up and tried again with no better luck. She slammed the receiver onto its hook a second time.

Kay went to Carla's side. "Tell me the number, honey."

Carla closed her eyes and got a running start at the cell phone number while Kay dialed. She listened for an answer before putting the receiver to Carla's ear. Everyone in the room heard the electronic singsong of a recorded message and held their breath.

"Vern, where are you? Pick up the phone!"

Carla's face crumpled as she waited. Kay put her arm around the woman's shoulders, murmuring words of encouragement, until Carla groaned and dropped the phone onto the counter. Kay put the receiver onto its hook and led the woman back to the floral sofa.

"He's not answering." Carla bowed her head and sat before the detective as if confessing a mortal sin.

Teig shifted his feet, leather creaking, and interrupted the awkward silence. "Do you have a recent photo of your husband, Mizz Baker?"

An aura of doom surrounded Carla, isolating her from the tropical paradise outside her balcony, but she hoisted herself from the sofa. She removed a frame from the bedroom wall and brought out an album. "This one was taken on our twentieth wedding anniversary," she said, displaying an eight-by-ten of a younger version of herself and her husband. Carla flipped through the album. "These are more recent. Here, this is Vern." She removed two photos from the book and handed them to the investigator.

Detective Leland studied the photos and exchanged a glance with Teig. Packi's heart sank. Too distracted with her album, Carla didn't see the tic of Billy's eyebrow. She pointed out a picture to Kay of her and Vern at a mixed-doubles tennis tournament last year.

"Mrs. Baker," Leland said, "we want to rule out that the victim found in the pond is your husband. Will you come with us to view the body?"

Stricken, Carla fell back into the sofa cushions. Kay glared at the cops and bared her teeth, but opted to comfort Carla.

Mrs. Baker sobbed. "I can't. I can't! It's not Vern. I know it's not."

"Billy." Packi touched his thick forearm. "Deputy Teig," she said louder and tugged his sleeve.

As if she was a nuisance, Teig glanced down and raised his eyebrows. "Let's step outside, Mizz Walsh."

He held the screen door open for her and pulled the heavier door closed behind them. He led her to the railing overlooking the parking lot three floors below. "Why are you here?"

Packi's throat dried out. She tried to make eye contact with the deputy, but the afternoon sun behind his shoulder blinded her. "I knew, I mean, I know Vern Baker," she said, stepping in to the shadows. "May I view the body instead of poor Carla?"

Teig frowned and crossed his arms over his chest. "It's not a pleasant task." He took his dark glasses out of his pocket and slid them on.

"I'm not a busybody, Billy," Packi said. "I can help. I've done this before."

She intended to get her way. Her own experiences could help Carla Baker, help solve the detective's case, and could even help Big Joe. If she had to pad Deputy Teig's belly with a thousand extra calories a day, she'd do it.

"There are homemade cupcakes for you in the car, Billy."

The deputy suppressed a smile. "Mizz Walsh, you're a real pistol."

11

Deputy Teig turned his cruiser onto Metro and headed toward downtown. The high-rises on the river towered in the distance over the landscape of shops and light-industry businesses. *You want something done,* he thought, *you find it on Metro—tile, electrical, tow hitches, patio brick.* The snowbirds kept his friends in business, so Teig accepted the crowds and traffic. He remembered ditching school to hunt deer out here. *Back then, nothin' was east of 41. Now... at least Russell's got customers parked in his lot.* Teig whooped his siren and Russell raised his hand without taking his head out from beneath the hood of a car.

Mizz Walsh flinched at the sound of the siren.

"Sorry. Friend of mine."

She'd been eyeing the gear and communication equipment crammed into his cruiser, but hadn't asked one question. She stared hard at the shotgun in its rack. He wondered what was going through her head and what possessed her to volunteer to identify the body.

A chill bristled his neck hair as Teig remembered his first time at the morgue. He'd been fifteen, when Harlan Teig walked into the swamp with a bottle of Jack and a shotgun. Arletta Teig identified her husband's body, while Billy stood at her side and cried like a baby.

"You okay with this, Mizz Walsh?" Maybe she needs a way out, he thought. "You know, the medical examiner doesn't much trust visual IDs. Too unreliable. You don't have to do this."

Her eyes flicked at him and then focused on a pickup truck doing a U-turn. "I'm okay."

Somehow Mizz Walsh reminded him of his mother. Arletta Teig loved a cold beer after a deer hunt and fished for mullet with a cigarette between her fingers. She loved the Lord and waited tables to keep the family fed. His father had been too discouraged to help, but she never gave up on him. Lung cancer took her ten years ago.

Beneath the soft pink stuff, Mizz Walsh had his mother's steel.

"What'd you mean when you said you'd done this before?" They stopped at a red light, while traffic streamed across Metro. He turned to watch her reaction. "Have you had to ID a body?"

She flinched like a doe hearing the click of his trigger.

"I've been to the morgue."

"A family member?" He pushed her. There was something she wanted to say.

"My husband," she whispered with a sigh. "Five years ago."

He assumed an illness or a car accident. "What happened?"

She turned toward him, straining her seat belt. Her eyes hurt him with her pain. "My husband had cancer." The pronouncement sizzled like fat on a grill. "He walked into Lake Michigan and shot himself. Washed up on the rocks three days later." Mizz Walsh jerked back in the seat, crossed her arms, and scowled out the window.

"My father shot himself in the swamp." He winced when the words fell from his mouth. *Why did I say that? My loss doesn't compare to hers.* His knuckles whitened on the steering wheel.

A light touch to his shoulder caused him to turn toward his passenger. Fierceness had drained from her face, leaving her as soft and vulnerable as she had been at the slough. Her eyes held more sadness than his mother's had. He looked away.

The light turned green. With her hand still on his shoulder, he pointed the cruiser toward the morgue.

* * *

At the morgue the technician in a white lab coat wheeled a stainless steel table into a small windowless room. Packi hadn't expected the smell. She pressed the face mask Teig had given her against her nose and chewed her minty gum. The odor of raw, rotting chicken and formaldehyde transported her thoughts back to the sterile room in Chicago.

She had looked then, needed to, with her brother at her side. The bloated body in the Chicago morgue bore little similarity to her husband, but she'd known his cleft chin, his ear, the curve of his shoulder. Her grief must have masked the stench.

Packi clenched her teeth and placed her hand in the crux of Deputy Teig's elbow. *Please God, don't let me faint. Let me get through this.*

The harsh sound of the body-bag's zipper echoed off the white tiled walls. The odor of garbage escaped. She refused to gag. Inside the paper mask, Packi chewed her gum faster and blew minty breath to her nose. She forced herself to look. There he was. Terror rigid on his face. No shirt. Balding head, long nose, angular jaw.

Packi bobbed her head once and stepped back. Teig grasped her upper arm and steered her through the exit door. She loosened the mask and took a deep breath of basement air.

"You okay, Mizz Walsh?" the deputy asked. "You're fish-belly white."

"Fine, Billy. Yes, thank you." She dabbed her upper lip with a tissue. "Can we get outside? I need daylight."

Out in the fresh air, Billy's eyes were on her. *He expects me to faint,* she thought. Determined not to give him that satisfaction, she focused on an oak growing alongside the long, low building and negotiated a straight line toward the bench in its shade. The hard seat made her feel safe again.

"You did real good, Mizz Walsh. Folks, even cops, lose their cookies from that smell." Deputy Teig dumped himself onto the bench next to her and balanced a clipboard on his thigh. "Okay, just sign this statement, and I'll get you back home." He held out a pen. "I'll inform Detective Leland, and she'll tell Mizz Baker."

"No, don't do that." Packi refused the pen and closed her eyes to collect her thoughts. "Forgive me, Billy." The gum in her mouth tasted like morgue. "I don't know who that dead man is, but it's not Vern Baker."

The small bench wobbled as Teig shifted to face her. "Are you sure? The description matches," he said, "and I thought your nod meant you recognized him."

"I don't. I'm sorry. That man resembles Vern, but Vern had a cleft chin, just like my husband. I think that's why I enjoyed talking to him." Packi spit the morgue gum into a tissue and took a long, cleansing breath. She stared at the leaves fluttering above her head. "The dead man wears glasses. Vern didn't."

Deputy Teig tapped the end of his pen on the clipboard before speaking. "He wasn't wearing glasses when we found him."

"No," she said, "I suppose not, but he must ordinarily wear glasses to leave that indentation across his temple."

"Good catch, Mizz Walsh, but Detective Leland won't be happy. That business card was her only lead." Teig got to his feet with a groan. "Wait right here while I finish this paperwork and let them know we still have a John Doe."

When Teig disappeared behind the glass doors, Packi pulled out Ron's old iphone and dialed Kay's number. While it rang, she raised her face to the filtered sunlight; glad to be alive, glad to be out of the morgue, and glad to tell Carla Baker that her husband was not the man zipped into that body bag.

"Packi?" Kay whispered. "Let me get into the other room."

"It's okay," Packi said. "I'm almost certain the dead man is not Vern Baker."

"Really? Oh, gad, I'm so relieved."

"Wait, Kay," Packi hurried to say. "Before you tell Carla, get a peek at that framed picture. This man looks very similar. Make sure

Vern has a cleft chin, like I remember, and then ask Carla if he wears glasses, possibly sunglasses, that are tight to his head."

"Okay, Okay. I'll be right back."

The phone on Kay's end clunked onto a table top. Packi listened to muffled voices and worried. *Is it possible I got it wrong? What if I don't remember Vern as well as I thought?*

"Packi!" Carla came on the phone. "Is it true? They didn't find my Vern? Oh, God, Packi. Thank you. Thank you."

The woman's joy added to Packi's fear that her brief glance at the man in the morgue wasn't enough. "What about the glasses, Carla?"

"Just reading glasses, and they're always sliding off his nose, and yes, of course, he still has a cleft chin, as handsome as Cary Grant's."

Packi imagined the woman dancing around her kitchen and throwing her arms around Kay. "I'm so relieved I don't have to tell my children." Carla's voice broke. Her laughter dissolved into sobs. "Where *is* Vern?"

Packi wondered the same thing. *And who is the dead man? Why is he so familiar?*

12

Packi ran to her shower the minute Billy dropped her off at Paradise Palms. She disinfected herself under hot water with every soap, body wash, and shampoo within reach, scouring every pore with a harsh bristle brush. When the hot water ran out, cold water shocked her skin.

Why am I alive? The two morgue visits twisted into one memory, bringing grief as real as her raw skin. She turned off the icy water, but stood in the glass enclosure, dripping. Tears, which she thought had run dry years ago, flowed.

When the fog cleared from the bathroom mirror, Packi stepped from the shower stall and scrubbed at her skin with a rough towel. *That's enough, Patricia,* she thought and shook her wet hair to clear her mind. She brushed her teeth and gargled deep into her throat to rid herself of the morgue scent that clung to the back of her tongue.

* * *

Cleansed and dressed, Packi settled in the shade of the lanai with a soothing cup of Earl Gray tea. She propped her feet on the opposite chair and watched a kingfisher swoop low across the surface of the pond. Ron had chosen the building lot for the long, lovely view. A pang of guilt hit her. *Was I disloyal to Ron by divulging his suicide to Deputy Teig?* She dunked her tea bag several times before she could usher in more pleasant memories.

The house phone jangled. *I've had enough for today*, she thought. *Let the machine answer that.* She took another sip of Earl Gray.

An excited, apologetic tone reached her and urged her out of her chair. She slid open the lanai doors to listen. Packi leaned her head against the door jamb, while Marilyn Scott's voice reminded her of the scheduled radio interview.

"Steve Stearns will call you." Marilyn said. "Don't forget, Packi. Are you there?"

Driving downtown, or wherever, for an interview was the last thing Packi wanted to do, but she reminded herself that Big Joe needed the publicity. She reached for the phone. "I'm here, Marilyn."

"Packi! Hi. I'm sorry, but Steve Stearns wants to interview you over the phone," Marilyn said as if the news would crush Packi. "He'll call you at four-thirty. Is that okay?"

Good news, bad news, Packi thought. "Sure, I'll be here. All I have to do is run up to the strip mall to get a replacement phone. Is there anything special I should do for the interview?"

"I don't think so." Marilyn paused. "Just answer questions, I guess."

Marilyn hung up and Packi rushed out on her errands so she'd be home on time for the dreaded phone interview.

* * *

Steve Stearns called precisely at four-thirty. He had earned his spot on Fort Myers morning talk show with his enthusiastic assertiveness, made interesting by a kind, conversational tone. Within minutes, he had Packi talking. Packi found herself drawn into a robust discussion and made an emotional plea for Big Joe's life. Steve anticipated his listeners' reaction and was smart enough to avoid humanizing the body. He insinuated that the man drowned or otherwise foolishly endangered his own life. He let Packi paint the alligator as an innocent creature.

The interview lasted only ten minutes, but drained Packi. She hung up, brewed another cup of Earl Gray, and curled her feet under her on the chaise lounge just as the phone rang again.

Dang it. I'm not answering if it's Marilyn checking up on the interview. She vowed to let the call go to the answering machine. When she heard the urgency in Beth's voice, she jumped up and rushed inside.

"Hey!" said Beth. "Big Joe's campaign is going great, but I have more ideas. Can we talk about it at Buncotini tonight?"

That's the big emergency? Packi sighed. "I don't know what Buncotini is," she said, though she knew. She'd seen the event advertised in the Paradise Palm's newsletter.

"Bunco. You've played bunco!" Beth's laugh hurt Packi's ear. "You throw the stupid dice and drink martinis. I reserved two tables for the team. You need to come."

Packi never imagined herself playing such an inane game, but lacked the strength to withstand her team captain's forceful personality. Besides, she reasoned, another brainstorming session would move Big Joe's campaign along.

"What time?"

"Seven o'clock. Casual dress. See you there." Hurricane Beth hung up, leaving a shock of silence in her wake.

As Packi returned the phone to its cradle, tension eased from her shoulders. *I'm part of the group,* she thought, *part of the team.* In a surge of girlish happiness, she rushed to her closet to choose a Buncotini outfit.

Across her bed, Packi spread clothes she hadn't worn in years and opted for a pair of capris. Embroidered flip-flops embellished the bottom hem. They had been a favorite for dinner on Fort Myers Beach where anything more than a bathing suit was considered dressy. She dragged the ironing board to the living room and turned on the TV for background noise.

As water perked and steam hissed from the iron, a familiar jingle caught Packi's attention. The TV commercial flashed pictures of houses, townhomes, and high-rise condos on beautiful golf courses or waterfront lots, all with price tags slashed. Like a used-car salesman, a man in a tropical shirt pushed people to buy foreclosed properties.

"Call Danny Golden at 239-555-9000. There's a Golden deal waiting for you!"

"Oh, my God." Packi gasped and stared. *That man could be Vern Baker's brother.* Suncoast commercials aired a dozen times a day, but Packi had never paid attention, never saw the resemblance until now. She studied the screen. The real estate salesman wore glasses, lacked Vern's cleft chin, and had a full head of sleek, dark hair. She liked his smile. His assertive sales techniques should have been off-putting, but somehow made him endearing, fun.

Too much hair, Packi thought. She grabbed a pen and wrote in the white border on the front page of the newspaper. *Danny Golden, Suncoast Realty.* She added the phone number, tore off the scrap, and dialed Deputy Teig's number.

"Billy!" she said when he answered. "It's Patricia Walsh—from the morgue today?"

"Hey, Mizz Walsh. You feeling better?"

"Yes, yes." Packi clucked her tongue at the wasted time. "I just saw a commercial on TV for Suncoast Realty. Danny Golden. It's him. I know it."

"Slow down, Mizz Walsh. Who did you see?"

Packi composed herself and enunciated her words. "Danny Golden is the man in the morgue. I know it. He looks like him anyway, but with more hair."

Packi waited, listening to heavy breathing on the other end of the line. "Billy, are you there?"

"That's not a lot to go on," Deputy Teig finally said. "Someone would notice a man like Danny Golden was missing."

"You saw the body."

"I did," admitted Teig, "but had to watch you in case you fainted. I'm not saying you're wrong. No one has identified the man yet. There's no missing person report."

The fainting remark miffed her, but she let it go. That odor and thoughts of Ron may have thrown her off. "I guess I could be wrong." A sudden pang of sorrow for the man on TV told her to push the issue. "I have good instincts, Billy. Will you at least visit his home to see if he's alive?"

"We can't barge in on private citizens." Deputy Teig huffed, but paused. "Let me make a phone call."

13

Packi stood in the clubhouse's main dining room, wondering why she had agreed to come. The din from a room full of bunco players almost drove her back to the parking lot. She considered retreat until Beth's voice cut through the noise.

Packi waved and threaded her way to the back of the room through a maze of tables, chairs, and women enjoying foo-foo drinks. Seven teammates greeted her as if she was a long-lost friend.

Grace, Kay, and Marilyn toasted her with raised martini glasses. From another table, Beth rose to thump her on the back. Helen even smiled and introduced her to Valerie, a player on the injured list.

"The first one's on me." Grace pushed a fruity martini across the table and laughed as if she'd had a few already. "Welcome to Buncotini."

"Oh, no thanks." Packi waved away the drink. "I seldom drink."

"Come on, girlfriend." Kay slid the glass closer. "After the day you've had, you can try one."

Packi suddenly wanted to let loose and join the camaraderie. She took a sip of the pomegranate martini. "Not bad." *In fact, pretty good.* She toasted the team. "Thanks, Grace."

Bunco turned out to be fun—throwing the dice and cheering when the right numbers came up. Between games, as they moved from table to table; the tennis team discussed Packi's visit to the morgue; poor Carla still waiting for Vern to come home; and Big Joe's publicity campaign.

Packi withheld her thoughts about Danny Golden. She needed Teig's confirmation before making that suspicion public. She frowned, but set the thought aside when the woman next to her passed the dice. On her second toss, Packi rolled all fives. "Bunco!" Her excitement surprised her. She enjoyed the thrill of the win and ordered a chocolate martini to celebrate.

While she and Beth waited for points to be recorded, they chatted about their lives beyond tennis. Packi's lack of knowledge about her team captain's life shocked her. She found out that Beth's second husband, Rex, could fix anything; they were childless; and they both loved to race swamp buggies in the Everglades.

How'd I miss so much? Packi licked the chocolate from the rim of her glass and listened to Beth's stories. Engrossed in the conversation, she didn't notice when the waiter whisked the empty glass away. She searched for it on the floor. When she straightened back up in her chair, her head spun with a pleasant, gauzy buzz.

"It's gone," laughed Beth. "Order a new one. Apple's the best."

"Good idea," Packi said as she absentmindedly stacked and rearranged the dice. "I'll buy for both of us."

"Not for me. I have to work in the morning," Beth said. "You go ahead. I'll drive you home."

"You work?" The news surprised Packi, but shouldn't have. Many retirees held part-time jobs to supplement their pensions, while others were too young for medicare and needed the benefits. Packi wondered which was the case for Beth. "What kind of job?"

"Part-time office at Suncoast Realty."

"Suncoast?" Packi tried to recall where she'd heard that name. When she remembered the tropical shirt, she gasped. "Do you mean that Danny Golden guy on TV? He's your boss?"

Beth dismissed the man with a wave. "Nah. He's in the office downtown. I work for his partner in the rental office on Daniels Parkway."

A rush of energy cleared Packi's thinking. She vowed not to give away her suspicion that Danny Golden now lay at the morgue. Not even to her team captain. "But what do you know about the one on TV?"

"Smart businessman, but one of those frantic, type-A guys, always moving, talking. Lives over at White Egret Marina. Wears those stupid tropical shirts."

Their new bunco opponents, Valerie and a woman Packi didn't recognize, joined them at the table. Packi greeted them with a smile, but pressed Beth for information. "What else?"

"I don't know. He's got plenty of money and buys all the toys—boat, motorcycle, sports cars."

"Play the game, ladies," Valerie commanded. "You're rolling for ones."

Beth scooped up the dice and shook them in her cupped hands. "What's with the questions? You got a crush on the guy?" She threw the dice.

Packi's jaw dropped. "Of course not."

Beth did her Groucho eyebrow thing. "Cuz Danny's got a wife—a trophy wife. You've seen her." Beth passed the dice to Valerie, who held them in her hand, waiting for juicy rumors.

"Me? I've seen her?" Perplexed, Packi took a long sip of martini.

"Yeah, she's that young thing Collin gives private lessons to twice a week. She used to bartend at a place on the beach."

Packi vaguely remembered seeing a girl with the club's tennis pro. She had been out of place among the residents of Paradise Palms—late thirties, cute, long-legged. It irked Packi when older, successful men divorced and bought young wives. Foolish. She wondered about the first Mrs. Golden and motioned to Valerie to throw the dice. "Tell me more about Danny Golden."

"That's all I know," said Beth. "It's only been three months since Carla got me the job."

"Carla?" Packi's apple martini sloshed out of her glass. "You mean Carla Baker?"

"Well, yeah, from the 2.5 team." Beth mopped up Packi's spill. "Vern Baker is Danny Golden's golf partner. They've been playing together for years—here, White Egret, all the best courses."

Packi saw dots that should connect, but the alcohol fogged her thinking. A room full of women laughing, chatting in loud voices, and yelling Bunco, made it too difficult to think of the body at the morgue, or murder, or ex-wives who may or may not have held a grudge.

"Bunco!" Someone at the next table screamed as if a big money prize rode on the outcome of the game. Time to change table partners and take a ten-minute break. Packi stood, smoothed wrinkles from her capris, and headed for the bathroom. Along the way, the camel-brown leather chairs in the quiet clubhouse lobby invited her to sit. She decided to make a phone call, fell into a cushioned chair, and tried to read the scribbled number on Deputy Teig's business card.

"Hello?"

The youthful voice surprised Packi. "Hello." She glanced at the number again, wondering if she misdialed. "May I speak to Deputy Teig?"

"Dad! For you!" The boy dropped the phone. Packi heard his running footsteps. "Dad!"

Oh, no. This is his home phone. Packi tried to clear her thoughts and hoped the deputy wouldn't be angry. *I should hang up. Dang. He'd have caller-ID.*

She glanced at her watch and groaned. Nine o'clock. Too late for phone calls. She formulated her apology and waited until the sounds of heavy breathing came over the line.

"Teig here."

"Billy? Hello. This is Patricia Walsh." She fought to keep her eyes open and rushed to speak. "I hope it's not too late to call, but I wanted to tell you that Danny Golden probably wears a toupee on his TV commercials. I'm certain he's the victim and..."

"Mizz Walsh, you're slurring your words. Are you drunk?"

Packi gasped. *Am I?* "Sorry, Billy. I never drink." She thought of the crystal glasses lined up on the table. "But I tried two new martinis or maybe three, and we're playing Bunco at the club, and we're talking about Danny Golden."

"Do you have someone to drive you home?"

"Got my car."

"Don't drive yourself. Find someone who hasn't been drinking."

"Yes, Deputy."

"Promise me, or I'll come get you myself."

How cute. He's worried about me. "I'm okay, Billy. Beth will drive. But I want to talk about Danny Golden."

A heavy sigh sounded in Packi's ear. "Thanks for that tip today, Mizz Walsh. Detective Leland brought the wife in to identify the body, so you can forget the investigation and let the sheriff's department do its job."

"Oh, no, Billy. I can't. Not until we prove Big Joe is innocent." Her head was spinning with possibilities. "So, it is Danny Golden. You never said what killed him. What'd the wife say? Was it murder? I have a suspect."

"Be careful going home, Mizz Walsh," Deputy Teig said. "You can call me later in the week."

14

Packi awoke at four the next morning, took an ibuprofen, and went back to bed. Three hours later, her headache backed off and the day promised to be more bearable. In a half-dream state, she thought about Big Joe's campaign. Beth talked last night about mobilizing her troops. Fifth-graders distributed flyers in front of the grocery store. Friends told friends on Facebook. Grace posted pictures of Joe on Pinterest. Lee County offices had been inundated with calls and e-mails. The County Manager released a statement in political-speak touting his support of wildlife and the many outdoor opportunities available to the citizens of Fort Myers.

Packi worried about the man in the tropical shirt, but put that aside to think of her responsibility to the alligator. *Today, I'll prove a person, some human with a motive, killed Danny Golden.* She rolled out of bed, staggered into the kitchen, and plugged in the coffee maker.

A high-pitched trill fractured the quiet and sliced through her head from one ear drum to the other. She lunged for the phone before it rang a second time. Her early morning voice allowed her nothing more than a grunt as a greeting to the caller.

"Packi? It's Marilyn. Did you see it? I'm so sorry. They buried my article on page seven."

"Wait, wait, Marilyn." Packi pressed her hand to her achy forehead. "What are you talking about?"

"The Fort Myers Gazette has Big Joe on the front page. They make him sound monstrous."

"Who's the reporter?" Packi's anger woke her instantly. "What's it say? Never mind. I'll get my newspaper."

"Sorry, Packi," Marilyn said. "See you in an hour."

"What?"

"We leave for the match against White Egret at ten o'clock. We're partners on court four."

She'd forgotten tennis. *A body is in the morgue and life goes on. And Big Joe needs saving.* Packi rushed out to her driveway to retrieve the newspaper, planning to dash back in before any neighbors spotted her in her pajamas. Only Mr. Army, walking his two golden retrievers, noticed and waved.

Packi dumped the paper out of its plastic sleeve and spread it on the coffee table. She didn't need her reading glasses to see the headline. "Gator attacks man at Hammock Preserve." Her heart sank and her temper flared. She grabbed her bifocals and skimmed the article, searching for hope. Victim unknown. Swimming in Gator Lake. Body retrieved by divers. Third alligator attack in Florida in five years.

She squinted at the byline. *Kevin Mitchell.* The WFMK TV reporter? The circle she drew around his name tore through the paper. *He promised he'd spin the story so Big Joe wouldn't be the villain.* Packi dug Kevin Mitchell's card from her purse and dialed the number. "Kevin." she said when he answered. "What are you doing in the newspaper? You promised that you'd tell Big Joe's story. You promised to tell the truth."

"Calm down, Ms. Walsh. The article is all true, all facts. Please read it again."

Ink smudged her hands, when she flattened crinkles from the paper. The story he'd written turned out to be fair, but she didn't want to let go of her anger. "What about that headline?"

"Out of my control. I'm just a stringer for the Gazette. The editor added that headline to grab attention, to sell newspapers. I had to fight to keep in the last part about the raft. It's my job, Ms. Walsh. I have bills to pay."

Packi realized that berating the young man wouldn't help the alligator's cause. "Okay, Kevin." She'd lost her steam. "Will you at least do a follow up story about how the children and the visitors all love Joe?"

"I can try, but it's all up to the editor."

"His scare tactics are despicable." Packi gritted her teeth and tried to think of how to handle the editor. How to win him over. "If you break a big story," she asked the young reporter, "would your boss publish a story favorable to Big Joe?"

"He might. What do you know?"

"You'll get his assurance first?"

"I will. I will," he said, like a four-year-old making promises to Santa.

"The victim's name is Danny Golden."

"No shit!" He gasped. "Excuse my language, Ms. Walsh. Suncoast Realty? The salesman?"

"I saw the body at the morgue, but call Deputy Billy Teig or Detective Leland at the sheriff's department for confirmation."

"I'll do that." His voice broke as if his adolescence had returned.

"I'm working on this, too, Kevin. If you figure out what really killed Mr. Golden, call me."

"Okay. Will do, and you'll tell me, if you get more details."

"Yes." His excitement exhausted her. "If you convince that editor to leave Big Joe out of it."

"I promise, Ms. Walsh." He hung up without a good-bye.

* * *

Packi rushed through her morning routines, gathered her tennis gear, and wheeled her bicycle out of the garage. Humidity rose from the ground, but the day was not yet hot. A ride to the clubhouse would clear her mind, warm her muscles, and help prevent a strain or cramp during the match. Off-season league games wouldn't affect anyone's rating, but they could get intense. She hoped a breeze coming off the river at White Egret Marina would lower the temperature.

In the clubhouse parking lot near the library, a gaggle of women waited in matching uniforms, white with accents of black and tangerine. Mary's SUV hatch yawned open, waiting for their tennis gear.

"There she is," Beth said as if they'd been talking about her.

Six faces turned in Packi's direction, bright with anticipation, smiling, even surprised. Under their scrutiny, she propped her bicycle in the rack and shouldered her tennis bag. *What do they expect from me?* Packi preferred to sidle up to the group and merge into the team unnoticed. But here they were, wanting something from her. She fidgeted under Beth's friendly, but intimidating gaze.

Kay peddled through the parking lot and saved Packi from the group stare. "Hi, everybody. I talked to Carla this morning. Vern got home last night."

During a chorus of exclamations, Packi slipped into the group. Kay was inundated with questions about the pharmacist's whereabouts until Beth's voice rose above the gabbling.

"Let's go, ladies." The team captain slammed the trunk of her car. "Load 'em up."

No one ever argued with Beth. The Paradise Palms team piled into two vehicles for the drive to White Egret. Grace, Valerie, and Helen loaded into Mary's SUV. Kay grabbed Packi's arm and nudged her into the backseat of Beth's Lexus. "We gotta talk. What happened at the morgue? If it wasn't Vern Baker, who was it?"

Beth and Marilyn in the front seat sat up straighter and cocked their heads to hear the conversation.

"I'm not supposed to say anything," Packi said. "Deputy Teig and that reporter, Kevin Mitchell, are investigating. The news will be out this evening, I suspect, after they verify."

Beth frowned into the rearview mirror. Packi turned toward the window, away from her teammates' disappointment. "Next of kin and all that," she said.

Fifteen minutes later the two vehicles arrived at White Egret Marina's gate house. The guard examined Beth's license before raising the barrier to allow them to enter. They followed signs toward the tennis courts. Tall masts rose above the tennis shop from fifty-foot sail boats and yachts moored at the dock. Beyond, a sparkling waterway led directly to the Gulf of Mexico.

In awe of the gorgeous clubhouse and expansive gardens, Packi scanned the opulence from under the brim of her cap. "I don't belong here."

Beth snorted. "None of us do, but remember that they put their pantyhose on the same way we do."

"I haven't worn pantyhose in years." Kay stopped in an exaggerated pose to display her tanned leg. She laughed and ran to keep up with the team. "No way I'd live here. Too many snobs."

"Here's the rest of our team." Marilyn waved to Grace as if she hadn't just seen her fifteen minutes earlier. Packi welcomed the reinforcements.

"Game on," said Beth. "Let's find our courts."

The women followed the sidewalk lined with manicured shrubs and bright flowers. The busy tennis complex spread before them with twice as many courts as Paradise Palms. Packi told herself to focus on tennis and ignore the intimidating surroundings, but confidence slipped away. Hope for a win dwindled.

League etiquette suggests that the host team greet and welcome the visiting team. There was none of that. Beth and team filed onto the bleachers and dumped their gear and purses.

"Maybe they don't realize we're here." Packi tried to be generous, but felt the unwelcoming air.

"They know," Beth said. "That's the team captain there, warming up on court one." Beth grabbed her clipboard and marched to the side of the court to force the captain's attention.

"Where are we supposed to warm up?" asked Grace.

"I guess we don't." Helen clucked her tongue. "That's how they stay in first place. They play mind-games with their opponents." Helen plunked herself next to Packi and continued her litany of complaints.

Packi couldn't place Helen's accent, but could picture her berating a deli owner in a New York neighborhood. The rest of the team distanced themselves and ignored Helen's sniping. Packi fabricated a smile and watched the girls warming up on the courts, trying to spot a weakness to exploit during the match. Their youth and the quality of their haircuts, clothing, and jewelry rubbed Packi the wrong way. Disgusted with herself, she realized she was losing the mind-game.

Beth's laugh carried across the courts from the sheltered bleachers on court one. She and the other captain compared lineups and chatted amiably. Kill 'em with kindness, Packi thought.

"Good Lord." Mary whispered from the bleacher seat behind Packi. "All those store-bought boobs. They must have their plastic surgeons on speed-dial."

Packi studied the opposing team's strengths and weaknesses and listened to her team rip into them, relieving their pre-game tension in their own ways. The chattering continued until Beth returned with her clipboard.

"Change of plans, Packi. Kay's ankle is bothering her, so she's on court four with Marilyn. You're on three with Helen."

The announcement surprised Packi. With more enthusiasm than she felt, she said, "That's okay with me." She flashed a smile at her new partner. Helen was in shock.

"They'll give us time to warm up in a few minutes," Beth said, "so go to the bathroom or whatever now."

Helen jumped to her feet and dogged Beth's footsteps. "I've never played with her." Helen's strident voice could be heard from fifteen feet away. "How can you expect me to win with a little girl like that?"

Packi pretended not to hear. She turned her attention to the opposing team running around the courts. She promised herself not to expect too much from the match. After all, her partner didn't want her, the opponents were surgically enhanced, and her own mind wandered to the morgue and to the problem of saving Big Joe.

Kay slid onto the metal bleacher seat beside Packi. "Sorry," she whispered.

Packi glanced at Kay's ankle. "Sudden fracture?"

"I'm sorry, but I can't play with Helen," Kay said. "She's so pessimistic and she hates me. You can win her over."

Packi looked over Kay's shoulder to watch Beth with her pen in her mouth and Helen gesturing with wild arms. "It hasn't started well." Packi liked Kay too much to give her grief about dumping an unpleasant partner on her. "This is just a game." A big psychological game, she thought and refused to get mired in negatives.

Kay's relief brightened her face. "Thanks, Packi. Now remember, Helen's not as good as she thinks she is, and she never runs."

"That's just great." Packi groaned, but took a deep, cleansing breath. *It's only a game.* She calmed herself by picturing wildflowers in the slough, osprey overhead, cypress knees, Big Joe. *No, don't think about him.*

Kay nudged Packi's elbow. "Here's the player they've been stalling for."

A willowy blond with a finely crafted hairdo and store-bought body dumped her tennis bag next to court one and rushed toward the White Egret captain.

Packi studied the woman, recognized her formfitting, low-cut tennis dress. "Isn't that the girl who takes lessons from Collin?"

A spectator seated on the bleacher in front of them turned to confide to them, proud of her superior knowledge. "That's Lyla

Golden. Her husband is Danny Golden. You've seen them on television."

Kay winced. "She's your opponent on court three."

Shocked, Packi stared at the late arrival. *How can she be here with her husband dead in the morgue?* Packi watched for signs of grief or hysteria. She expected the woman's team to gather around her, give her hugs and condolences, but they called her onto the court and urged her to warm-up. Lyla Golden unpacked her racquet and loped onto the court.

I must be wrong, Packi thought. Oh, God! I told the reporter the dead man is Danny Golden. Didn't Deputy Teig say Mrs. Golden identified the body? Packi put her head in her hands. "I'll never touch another martini."

"Come on. You'll work off your hangover." Kay tugged at her arm. "Beth wants us to warm up."

Helen was on court three, talking with the dark-haired player from the opposition. "We'll try to give you a good match," Helen said, "but she's new to the team."

The White Egret player's eyes darted to Packi approaching from behind Helen.

What is Helen thinking? Dissension between us gives the opponents a huge psychological advantage. Packi broadened her smile and held out her hand. "Hi, I'm Packi."

"Sandra. Welcome to White Egret." The woman seemed relieved that Packi ignored Helen's faux pas. "And this is Lyla."

"Nice to meet you." Packi shook the younger woman's soft, pampered hand. "You look familiar, Lyla. Do you take lessons from Collin at Paradise Palms?"

Lyla pulled her hand out of Packi's grasp and took a step back. She shot a look at her partner, and Sandra paused to listen.

"I've been there," said Lyla. She tore the aluminum seal off a new can of yellow balls and handed two to her partner.

Packi had a different game to play. "So you're Danny Golden's wife," she said in a pleasant, conversational tone. "I've seen you on the commercials with him." Packi hated gushing, but wondered how this widow could be so heartless. *What makes her tick?*

Lyla flicked a sharp glance at Packi. "Yes, probably." Her coral pink lips pulled into an upward curve, uncovering bleached white teeth. She examined the third fuzzy ball and bounced it on the gritty court as if testing the ball's quality.

Packi waited for a hint of courtesy or sportsmanship and looked Lyla up and down, wondering if any part of her was genuine. *Is it possible she doesn't know her husband is dead?* Packi noticed a slight tremble in the young woman's hand. If she knows, thought Packi, she's one hard …

"Let's spin for serve," interrupted Helen, "and get this match over."

"Have fun, ladies," Sandra said in a humorless chirp.

The first game got off to a poor start. Helen double-faulted her second serve and complained about trees shadowing the court.

"You'll get this one, Helen," Packi called back at her partner. "You've got a great serve."

Helen humphed, but whistled a bullet into the serving box. The games seesawed between the teams. Packi didn't mind running down the balls Helen didn't try for and was happy when her partner put away shots within her reach. They lost the first set in a tiebreaker.

During the two-minute rest, Packi heaped praise on Helen for her bullet serves and well-placed drop shots. No need to point out her three double faults and her lazy feet. She figured that a confident Helen made for a winning partner.

"You were fabulous, Helen. Keep it up."

"You know, they're picking on you because you're the weaker player." Helen's brows met above her nose. "Put some power into your volleys. You're killing me at the net."

Packi hid a sneer behind her towel and mopped the sweat from her face. She couldn't control her glare, so she bent to get a drink of water. Helen maddened her, but might be right in one sense. Packi had targeted Sandra, trying to be kind to Lyla. She couldn't shake the idea that Lyla might be a recent widow.

The image of the body on the steel table entered Packi's mind and changed her perspective. *If Lyla knows her husband is stretched out in the morgue, and she's playing tennis...* Packi grabbed her racquet. "Helen, let's slam it at Lyla. She's having a bad day."

"Which one is that?"

"The blonde," said Packi. "You pick them off at the net, and I'll cover the rest of the court."

The Paradise Palms team sailed to a second set win. Sandra tried to cover Lyla's mistakes and became livid when they dropped the last game. Lyla withered under the disapproval.

As Packi waited for their opponents to get on the court for the third-set tie-breaker, Kay and Marilyn finished their match and arrived to sit on the benches to watch. Helen still basked in the glory of taking the second set. "I told you my net shots would break them."

Marilyn and Kay cringed at the braggart's bravado. Packi signaled her agreement to her friends, but patted her partner on the shoulder. "You were great, Helen. Let's do it again."

And they did. At 0-3 Lyla lost her composure. At 0-5 Lyla threw down her racquet and ran from the court. Teammates caught her at the tennis shop and tried to soothe her, but she would not return to the court.

Sandra approached the net and stuck out her hand. "Sorry. I guess this means we forfeit the game." She shrugged. "Something must be bothering Lyla."

Something indeed, thought Packi. Why would she hide her husband's death from her friends? Did *she* murder him? What's going on in that girl's luxurious life?

* * *

Beth opened the windows and cranked up the AC in the Lexus, while Kay, Marilyn, and Packi piled in. Packi spread a tennis towel out to protect the seat from her sweat, and her legs from the burning leather. Before she got her seat belt buckled, Beth revved the engine and sped out of the parking lot without waiting for Mary's SUV to follow.

Beth took a detour through the community to check out the houses and exclaim over the mini-mansions scattered along the two golf courses. Packi didn't comment. Interesting architectural lines, she thought, but I'm done with big houses—the headaches, the taxes, the waste. The guard shack's automatic arm released them from White Egret, and the conversation turned to their opponents.

"Great win on three!" Beth's volume filled the small car and brought other discussion to a halt.

"Thanks," Packi said. "Helen has a great serve."

"Helen?" Kay sniffed. "I watched that tiebreaker."

Their team captain adjusted the mirror to catch Packi's eye and changed the subject. "Why is lovely Lyla all bunged up?"

"Yeah. What brought that on?" Kay said. "I saw it, but couldn't believe it."

Packi shrugged, not ready to accuse Lyla of murder. "She seemed flustered or angry from the beginning. It went downhill after I asked about her husband, Danny Golden."

Beth snickered. "She didn't crow as if marrying money was an accomplishment?"

Packi let the remark slide. She'd heard of too many such money-motivated marriages right in Paradise Palms, mostly among the beginner golfers.

"What's going on with lovely Lyla?"

Packi wanted these women as her friends, to be a part of their group. She also wanted to share the burden of her suspicions and hoped the team could suggest the next move. She needed to trust them. "Can you keep a secret," she asked, "at least for the rest of the day?"

"Lay it on us," Beth hooted.

Packi exhaled and plunged ahead. "The guy at the morgue is, I think, Danny Golden."

Kay grasped Packi's arm and gaped at her.

Marilyn turned herself around in the seat with the seat belt straining against her neck. "But his wife just played tennis with you."

"That's cold," Beth said, her eyes wide in the rearview mirror.

"Exactly," said Packi. "Now you see why I doubted my identification of the man."

"But what did that deputy tell you?" asked Kay.

"That the wife came to the morgue." Packi shrugged. "But after two martinis, I may have heard wrong."

Kay held up three fingers.

"Even worse." Packi groaned and held her palm against her forehead. She wondered what other evidence the deputy may have shared with her. "I'd better call Deputy Teig."

She powered on her new phone and reviewed the call log for Teig's number. An unnatural silence filled the car while the occupants waited for the deputy to answer.

"Hello, Billy? This is Patricia Walsh, the witness from Hammock Preserve?" Packi shrugged at the women in the vehicle. "I'm sorry to disturb you again, Billy, but did you tell me that Danny Golden's wife identified the body?"

The tennis players strained to hear the faint sound of Teig's deep bass, but heard only the purr of the Lexus.

"Ohhh. I see," said Packi. "Well, I know where she is." She listened. "I just beat her at tennis."

The driver in the car behind the Lexus beeped to remind Beth that green means go. She waved him around and growled as he passed.

"Yes. Lyla Golden." Packi gave the tennis players a thumbs up. "Probably."

Packi raised her right hand. "No, I didn't tell the reporter anything else. I swear." She listened and bobbed her head. "Okay. You're welcome."

92

Beth made a left-hand turn and braked hard in a restaurant parking lot just as Packi ended the call. She threw the car into park and turned toward the backseat. "What'd he say? Is it Golden?"

"Yes, I wasn't hearing things. The wife identified Danny Golden." Packi paused for effect. "His first wife. They couldn't locate Lyla yesterday or this morning. They'll go to her home and break the news to her. Poor thing."

"Now I feel bad," said Kay. "She was playing tennis without even knowing her husband is dead."

"Yeah. But why wasn't she at home?" asked Marilyn. "How could she not know her husband was missing?"

"You don't suppose we should go back to comfort her when the police get to her door?" Packi raised both her eyebrows and waited.

"She may not be happy to see *you* ever again," said Beth. "I'll call their team captain and give her a heads up."

"You're right. Her friends will help her." Packi remembered Lyla's emotional state on the tennis court and predicted another melt down when the police paid her a visit. She pitied the woman. "I need to talk this out," Packi said. "Can we discuss this over lunch?"

"Let's eat," said Marilyn as she pushed open the door. "And we can figure out who killed Danny Golden at the same time."

"No way. Teig warned me again not to get involved in the investigation." Packi scooted out of the car and closed the door quietly while Beth made the call to Lyla's captain. "Besides," Packi said, "nobody said Golden was killed."

When an idea hit her, she paused. "But if I can convince the judge it *was* murder, Big Joe will be off the hook." She cringed at her choice of words and pictured the gator with a hook skewered in his throat. Worry over the body in the morgue had overshadowed the campaign to secure a reprieve for Big Joe. She needed to let the police do their job and get herself back on track.

"But wouldn't it be great if we could do both," said Kay. "We'd be heroes."

Packi heaved a long sigh. In spite of Deputy Teig's warning, she was pulled into the ugly business. Evidence kept popping up. Was this a murder investigation, an accident, or a sad case of suicide? Packi wished she hadn't seen the body and hadn't felt compelled to protect the alligator. But she had. At least she didn't have to face it alone now. She followed Marilyn, Kay, and the aroma of grilled onions into the restaurant.

The women settled in at a table and luxuriated in the breeze from an AC vent. Packi's mood lightened with the promise of food, and as her body temperature cooled. They treated themselves to chardonnay and ordered a beer for Beth.

Just as the waitress served the drinks, Beth joined them. She plopped onto a chair and reached for the frosted glass. "Their captain's on her way over to Lyla's now. Don't worry. Her team will take care of her."

"I hope so," said Kay, "but none of them looked like the nurturing type."

"Their stuck-up attitude is all for show," said Beth. "When one of their own needs help, they'll pull together. I think." She thunked her half-empty glass on the table. "Those trophy wives are a different breed."

While the tennis team discussed the dangers of wishing for too much money, Packi made a list on a paper napkin of possible murder suspects. "By Thursday morning at nine…" She got their attention. "I have to be in front of a judge at the Lee County court house."

"We have a match that morning," Marilyn said. "How can we…"

"We could forfeit," Kay said. "Not like we're anywhere near first place in the league."

Packi appreciated the thought, but shook her head. "Go play, but don't schedule me." She waited for Beth's nod of agreement. "Right now, help me think of a plausible scenario to give the judge, something that says Big Joe didn't kill Danny Golden. I need suspects and motives."

"What do you have so far?" asked Marilyn.

Packi tapped the pen on the napkin. "The oldest motive in the world—jealousy. I've got an ex-wife and a trophy wife." She groaned and tore up the napkin. "I've got nothing. I don't even know how he was killed."

"Now wait a minute," Beth said. "It's possible the ex-wife didn't appreciate being put out to pasture, and *she* banged him over the head with a frying pan. I used to play against Catherine before Golden traded her in for a younger model. She's as big as me and a strong net player."

Packi pictured a hulking woman throwing the man's two-hundred-pound body over her shoulder and making her way through the woods toward Joe's pond. "Not likely. No woman could dump a body alone."

"Here's a theory," Kay said, getting excited and leaning forward in her chair. "Trophy wife wasn't happy with the older man. She gets her boyfriend to strangle him, they throw him in Joe's pond, and she gets his insurance money."

"We'd have to find the boyfriend." Marilyn picked at the label on her beer bottle. "Maybe Lyla spent last night with her lover."

"But who would that be?" asked Kay.

"She spends an awful lot of time with Collin." Beth's voice carried authority no matter what she said.

"Collin, our tennis pro?" The women paused their forks above their salads. "Our Collin?"

"Let's be careful here," cautioned Packi. "We can't let gossip ruin a man's reputation."

Kay raised her hand to signal she had something to say. "That *is* Collin's reputation. My husband hears all that stuff when the tennis pros get together at the exhibitions." She shrugged her thin, brown shoulders. "My Mike is the pro at Orchard Creek, you know. He's mentioned a red Porsche in Collin's driveway on many evenings."

"Wow." Packi heaved a troubled sigh. Collin had always been pleasant to her. A few of the women were gaga over him, but Packi thought the handsome young man was too neatly packaged, too suave to be real. "We need a whole lot more evidence than a red Porsche before we accuse anyone of murder."

Packi pushed a tomato around her plate and listened to her teammates brainstorm about possible boyfriends, the weight of the body, the murder weapon. They gesticulated to make their points, threw out ideas, and laughed at the more preposterous theories. Their enthusiasm stimulated her own imagination and a plan fell into alignment. She interrupted the would-be Miss Marples. "Beth, when do you work at the real estate office again?"

"This afternoon, four hours."

"The employees will discuss Danny's death. Listen for their speculations. Poke around the files or something. Was there any business reason someone might kill him?"

"I'm not in the main office," Beth reminded her.

"I know, but the business partner may say something." Packi gasped at a thought. "If the police come to interview him, try to eavesdrop."

"I'd love to." Beth waggled her eyebrows, Groucho Marx style, grabbed a napkin, and wrote out ideas of her own.

Packi tapped her fingertip on the table in front of Kay. "Ask Mike about that Porsche and pick his brain about Collin. Men are worse gossips than women. He'll know something."

"Yes, boss." Kay grinned and sat back, satisfied with her assignment.

"What can I do?" asked Marilyn.

Packi thought. "How are you with finding public records? Divorce papers, prenuptials?"

"I can try." Little lines gathered on Marilyn's forehead. "I did an internet background check on my husband before we started dating. You'd be surprised how many guys have drug arrests or financial problems. I'll get Mary to help."

"Good," said Packi. "That reminds me. Deputy Teig asked if I'd told the reporter that Danny used drugs. Now how would I know that? How would Kevin Mitchell know that?"

"Drugs?" said Beth. "Now it's getting ugly."

Kay's fork clattered onto her plate. "Aren't murder and getting eaten by an alligator ugly enough?"

"Hey," interrupted Packi. "Joe didn't kill anybody. He's innocent."

"Okay, okay." Kay raised her hands in self-defense. "Sorry. I keep forgetting how this started." She laughed at Packi's fierce glare. "Don't worry, partner. With all the public support you've drummed up, they wouldn't dare kill your alligator. He's famous now."

15

The next morning the 3.5 team gathered on the bleachers under the awning. They had ten minutes before their regular nine o'clock tennis clinic to report their progress in the murder investigation and the campaign to get amnesty for Big Joe.

"Any luck with eavesdropping at the real estate office, Beth?" asked Packi.

"Nope. The police interviewed Arthur Maddox, Danny's business partner, at his home." Beth absent-mindedly repositioned the strings on her racquet while she spoke. "Everyone at the office shut up when I walked in, like they were afraid to talk in front of me." Beth pretended that being shunned by the group didn't hurt. "So I volunteered to work the desk this evening. After the others go home, I'll get a look at the files."

Packi admired Beth's resilience. "Keep listening," Packi urged. "Employees always know, or think they know, what's going on behind the scenes: bad company policies, angry clients, financial problems."

Four women, who had been practicing doubles on court two, came into the shade of the awning to retrieve their gear from the benches. Kay nudged Packi and pointed to the pale woman with freckled arms who stopped to brush grit from her shoes. Packi had to look twice to see Carla Baker under the straw visor with the extra large brim.

"Carla," Packi said as the woman zipped her racquet into its case. "I'm so glad Vern got home okay last night."

Carla's shoulders twitched, and she dropped her sunglasses. "Oh," she said in a low voice. "I didn't recognize you in your tennis clothes." She glanced at the others busy in their own conversations. "I've told no one about—about what I was afraid of yesterday."

"No, of course not." Taken aback, Packi lowered her own voice. "I'm sorry." She bent to pick up the sunglasses. "I won't spread it around."

Carla nodded and joined her tennis partners at the other end of the bleachers.

Spread what around? Why did I apologize? Packi wondered at the woman's odd behavior and her own response, but was distracted by Grace bustling toward them.

"You've got to see this!" She waved a cell phone over her head while she was still yards away. "I worked on it all evening. Big Joe has his own Facebook page." Grace shaded the screen from the sunlight and put it up to Packi's nose.

"You're kidding. Wow, Grace." Packi squinted, but without her glasses, saw nothing but blur.

"I posted this on my page and linked to nineteen different web sites asking people to flood Lee County officials with e-mails telling them to fight for our alligator." Grace jostled Packi's shoulder for emphasis. "We have 567 likes in less than twelve hours."

"That's great." Packi didn't know whether the numbers were great or not, but she didn't want to dampen Grace's enthusiasm.

"Sorry I'm late." Grace fanned her flushed face and plopped herself on the bleacher. "I just came from the grocery store. You've got kids out there with signs and a donation jar. Their class set up a defense fund for Big Joe."

Marilyn raised her hand. "I talked to the County Manager's secretary. Her office is swamped with phone calls and e-mails in support of your alligator. They're not happy." She tilted her head toward her teammate. "And I asked our resident real estate lawyer to find that legal stuff for you."

"I'm working on it." Mary feigned overwork with her wrist held to her forehead, but laughed. "Nothing yet, but I'll find an angle."

Helen grunted like one of the wild pigs at the preserve. "Are we playing tennis or what?"

The team met her glare with bewildered silence. Stalemated, Helen wagged her head in disgust and stomped out to the players' bench between the courts.

"What a…" Kay stifled a laugh and threw her hand at Helen's back. "An article in today's paper featured the science class that built the alligator raft. Your buddy, Kevin Mitchell, must've won over his editor."

"Great work, everyone." Excited by the team's successes, Packi wanted to brag too. "I baked coconut bars yesterday afternoon," she said, "and tracked Deputy Teig down after his shift."

"Do tell, girlfriend." Kay scooted closer. "What did you get out of him?"

Packi glanced at the clock. Five minutes before Collin started their lesson. She'd explain quickly. "No suicide note has been found, and he didn't drown," she said. "The medical examiner says the cause of death was blunt trauma to the back of the head together with a drug overdose."

She paused for a moment to let the tennis players absorb the facts. Several of the women had ideas flashing behind their eyes, others curled their lips in distaste.

Beth stood against a post with her arms crossed over her chest. "So he got high, stumbled into the water, and the alligator whacked him in the head? With his tail?"

Packi pursed her lips. "I asked Deputy Teig a similar question." She turned toward the group to emphasize her point. "The medical examiner said Danny was dead before he went into the pond. The divers retrieved the body before much damage was done, but his leg and foot were shredded."

Grace covered her ears while the others winced or frowned.

Too much information, Packi thought, and hurried to reassure them. "Joe didn't kill him."

As if trying to unravel the implications, Kay ran her hands through her chestnut hair. "You mean someone threw him into the water."

"That's what I think," Packi said. "The toxicology report showed a high level of oxycodone." That fact came out before she could stop herself. She hadn't intended to broadcast such personal information.

"Danny Golden must have had serious pain issues," said Kay. She leaned over to catch Marilyn's eye and get corroboration.

"I don't understand," said a woman with a lilting British accent from the far side of the bleachers. "Was it a drug overdose?"

Packi didn't recognize the owner of the accent and shrugged. "Could be." She then realized a small crowd had gathered, listening; women waiting for the tennis lesson, players coming off the practice courts or just arriving, a few supportive spouses, and Collin, the tennis pro. Broad shouldered, six-three, smooth tan, and dressed in crisp white, he eyed her from behind the bleachers. Packi's instincts told her to run.

Without a word, Collin strode onto the court, pulling the ball cart behind him. Half the tennis players dispersed, some followed him to the court, others left for the showers. Packi heard her heart throbbing in her veins and a hiss from the back row.

"You people sicken me." Carla sat alone with her anger, gripping the bench and leaning toward Packi and her partners. "A real person is dead and you make a game of it! Pretending to be detectives, dissecting it like one of Kay's idiotic reality TV shows."

Kay's eyes popped open. She jerked around to face Carla, but said nothing.

"Shame on you." Carla sprang to her feet. "Making a fuss over an alligator when a woman's husband is dead. Shame!" She pointed her finger at Packi. "Don't forget curiosity got the cat killed." Her racquet clanked against the metal seat as she grabbed her bag and stalked off.

"I'm sorry, Carla," Packi called after her. "I didn't…"

"I'll go calm her down," said Kay, trotting after the angry woman. "Be right back."

Packi felt alone though four team members sat on the same bench. Drained and chastened, she propped her elbows on her knees and put her head in her hands. *Is Carla right? Am I playing a game with the investigation?* "We should stop all this. Leave it to the police."

"Oh, no, Packi." Marilyn put her arm over Packi's shoulders. "Don't listen to Carla. She's still emotional after the police visit yesterday, and she's upset with Vern."

"Think about Big Joe," said Grace.

Packi looked up into her round, Irish face and wanted to do whatever the motherly woman asked. "You have a court date tomorrow," Grace said, "and have many people supporting you."

The prospect pushed Packi's shoulders lower.

"Listen, girlfriend." Beth softened her voice, but it still carried across the tennis court. "If you help your gator by finding evidence of a murder, isn't that the right thing to do? Hell, you gave the cops the man's identity."

Packi pictured the floating body, the morgue, and Danny Golden's quirky commercials. It's not a game, she thought. Someone murdered the realtor, threatened Big Joe, and is playing havoc with my peace of mind. I have to find out who.

"Carla's right about one thing," Packi said, sitting upright. "We should support Lyla. Innocent until proven guilty, right?"

Her teammates patted her back and took up their tennis racquets.

"I planned to bake blueberry muffins for Deputy Teig," said Packi, "but I think I'll bring them over to Lyla. She'll have visitors to feed. Who will go with me?"

Beth picked up Packi's cap from the bleachers. "Can't. She hates me." She patted the hat onto Packi's head and strolled on to the tennis court.

Marilyn nodded at Beth's bland statement. "I'll visit Lyla with you."

"What did she mean?" asked Packi, grabbing her racquet.

Marilyn shrugged. "Collin won't wait for us. Let's get on the court."

* * *

Collin skipped the warm-up routines and had the team running cardio drills within five minutes. The older women protested by throwing their hands at any ball out of their reach. Even Helen, Collin's biggest fan, complained and walked off the court for a drink, muttering under her breath.

"Did I miss something?" Sweat glistened on Kay's collar bones. She had spent time with Carla and missed the first ten minutes. "Collin is trying to beat us up," Grace said. Team members nearby groaned in agreement, but focused on the drill.

Up next, Packi ran down a short feed to her forehand and missed a backhand lob to the service line, but returned the overhead with a weak blooper. She hustled to the end of the line, out of breath. "Is Carla all right?" she asked Kay.

"Yeah, but she's upset about the funeral. Thinks we should go to support her and Lyla. Vern was Danny's golf partner, you know." Kay took off running after a forehand approach shot.

Huh, thought Packi. Everyone on her suspect list would be at the funeral. She analyzed her list while bouncing on the balls of her feet, awaiting her turn. She put her next crosscourt ground stroke back on the baseline, but drove the approach shot out of bounds.

"Get your head in the game, Packi," the pro yelled. "Get to the net."

Packi swore Collin hit the balls especially hard at her, feeding them at her feet or just out of her reach, so she'd look like a fool. What's he trying to prove? She lunged at a drop shot with spin on it, but the ball skipped away from her racquet. Packi glared at her tormenter. Rough workouts usually exhilarated her, but this was something different.

"Come on, ladies!" A smirk tightened Collin's upper lip. "You think your opponents will be easy on you?"

Why is he so hostile? Packi glanced at her teammates just as Collin humiliated Grace with a hard-driven baseline shot. *Did he hear comments about the morgue? Is he ticked off about the investigation?*

Beth, grim and determined, smacked an overhead back at Collin, making him flinch and protect his private parts.

"Is that all you got?" he taunted.

The team cheered Beth on, but she went down in defeat, as they all did, time after time.

Up next, Packi vowed not to let Collin's bully tactics intimidate her, but sweaty hands made her racquet slick. She gripped tighter and forgot about murder, Big Joe, and the smell of the morgue. She wanted only to drive that ball past Collin.

He fed a lob over her head. She sprinted to the back fence and leaped to return the ball.

"More follow through, Packi," Collin scolded. Next, he dropped a soft shot near the net. "Move your feet!"

She refused to quit and ran as if she could reach the ball. Before the ball bounced a second time, he turned his back to her and the court. "Let's pick up balls, ladies."

Packi gasped for air. Her heart pounded against her chest, but she refused to let him see he had run her into the ground. She hated that Collin had toyed with her. *So what. A pro beat me at tennis.* Packi gritted her teeth, leaving no escape for vulgar words. *What's his problem?*

She grabbed a plastic pickup tube and stabbed at balls along the back fence away from the others. She groused to herself and vowed to move Collin up on her list of suspects. *Perhaps the red Porsche in his driveway did mean something.*

Kay joined her and gathered a pile of balls onto her racquet. "Geez, what got into him?"

"Don't know." Packi blew sweat off her upper lip and glared at the tennis pro's back. "I intend to find out."

* * *

Collin eased up during the last half of the workout. Maybe he had proved his point or maybe Helen's whining got to him. After the lesson, the team grasped their water bottles with shaky hands and slumped onto the bleachers. They talked about groundstrokes, drop shots, their next match. Anything but the murder.

Packi dampened a towel and draped it around her neck, welcoming the icy shock. "Thanks for agreeing to visit Lyla with me," she said as Marilyn slid onto the bench.

"No problem." Marilyn took a long guzzle from an insulated cup. "Can we stop by the mission afterward?"

Packi mopped her overheated face and searched her memory for an earlier mention of a mission.

Marilyn looked over the rim of her cup. "The golf league's food drive. You don't mind, do you?" She looked startled or hurt. "I volunteered to deliver a load to Morning Star down on Edison Street."

"No," Packi hurried to reassure the woman. "That's fine." She bent to tighten her shoe laces, not because they were loose, but to give herself a moment to think. *Is this what it means to be part of the tennis team group? People assuming, filling your schedule for you? Buncotini, now a food drive.* Packi tugged at her laces and decided she liked her new status. Besides, hadn't she assumed the team's help with Big Joe's campaign?

Packi straightened up and smiled at her teammate. "Lyla's house is on the way downtown." If we drive in a big circle, she thought. "I'll pick you up about eleven-thirty?"

16

Packi pulled up to 2241 Spoonbill Lane to find Marilyn dragging donation boxes, the size of dog houses, from her garage. "Oh, no." She pictured driving up to White Egret Marina's security gate with the boxes strapped to the car and bulging from the trunk. She waved and exited the sporty little Audi.

Marilyn straightened up with her hand on her lower back. "Hey. You're early. I'm almost ready." She caught a plastic grocery bag that threatened to blow away and tucked it under a can of corn.

"Good job with the food drive, Marilyn. The golf leagues were very generous." Packi poked through the nonperishable groceries, impressed with the quality of the donations. "We have a problem," she said, motioning to the car.

Marilyn's eyes got bigger than her glasses. "Good Lord." She dropped her chin to her chest and studied the compact car. A grin tugged at the woman's lips, erasing tiny wrinkles around her mouth. She hooted and slapped Packi's shoulder. "We'll be the Beverly Hillbillies."

Packi couldn't resist Marilyn's laugh. Her own giggle started small, but grew to a full-blown belly buster. Soon the two women wiped tears from their faces and hung on to each other.

"I guess I needed a good laugh." Packi groaned and wiped the back of her hand across her cheeks.

"Can the boxes fit in the back seat, and we'll leave the top open?"

"Nope." Packi took a deep breath to regain her senses. "Too windy. We'd leave a trail of groceries on the highway."

Sober again, Marilyn glanced back at her empty garage. "I told Pete he could take the Chrysler. What was I thinking?"

"We'll figure it out." The crazy laughter left a heady optimism in its wake. Endorphins, Packi thought as she swelled with new hope for the groceries, for the investigation, for her life.

* * *

Packi showed her driver's license to the guard at White Egret and told him they were there for lessons with the club's tennis pro. No doubt bored with the parade of cars, he waved them through the gate. If he noticed the bags of groceries stuffed under Marilyn's feet and into every corner of the Audi, he didn't comment.

Marilyn juggled Packi's fresh blueberry muffins in her lap along with the tennis league directory. Her finger kept her place in the 3.5 team section, pointed to *Lyla Golden.* "We're looking for 921 Gulfview."

Packi already guessed the house. The one with massive stone pillars on either side of the grand entrance, copper flashing on the roof, a sleek white yacht anchored at the private dock in the back, and two squad cars parked in the circular driveway.

Oh no. Not again.

"Is that it?" asked Marilyn. "We should leave."

Packi groaned, thinking of Carla's reaction to a visit from the cops. "We'll leave, if she has friends there to support her, if not..."

The door chimes sounded hollow within the big house. Packi and Marilyn waited in the cool entryway shuffling from foot to foot until heavy footsteps echoed inside. A blast of air conditioning met them, and Deputy Billy Teig's silhouette filled the doorway.

"Mizz Walsh, I told you to stay out of this investigation."

"I know, Billy." Packi waved her hand to stop him. "We play tennis with Lyla and thought she could use friendly support." She held up the plate of muffins. "For Lyla."

Deputy Teig's huge chest rose and fell with a deep huff. "Detective Leland is almost done here. Maybe you can settle Mizz Golden down a little."

Packi heard keening coming from a distance, somewhere beyond the marble foyer.

Teig led the Paradise Palms women into a sunlit great room with a soaring expanse of windows and a view stretching to the Gulf of Mexico. Designed by Robb and Stuckey, Packi thought, up-scale Floridian in a Caribbean motif.

Lyla Golden sat on an overstuffed, leather sofa slumped against a man with her face buried in his chest. He stroked her hair more gently than his large hands would suggest. An uncle or older brother, Packi thought. She wondered if the widow learned sobbing in a high school drama class. Detective Leland raised her eyebrows at Teig and rose to her feet.

"Excuse me, Mizz Golden," Teig said. "You have visitors."

Lyla lifted her head and straightened her spine. She stared at Packi and Marilyn until recognition dawned. "What are you doing here?"

"Hello, Lyla," said Packi. "We came to offer our condolences and thought you'd need company after the officers leave."

Lyla pushed away from the man and leapt to her feet, knocking an ashtray off the table onto the white rug. She advanced on Packi with her finger pointed in accusation. "You're the one trying to save that alligator. How dare you!"

Dumbfounded, Packi's smile died on her face. She stopped at the edge of the area rug while Marilyn ducked behind Deputy Teig. Detective Leland moved her body into Lyla's path. The man tried to pull Lyla back into his arms, but she shoved him away. He retreated into the cushions.

Mrs. Golden continued her accusation from behind the coffee table, penned in by the officers. "That monster killed my husband, and you're trying to protect it?" After long seconds of shocked silence, the distraught woman lost her fire. Her pointed finger wavered. "Nobody cares." She moaned and sank back into the massive sofa.

At least her anger is sincere, Packi thought. "I'm sorry, Lyla. It's true I believe Big Joe is not a danger, but we're here as your friends."

Lyla pulled her knees up to her chin and hid her face in the crook of her arm.

In spite of the theatrics, Packi felt a kinship to the grieving woman. "We came to let you know that many people are praying for you. I'm sorry for your loss." She stepped forward to place a light touch on Lyla's arm. "My own husband died not long ago. I understand your pain."

The new widow looked up as innocent as a child. Real tears stained her pale face. "How could you know?" she hissed. "You're old. Your husband was old, not young, like my Danny. I'll see your alligator slaughtered and made into my new purse!"

Packi stumbled back, astonished and stung by the rebuke. A warm hand on her shoulder blade steadied her, comforted her. She turned to give Marilyn a thanks, but found Billy Teig behind her instead.

Teig stepped in front of Packi. "Are we finished here, Detective?"

"I have no more questions," Leland said. "Will you be all right, Mrs. Golden?" The detective shot a look of disapproval at Packi.

"I'll take care of her," the man said as he resumed his position next to Lyla.

"Thank you, Mr. Maddox," said Detective Leland. "We'll keep you apprised of any developments."

Though dismissed, and with Marilyn at the door ready to escape, Packi resolved to complete her mission. She sidestepped Deputy Teig to offer the plate of baked goods. "You have our sympathies, Lyla," she said with funeral-parlor kindness. "I baked these muffins for you or for your visitors. I'll leave them in the kitchen."

Lyla recovered herself and stood to escape Maddox's embrace. She tossed her mane of ash blond hair over her shoulder. "Don't bother." She screwed up her face as if to say, "Duh!" and pointed with both index fingers to her hips, her waist, and to her silicone breasts. "I don't eat muffins."

Packi narrowed her eyes and withdrew the plate. "Ah, I see." She smiled. "Some people *do* have that problem."

Deputy Teig coughed. Before Lyla's confusion cleared, Packi turned her back. She gestured for the deputy to follow her into the foyer where Marilyn waited with her hand on the doorknob, ready to bolt.

Packi glanced back into the great room where Detective Leland distracted Lyla with a last minute review. "Is that man a relative, Billy?" Packi asked.

"Art Maddox, a Suncoast Realty partner," Deputy Teig said. "And don't even think about it."

"Of course not, Billy," Packi said, protesting her innocence, "but I have a question. Was Lyla here when her husband left the other night?"

"Leave the investigation to us, Mizz Walsh."

"I know, I know," she said, "but did she see him leave?"

The big man groaned. "Mizz Golden wasn't here."

"Was there a fight, maybe an intruder?" Packi asked. "Did he leave voluntarily?"

They both turned to survey the pristine room staged like a model home: bamboo flooring, cream-colored rug, fresh flowers, artwork.

"What are you getting at, Mizz Walsh?"

"Did you notice the glasses and the man's wallet on the mantel above the fireplace?" Packi asked. "Danny Golden wore glasses tight enough to leave an indentation on his face. Why would he leave the house without them?"

Teig's head whipped toward the stone fireplace. His eyes became slits above his chubby cheeks. "And Mr. Maddox has his glasses on. I'll check it out." He motioned a thumb toward the door. "Please go."

"Yes, Billy." Satisfied that she'd helped the investigation, Packi turned to the exit. She offered the plate of muffins to Deputy Teig. "Do you want them?"

He pointed with two stubby index fingers to his belly. "Not with this body."

"Blueberry," Packi teased, putting a twinkle in her eye.

Teig opened the door for the women and glanced back at his fellow law officer. "Stick them in my cruiser."

17

Towering royal palms, imported to Fort Myers by Thomas Edison himself, lined McGregor Boulevard and greeted visitors to the City of Palms. Elegant, old homes, behind lush vegetation, and the occasional modern mansion, lined the north side of the street, hoarding the view of the sparkling Caloosahatchee River.

Packi drove past Henry Ford's winter home, Edison's estate next door, their expansive gardens, and the great inventor's laboratories across the street. Tourists queued up in the shade of an ever-expanding banyan tree, one of Edison's one-hundred-year-old experiments, to buy tickets to the must-see museum. Packi always felt if she looked hard enough, she'd see Tom in his white suit, sitting on the porch swing with Myna, or tinkering in Ford's garage.

"Turn here," Marilyn said, pointing down a less prosperous street, away from the riverfront and tourists.

Packi drove on as directed, but on alert, feeling out of place. They navigated the Audi through narrow, potholed streets with historic names in a neighborhood left behind by history. Men with white whiskers bristling in contrast to their black chins watched from sagging porch steps as if they had nothing better to do. Children, too young to be in gangs, played in the bare yards.

"Where are you taking us?"

"Don't worry. We're okay during the day," said Marilyn, leaning forward, turned off the radio, and tapped her nails on the console. "Almost there."

Morning Star Food Pantry turned out to be an old corner store with bars on the windows in a row of squat houses in need of paint and everything else. Leggy impatiens planted in the thin sandy soil along the broken sidewalk struggled to brighten up the place.

Packi pulled to the curb and popped the trunk.

"Hey, Marilyn!" A man greeted her from the doorway with an exuberant wave. He could have stepped out of a Naples yacht club. Khaki shorts, a blue fishing shirt in the Hemingway style, a full head of hair, bright teeth set in a tan grin. He bounded off the porch and took bags of groceries out of Marilyn's arms.

"You're a godsend," he said while grabbing another bag from the trunk. "The shelves are almost empty."

Her husband had been like that in their early years. Running, in charge, athletic. Hidden in the shadow of the Audi, Packi enjoyed the wash of memories. Surely, Ron had some of this man's smile, his joy of life. She peeked over the top of the car to survey his broad shoulders. He held the door open for Marilyn and disappeared into the building.

Packi blamed the extra heat on the midday sun. Her heart beat like an infatuated high school girl's. She dismissed the foolishness and remembered her mission. And her manners.

The man in the Hemingway shirt jogged back to the car for another load. She met him at the open trunk with an outstretched hand. "Hello, I'm Packi, Marilyn's chauffeur."

Surprised, he juggled a box of canned goods and took her hand. "Mark Hebron." He made a slight bow. "Marilyn's butler, servant, and valet." He enjoyed his joke.

Mark's calloused hand engulfed hers. A carpenter, she thought. Retired. He watched her eyes with his head cocked like a Doberman waiting for a command. She blushed beneath his long stare and pulled her hand away.

Inside the food pantry Marilyn took charge, directing Packi to the labeled shelves. Pasta, Soup, Canned Vegetables, jello, Condiments.

The organizational task took her mind off the man working at her elbow. He reminded her of a gentleman sailor, a distinguished beach boy. She got a kick out of the juxtapositions. A sincere playboy. Ha. She controlled her rampant imagination by arranging jello in neat stacks according to flavor.

Mark knew the routine. He grabbed a step stool and organized boxed crackers and cereal on the upper shelves. Without referring to labels, he shelved cans of tuna, many jars of peanut butter, and several jars of salsa. He put the single package of ground coffee in amongst the boxes of tea.

As she sorted through the donations, Packi called out each item for Marilyn's inventory sheet. "Two oatmeal," she said as she handed Mark the boxes to go in the cereal section. He smiled down at her from the step-stool. A grin eased across her face. Uncomfortable with the connection, she knelt to stock the lower shelves and tried to keep her mind on the task.

She listened to the tune he hummed. *Nowhere Man*, she thought, from the Beatles. With peripheral vision, she watched him work.

Stop it, Packi told herself. You're a widow for cripes sake, behave. She concentrated on organizing groceries, but anxiety made her clumsy. She dropped a can of peas and chased it across the linoleum. Embarrassment added to the heat in the small room.

"I'll go check to see if we got everything out of the car," Packi said, attempting nonchalance. She escaped through the screened door without waiting for Marilyn's response.

Packi found a jar of jelly under the passenger's seat and bent into the car to search the driver's side. Flushed from the effort in the confines of the small car, she grunted and extricated herself from the Audi, butt first. As she straightened up, she backed into a man standing on the curb. Startled, she jumped away.

Trapped between the black man and the open car door, the three feet between them wasn't enough. Adrenaline pricked her armpits. She thought to hop into the car and slam the door, but that would be rude.

The old man with the white whiskers smelled of whiskey and stale cigarettes. His yellowed eyes studied her. Packi glanced down the street and wondered why he'd left his front porch.

"Hello," Packi said, her mouth as dry as lint. She held up the jelly jar. "It almost got away."

His chin pushed his lips up to his nose as if teeth no longer stood in the way. He nodded once and shuffled toward the door of the food pantry with the strap of a limp cloth tote bag clutched in his fist.

"Henry!" Marilyn called from within the store. "Come on in. We're ready for you."

Disconcerted by her own foolish response to the man, Packi marveled at her teammate's comfort in the shabby neighborhood and her ease with the people. On the tennis court and at club functions, Marilyn fidgeted and blushed, but here she seemed at home.

Packi leaned against the fender to mull over her friend's transformation. Heat from the metal fender burned through her shorts. *Dang!* As she jerked away and brushed her hand across the seat of her pants, Packi noticed two women trundling toward her in flip-flops. Each woman had two children in tow and empty cloth grocery bags swinging from their wrists. Packi hurried into the food pantry to offer help.

* * *

Over the next hour, as word of the new delivery of donated groceries spread through the neighborhood, many people signed in to shop for the free food. Clients, Marilyn called them. Most chose wisely, filling their tote bag with staples and nutritious foods. Mark pointed out the pound of coffee to Henry who breathed in the aroma and tucked the treasure into his tote bag. The old man then parked himself on a bench on the creaking front porch and greeted his neighbors.

Packi found goodie-bags of candy, leftovers from the golf league's event, and urged parents to take a few pieces for the kids. She rearranged shelves as they emptied and took in a donation from a man who arrived in a BMW. Between client visits, Mark and Marilyn chatted and laughed. After Mark's third bad joke, Packi relaxed and joined in.

"So where are you from, Mark?" she asked, noting his Midwestern accent. The question broke the ice at many club events and tennis matches. Most people who migrated to Florida's gulf coast were from the Midwest, but with a fair number representing the east coast, Canada, and Britain.

"I'm a Hoosier. Indianapolis." He slit the tape on an empty cardboard box and flattened it. "How about you?"

"Suburb of Chicago."

Icebreaker number two. "What kind of work did you do before retirement?"

His face tightened. Packi glanced at Marilyn to get a clue to her misstep, but Marilyn concentrated on her inventory. To cover her gaff, if it *was* a gaff, Packi gathered plastic bags and debris from the donation boxes.

Mark recovered his grin. "Home building, subdivisions." He shrugged off his accomplishments and turned aside to stack flattened boxes for recycling.

Packi liked him, his warmth, his humility. She wanted to normalize the conversation, get to know him. Perhaps Ron wouldn't mind. "So where do you stay while in Florida?"

Mark gave her a quizzical look and stooped to gather cardboard.

He thinks I'm prying, Packi thought, embarrassed by her inept attempt at personal conversation. *I stink at this. He knows what I'm trying to do.*

She froze when a new thought shocked her. *Is he married?* With a guilty conscience, she narrowed her eyes to check for a wedding ring, but his left hand hid beneath the stack of recyclables.

Mark straightened up and tucked the pile under his arm. No flash of gold showed on his finger. Just when she thought he'd ignore her and her question, he winked like a leprechaun.

"I have a little place downtown, near the river." He pointed vaguely to the east and carried the cardboard out the back door.

Where? Near Edison's estate? On a yacht at the marina? She wadded the plastic bags in to a tight ball. *A wink? What does a wink mean?*

Unnerved, she swore off inept socializing with the opposite sex and vowed to be content alone. Her marriage to Ron, their many years together had been enough. She banished her melancholy and busied herself with straightening up the half-empty shelves.

At the door in the other room, Marilyn said good-bye to the last clients. The two women lumbered away with full tote bags and trailed by the cute little girls with ribbons in their hair. Marilyn flipped the sign in the window from *Open* to *Closed.* "That's it for today," she said. "Let's get back to Paradise Palms. I've got things to do before book club tonight."

"Ready when you are." Packi retrieved her purse from under the counter and slung it over her shoulder.

The sound of wood scraping against wood came from the back room as Mark pulled the door shut and slid the deadbolt into place. Packi scolded herself for studying his profile and glanced away as he took a cloth bag from a hook near the door. From the grocery shelves, he filled the bag with canned vegetables, tuna, and a box of cereal.

"Nice working with you," he said as he passed Packi in the middle room. The dimple in his left cheek made her smile and forget her vow to swear off men. He paused on the porch with a mischievous look. "Marilyn, you find the most attractive volunteers."

Marilyn laughed and shooed him away. "See you next week."

Mark dislodged a bicycle from the side of the porch and tied the tote bag to the handlebars. As Marilyn locked the security door, Packi shaded her eyes and watched him pedal toward downtown in the scorched afternoon. His image warped in the heat waves rising from the road. He didn't glance back.

"Are volunteers supposed to take food?" Packi asked.

Marilyn stopped in mid stride, with the store keys still in her hand. "Packi. He's a client—homeless," she said. "What did you think?"

A muscle gripped her stomach. "Oh." Packi's emotions spun. *How did I misjudge him? He's clean and neatly dressed.* She defended herself. *He smells good.*

"Don't feel bad." Marilyn hooked her arm through Packi's and guided her toward the car. "He's different. I don't know the whole story, but I hear he lost everything. His business, their house. His wife left him."

Packi unlocked the car door as if in a trance. Now she understood. The scuffed shoes, worn collar, shaggy hair. She slumped into the driver's seat and turned the ignition.

18

"We're discussing *A Land Remembered*," said Marilyn. She'd called late afternoon to thank Packi for her help at the food pantry. "You'll enjoy the stories about Florida's early days even if you haven't read the book. Come on. I'm the moderator and need moral support. Beth will be there and a few others you'd know."

Packi sighed. *I guess I could use something intellectual to get my mind off Mark. And off murder and the court hearing for Big Joe tomorrow.* Her misstep with the homeless man had put her in a funk for several hours.

She agreed to meet Marilyn at the clubhouse library at seven o'clock and then rushed to whip up a tuna salad for dinner. With her plate on the desk, Packi Googled *A Land Remembered,* read excerpts on Amazon, and looked forward to the evening's discussion.

Packi wheeled into the club parking lot with five minutes to spare. She spotted Beth's Lexus convertible idling in the far corner, with the top closed and windows up. Packi parked nearby and waved. Good, she thought. I don't have to walk in alone.

Beth cut the engine and worked her long body out of the car, but then slouched against the front fender, waiting.

"Hi, Beth. What's going on?"

"Hey." Beth looked away.

Packi came nearer. "Is the book discussion canceled?" She circled around, trying to get a better look at her team captain's face. "Dang, Beth! What happened to you?"

Beth fingered her fat lip and bruised cheekbone and bent to examine her injuries in a car mirror. "I'm telling everyone I got hit with a tennis racquet."

"But you didn't?" Packi's nerve endings perked up. Her mind leapt to conclusions about domestic violence. *Beth should be able to defend herself, and Rex seemed so pleasant.* Packi wanted to cry. *That's how abusers get away with it.* "Your husband?"

"No!" Beth jerked up straight, darting a sharp, but short, glare at Packi. Her shock said she told the truth. "I got mugged while leaving work an hour ago."

Packi gasped. Relief over Rex's innocence mixed with a new fear for Beth's safety. "The real estate office? But that's a good neighborhood."

Beth shrugged as if befuddled by the incident, but willing to put the scare behind her.

"What did Rex say? Did you call the sheriff's department? Did they catch him?"

"Rex wasn't home. Thank God." Beth fidgeted with her short hair, pulling it forward as if she could hide the damaged lip. "That wouldn't go well and the guy warned me not to call the cops."

"You must call the police."

"Well, I won't." She pointed to her face. "This is embarrassing."

Beth's irritation surprised Packi. Was her anger aimed at the mugger or something else?

"Listen," said Beth. "If my husband hears about this, he'll go nuts. And nag me to quit that stupid job. We need the benefits." She stepped back and folded her arms. "So I'll tell him you whacked me with your racquet when we both went for the same ball."

"We didn't play this evening."

"We practiced this morning. Close enough." Beth stood over Packi like a grade school principal. "Besides I stayed late at the office, copying papers to save your alligator. You owe me."

"Oh, Beth, I'm so sorry." Packi pushed her hair back from her forehead as if it would help her think. "How did it happen? Did he have a weapon? What did he look like?"

"Don't know. He jumped out of the bushes and yanked my bag off my shoulder." Beth rested her rump against her car. "I grabbed it back and swung at him. He decked me." She patted her swollen lip.

Packi cringed. She couldn't picture anyone judging Beth to be the victim-type. "He must have been big. Can you identify him?"

"Bigger than me." Beth shrugged. "All covered: hat, sunglasses, a bandana of some sort over his face, and a hooded sweatshirt. In this heat." She threw her hands up in disbelief. "He got everything. My cash, my credit cards. The jerk. If I had seen him coming..." Beth balled up her fists and clenched her teeth.

Packi moved a step away from the angry woman. "Why don't we call the police?"

"No."

"Can I at least mention it to Deputy Teig? He may know the kids in that area and can get your stuff returned."

"It wasn't a kid," Beth mumbled through puffy lips.

"Really? I just assumed," Packi said. "If he was all covered, how do you know?"

"Just an impression. I was on the ground, seeing stars when he ran off, but he didn't move like a kid." Beth pushed herself away from her car and tugged her shirt into position. "Let's forget this and go inside. Remember, the story is—you hit me."

Packi felt as guilty as if she *had* swung a racquet at her. "Okay. I can take the abuse, but I still think you should fill out a police report."

They turned to walk together across the parking lot.

"Thanks, partner," Beth said. "You'll save my job."

"The least I could do."

"Hey. I found something for your murder investigation." Beth grabbed Packi's arm and pulled her to a stop. "Suncoast Realty was in big trouble. Danny Golden is, I mean, *was* selling his yacht and his house in White Egret. I found warnings from at least five different banks, stuff from bankruptcy court, foreclosure notices on Fisherman's Wharf."

"Wow." Packi's mind clicked through actions a desperate man might take to salvage his business. One of which got him murdered. "Is that the fancy marina subdivision south of Naples?"

"Yep. Skyview Towers, downtown Fort Myers, too."

"The empty building?"

"Yep. Gorgeous new place and no one can move in because of the bankruptcy. He had partners. About a hundred names were listed. I made copies for you."

"Great work." The news allayed Packi's fear of going into court the next morning. "The lawyer told me to bring some argument in Big Joe's favor. This will do it."

Beth groaned and held up her hand to cut short the celebration. "The copies were in my stolen bag. Sorry, Packi. I wasn't thinking. After that guy..." Beth seemed embarrassed by her fear. She jammed her fists into her pockets and hung her head. "I could go back to the office."

"No." Packi sighed and leaned against the nearest car to think. She hated that Beth seemed so vulnerable. "We won't do that. You don't need them hassling you." She watched an ibis sail from its perch in a coconut palm. *When did paradise become so complicated?*

"Hey," Beth grunted and pulled a wad of paper from her pocket.

"What's that?"

"My gum."

Packi moaned, wondering if she was in the fight for Joe all by herself.

"No, look." Beth uncrumpled the torn, half sheet of paper and laid it on the hood of the car. "This was an extra copy, part of one anyway." She offered a pair of reading glasses.

Packi peered through the lenses and focused. There it was, above the ragged tear, just to the left of a gray blob of sticky gum.

19

David Stanford unfolded his scarecrow frame from the bench outside the court room. He rose quickly as if she were a valued client. "Mrs. Walsh?"

She approached with a smile and appraised the man. Forty-ish. A roomy blue suit. Wispy hair, left long over his collar. Packi itched to feed him high-calorie food and take a scissors to his shaggy hair. More than anything, she appreciated that he hadn't dismissed her as a kook.

The lawyer shook her hand with a gentle press. He guided her into an empty side room and shut the door. "We may have a problem. There is a complainant present to argue that the alligator at Gator Lake is a nuisance and must be destroyed."

Packi's heart sank. "Lee County?" She had hoped that the public support was enough to suspend the usual policy.

"No. A woman." He offered her a chair at the conference table and glanced at his notes. "Lyla Golden."

"Lyla?"

"You know her?"

"Yes, well, no. Not really," Packi said. "We've met." I never should have questioned Lyla at the tennis match, she thought, or dropped in on her with muffins. Dang. I should have stayed out of her sight, under her radar.

"She's the victim's wife," Packi said and watched the lawyer's reaction, hoping he wouldn't abandon the case as hopeless. "The wake is tomorrow."

"Oh." The man's eyebrow twitched, but in the next instant, he regained his composure. "She will be a sympathetic witness."

"What can we do?"

Stanford stroked his angular jaw. "We'll ask for the preliminary injunction as planned, before the temporary restraining order expires this afternoon. It's been my experience that this judge will grant a preliminary injunction as a matter of course. With the woman present, I'm not so sure." He motioned to the Manila folder Packi clutched to her chest. "What do you have to argue in the alligator's favor?"

Packi glanced down at the thin folder and shrugged in apology. "Deputy Teig gave me a copy of the coroner's report." She slid the paper out and across the table. "It says blunt trauma was the cause of death."

The lawyer accepted the meager documentation with grace. "Can you prove that the blunt force wasn't a result of the alligator attack?"

"No, but Deputy Teig said the victim was dead before he was dragged under the water. I think that means he didn't have water in his lungs."

"Okay, that's good."

"He had a high level of oxycodone in his blood stream."

Stanford twirled a pen between his fingers like a miniature baton. "So he may have been impaired. Perhaps he fell and was knocked unconscious on the shore."

"Or somebody hit him over the head and dumped him in the pond so the wildlife would clean up their mess."

He stared at Packi from beneath his raised brows. "Why would you think that?"

"The victim owed a large amount of money. People lost their investments in his real estate ventures."

"Very good, Mrs. Walsh." He tapped the table with his fingertips as if thinking in Morse code. "You've been busy. Any other documents? Company reports? An investor directory?"

Packi hesitated. Last night, she and Beth had scraped much of the gum off the torn list. Worried that the judge would get sticky residue on his fingers, they'd made a duplicate on the club's machine. She slid both papers from her folder and passed them to the lawyer.

"I tried," she said. "My friend was mugged last night and lost the papers along with her purse. This scrap was all we salvaged."

Stanford grimaced. "Sorry to hear about your friend."

He studied the partial listing for a minute before slipping the documents into a Manila folder. He then scrutinized the wall for so long that Packi wondered if she should fill in the air space, tell him about the mugger or maybe her suspicions that Lyla Golden got more than tennis lessons from Collin Bainbridge.

"We'll go with what we have," the lawyer said. "Leave it to me."

* * *

Packi looked for a jury box and the little wooden fence with the swinging gate to separate the audience from the lawyers and their clients. Judge White's courtroom lacked that grandeur, but did have a judge's bench and an armed guard at the side, wearing the same sort of uniform as Billy Teig.

In the audience area, groups of twos and threes whispered together, seated in rows of stationary chairs. In almost every case, the one talking and gesturing wore a suit. Lawyers. Their listeners wore a variety of clothes: jeans and tee-shirts, khaki shorts and polo shirts, sandals. Too casual to give respect to the court. Packi had worried over proper attire and had chosen the navy blue suit she'd worn to Ron's wake, but paired it with a summery blouse to cut the austerity. She shivered in the government building's air-conditioning and tugged the jacket tighter across her chest.

All these people brought their own problems to the court, thought Packi. None came to support Big Joe. She scanned the crowd for teachers from the school or fellow volunteers from the slough. She checked her watch. The tennis match had just begun. No hope of Beth or Kay showing up. Packi sighed, accepting that she and the lawyer were Big Joe's only hope against Lyla Golden's demand for vengeance. *Where is Lyla?*

Packi swiveled in her seat to survey the room full of anxious people. Across the aisle, a big man with a dark beard hiding most of his face lounged back in his chair with his arms crossed over his chest. His obvious disdain for the court irked, yet fascinated her. A biker, she thought, judging from the chain hanging from a side pocket of his worn jeans and the red bandana tied around his head. His heavy, black boots extended beneath the chair in front of him. He wore a sleeveless denim jacket, flaunting well-muscled biceps. Packi narrowed her eyes to make sense of the tattoos darkening his forearms.

With a start, Packi realized she was staring at the man—and he stared back. She jerked her attention in the other direction and refused to turn around again.

The unsavory people in the room apparently had no effect on Dave Stanford. To let the biker know she was not alone, Packi leaned toward the lawyer as if listening to advice. Mr. Stanford kept his counsel, his scrubbed-clean face intent and serious.

Packi reined in her curiosity about the crowd and their issues and concentrated on her own testimony. She wished her lawyer would give her guidance. "Dave?"

He raised one finger to shush her and scribbled notes on a clipboard propped on his bony knee. She leaned her spine against the hard oak chair and waited.

* * *

"Walsh versus Lee County," the bailiff announced.

Dave Stanford rose, tucked a file under his arm, and motioned for Packi to follow. Afraid to say the wrong thing, speak at the wrong time, or stand in the wrong place, she stayed close to the back of the lawyer's loose-fitting suit jacket. In front of the judge's bench, Stanford took Packi's elbow and pulled her out of his shadow to stand at his side.

"Your honor, my client, Mrs. Patricia Walsh, requests that the court grant a temporary injunction against Lee County forbidding the destruction of the alligator known as Big Joe. She..."

Judge White held up a finger to stop the lawyer's prepared remarks. His sleeves billowed as he leaned across his bench. "Good morning, Mrs. Walsh. Please tell me your story." His level gaze confirmed that he would brook no nonsense, waste no time.

"Sir." She cleared fear from her throat. "Good morning." A light on the wall behind the judge glowed through his white hair like God's halo on Judgment Day. He's just a guy in a robe, she reminded herself. She imagined him making tennis errors dressed in white socks pulled up to his knees.

Packi relaxed and told the story of Big Joe. She talked about seeing the alligator during her morning walks and introducing slough visitors to him. She described the children's excitement over the gator, the science class, and the school's construction of the raft.

His Honor listened as if he had all day, so Packi continued. "Children have painted posters and collected money to help save Big Joe. People of all ages want the alligator to survive."

"*I* want that alligator dead!" The shout came from the back of the room.

The judge banged his gavel. Every eye in the courtroom turned toward the blonde struggling against a young man in a suit. Other than her curses and the judge's gavel, the room went silent.

"You have no right," Lyla Golden screamed as she struggled with the man who appeared to be her lawyer.

"Bailiff." Judge White's voice boomed from the bench. "Restore order."

"This is ridiculous! My husband is dead!"

The officer of the court grasped Lyla's arm and half dragged her, half escorted her to the double doors in the rear of the courtroom. She wrenched her arm free. "I'm going." Lyla set her jaw hard, straightened her dress, and patted her hair into place. Before stepping into the hall, she sent a glare at Packi that could have split atoms.

Packi chose not to take the widow's anger personally. She sensed real emotion behind the woman's outbursts, but was it grief or guilt? Either way Packi pitied her. She turned back to the bench to continue her testimony, but Judge White's scowl stopped her.

"Thank you, Mrs. Walsh," he said. "Counsel, approach the bench."

Packi retreated to the nearby table while Dave Stanford did a quick step to the bench. He was joined by the lawyer representing the county, a girl with frizzy, red hair, and wearing a gray suit with a string of pearls. The three of them spoke in low tones, His Honor asking questions, listening, frowning. Stanford produced the clean copy of the list of investors in Skyview Towers. The judge skimmed the document, returned it, and then dismissed the lawyers with a bob of his chin.

"Mrs. Walsh," Judge White said.

Packi got to her feet, using the table to steady herself.

"I am going to give you a thirty-day extension to the Temporary Restraining Order."

Packi flashed a look at her lawyer for an explanation, but he made a slight motion to keep her quiet.

The judge continued. "Lee County, as land owner of Hammock Preserve, has jurisdiction over the determination and disposition of nuisance alligators. You would do well to bring your case to them. Miss Curtis has agreed to give your position full consideration." He glanced toward the red-haired attorney.

"Request for Temporary Injunction denied." The gavel banged. "Next case."

* * *

"We did better than expected," Dave Stanford said. He and Packi sat on a backless bench in the marble hallway outside Judge White's courtroom.

"What did he mean by *jurisdiction*? Is Big Joe in the clear or not?"

"Not yet. Lee County has the say-so. It's up to them to decide whether your alligator is a nuisance or not."

Packi's heart sank. "We have thirty days."

"Exactly. And that was a gift."

"Now what do I do?"

The attorney considered the question and answered in his slow deliberate way. "Convince the county board members that Big Joe is no more dangerous than any other alligator and is more valuable alive than dead."

"I see." Packi's mind already rolled out a new twist in the campaign to protect Joe.

"For what it's worth, Miss Curtis seemed sympathetic," he said, "but it probably won't be her call. The county has their procedures. I'll help where I can."

Dave Stanford showed Packi to the courthouse exit, held open the door, and pointed toward the parking deck on Third Street. The judge's decision, Lyla's outburst, and the surly looks from people waiting their turns outside the courtrooms had her on edge and upset. She wished the lawyer would escort her to her car, but wouldn't think of asking. He rushed off to his next client like Ichabod Crane on a mission.

20

Parking garages reminded her of crypts. Low ceilings, empty echoes, dark. With Beth's mugger stuck in her mind, Packi marched up the garage stairs giving her best imitation of a non-victim. She gripped her nail file, flung open the door to Level Three, and held her breath to hear every sound. Street noise came from below.

Her heels clicked on the downward ramp, announcing her presence. She hurried to where she'd left her car. *Wrong way?* Packi retraced her steps, pressing the Audi's electronic key, listening, and pressing again. *Level Three, right?* She clutched her purse under her arm and kept walking.

A car engine revved on the level below. Its tires pulled at the cement as the vehicle took the tight turn onto the ramp. Packi thought of the driver. Someone just like her? Or a thug to drag her into his backseat? She slipped into the shadow of a support post.

The car ascended to Level Three and inched toward Packi's hiding spot. As the SUV approached, she spotted a female at the wheel craning her neck to find a parking spot. Packi chided herself for imagining the woman a menace and stepped from hiding. The sound of the car faded, leaving an eerie silence, except for...

Too late, her ears picked up another sound. Close. Footsteps, heavy boots. Between her and the exit. Packi froze and dared to turn toward the dark silhouette approaching her. She backed into the cement post. The edge of her nail file dug into her palm. The police will want details, she told herself. Six-two, two-hundred-twenty, beard. She caught her breath. The biker with the sinister glare came out of the gloom.

Run, she thought, but stood like a raccoon caught in headlights on a country road.

"Hey, gator lady," the biker said. His deep voice echoed off the low ceilings.

Packi faced him and stood as tall as her spine would allow. She looked him hard in the eye, determined not to flinch.

"Heard what you told the judge 'bout the gator." His ragged mustache covered his lips and moved as he spoke. "My kid loves that gator."

Packi's knees threatened to give way, so she steadied herself on the nearest car. "Oh."

"It ain't right some dude got himself killed, and they blame the gator." The biker crossed his bulging biceps over his chest and glared down at her.

She tried to withstand the force of his stare, but flinched, wondering if that woman in the SUV would hear her scream.

The bearded man hitched up his jeans, which clung to his slim hips, and slipped two fingers into his side pocket. He held out a crumbled bill toward her. Packi stared at the twenty, but couldn't move. Don't be a fool, she thought. This could be a trap.

He straightened the bill as if its appearance caused her reluctance. He folded it lengthwise and held it out again between his first two fingers. "For that lawyer you got." With a thrust of his beard, he urged her to accept his gift. "They ain't cheap."

"No. No, they're not." Still wary, Packi reached for the cash, ready to bolt if he tried to grab her. She pulled the bill from his fingers. "I'll add it to the fund."

He moved out of her personal zone and resumed his crossed-arm stance. A crooked smile emerged from within the beard. "Me and my kid helped build that raft."

Surprised, she smiled and looked into his face. He wasn't young, but he wasn't old, just weathered. "Thank you…"

"They call me Flanigan." He produced a business card from his back pocket.

Her hand trembled as she angled the card to bring the words into focus. "Two Veterans and a Truck," she read. "Furniture movers." That explains the biceps, she thought. Hard, honest work.

"Yeah," Flanigan said. "Been doing it for fifteen years." He pointed at the card with a calloused index finger. "You ever need help—anything."

Packi wrapped the twenty around his card and slipped them into her purse. "Thank you for the donation—Flanigan." The familiarity still didn't sit well. "And for the offer to help. I'll keep you in mind." She caught herself gawking at him, his clothes, tattoos, and chains, and tried to reconcile the biker stereotype with the good man beneath.

"Good bye, Flanigan." Packi pushed the button on her key fob and pointed it toward the next ramp. The Audi beeped from the level above. "There it is." She gave the biker a nervous shrug and scurried toward the ramp.

"I'll wait here till you find your car," Flanigan said. "I got your back."

* * *

As amiable as Flanigan had been, the incident had shaken Packi. Her pulse raced until she maneuvered the Audi out of the garage. She paused for a minute at the stop sign. The air seemed cleaner, the sunlight brighter than she remembered.

The exit sign forced Packi onto a one-way street. *Now what? Where's Cleveland Avenue?* With bravery leftover from surviving the garage and finding her car, she chose not to consult the GPS and nosed the car into the narrow street.

She shaded her eyes and peered down rows of sturdy, old buildings, some left over from a time when Fort Myers really was a fort, repurposed now into hotels, restaurants, and offices. A few people roamed the streets, poking into shops, carrying familiar mocha latte cups.

Packi oriented herself with the river on the north and circled the streets of downtown looking for directional signs. Orange barrels had replaced the street signs. Several roads were closed for a special event, others for construction. The road she wanted arched over an intersection full of traffic, but wooden barriers hemmed her in.

She started again at the river, driving along the sparkling Caloosahatchee, the marina, and the elegant high-rises, careful not to get pulled onto one of the mile-long bridges over the river and ending up in North Fort Myers and way off her route. She was most afraid of going too far east—into the area of town with street names listed daily in the Gazette's police blotter section. She parked at the curb near the old post office building to get her bearings and even considered dragging out the GPS.

Across the street, a tour group listened to a guide as he pointed out the columns of the abandoned post office and the two sculptures at the foot of the steps. Years ago, she and Ron had enjoyed that walking tour and had taken dozens of pictures of the post office's ornate ceilings and carved molding, all peeling and succumbing to years of neglect. Happy banners now fluttered outside, announcing that an art center had moved in. Scaffolding indicated that money had been found to refurbish the grand building.

A bicyclist stood behind the walking tour, apparently riveted on the guide's spiel. His shape looked familiar, his size. Packi squinted through the windshield, trying to separate the cyclist from the tour group and from the shadow of the banyan tree above them. She pictured the cyclist putting a box of oatmeal on the upper shelf, and a grin jumped to her face.

She stepped out of the car. "Mark!"

The bicyclist's head jerked up. He hopped onto the pedals, wheeled across the street, and bumped over the curb with a smile from ear to ear.

"Shouldn't you wear a helmet?" Packi allowed a twinkle in her eye to soften the reprimand.

"If I find one, I will," he said, brushing his hand over his shorn head. "This noggin can take a beating."

She wondered who had given him the buzz cut which made him look like retired military. They stood for a moment, sizing each other up, comfortable with the silence.

Mark watched her with that Doberman attentiveness. "Would you care to take a walk?" An ironic smile twisted one side of his mouth. "If you don't mind being seen with a homeless man, I'll show you a few sites visitors usually miss."

Packi pushed aside the guilt she felt for being a part of society that thought of the homeless as *them*. "I'd love to," she said. "After my morning in court, I can use the exercise."

They strolled with his bicycle between them beneath a canopy of trees hung with Spanish moss. He prodded her with questions about her morning. She told him about the tennis team's efforts to defend the alligator, the judge's decision, and Lyla's outburst in court. She even told Mark about her foolish fear of Flanigan.

"You were right to be afraid," said Mark. "Never trust strangers."

Packi looked sideways at the man she had met the day before. What an ironic thing to say, she thought. Something in the recesses of her brain rattled her good mood.

* * *

Mark and Packi left the traffic and tourist area behind and walked down quiet, tree-lined streets. The area had a historic feel though curbs were broken and weeds grew through cracked sidewalks. The shade and the breeze coming off the river made the hot day almost pleasant and helped Packi de-stress. She dominated the conversation for several city blocks.

Under a large banyan tree where green moss stained the sidewalk, Mark stopped and waited for Packi to take a breath. "Sorry to interrupt."

"Oh, God. I've been doing all the talking." Packi covered her mouth. "I don't usually… You're probably bored."

"Not me. I enjoy listening to you." A dimple showed in Mark's clean-shaven cheek. "But this park is worth seeing." He led her down a flagstone path and leaned his bike against a bench. "Every tree in the park is a palm."

"Oh, look. They're labeled." Packi hurried to the nearest tree to read the plaque. "Cabbage palm, Australia."

The next one read, "Bismarck palm, Madagascar…"

"This one's from India."

They moved from tree to tree. Packi became engrossed in the amazing variety of shapes and sizes and enjoyed the mental trip to exotic places. "Here's a monster. Banana…"

She screamed and staggered backwards. Two eyes stared from between the huge leaves. The rest of the man stood in the shadow of the banana palm's thick mass. Adrenaline urged Packi to run, but her feet did not obey.

"It's okay, Jake," Mark said, taking Packi's elbow. "The lady is with me."

Still on the balls of her feet, ready to bolt, Packi stared. A ragged suit coat hung from bowed shoulders. Whiskered lips folded over empty gums.

"Back away," Mark whispered. He put his hand to the small of her back and guided her away from the banana palm. "Jake gets agitated."

"You know him?"

"From the shelter. We see him once a week or so."

"He looks…" Packi glanced over her shoulder. An eerie presence lingered in the shadows, but the man had disappeared.

"Jake has issues," Mark said. "He should be hospitalized, but this is his choice."

"Is he dangerous?"

"Doubt it. He's more likely to hurt himself," Mark said, "though I'd better get my bike. It's my only transportation. Jake wouldn't know how to ride, but he might decide he needs it."

Packi's heart still pounded, but she figured her anxiety was her own problem. She surveyed Mark as he retrieved his bicycle. *How could he be homeless? Jake was the stereotype. Jake had issues.* Doubt crept in. *Could Mark have hidden mental issues? A history of drug use? A rap sheet?* Packi tensed her muscles and wished she'd stayed at Paradise Palms.

"I was lucky to find this baby." Mark kicked up the kickstand and rolled the bike toward another group of palms.

Find? As in stole? She scanned the isolated park and wondered where all the people were. How'd she let him lure her so far from the main streets? "Do you mind if we start back to my car? I've seen enough of the world's palms."

Mark followed her gaze around the park and seemed disappointed that her enthusiasm for the palms had died. As they walked into the sunlight toward the old post office, he pointed out the firefighter's memorial and the line of buildings that marked where the stockade walls of Fort Myers once stood.

She didn't ask questions. His words reached her ears, but withered there.

He stopped when her car came into view and leaned the bike against his hip. "I'm sorry if Jake scared you."

How could she say that Jake was only a fraction of her fright? My trust in you scares me, she thought, my gullibility. The sight of her Audi comforted her. She wanted to turn the ignition, slam the door, and leave this attractive stranger in the rearview mirror.

"That's not it," she said. "I'm distracted by the court stuff today and thinking about Danny Golden. Lyla blames…" The sentence died in her mouth as Mark scowled down at her.

"You know Danny Golden?" A storm raged in his eyes.

Packi fingered a button on her blouse and pulled the collar closed. She took a step toward her car. "No. No, I…"

Marks eyes narrowed and drilled into her.

"The victim," she sputtered. "He's the man in the pond."

Mark's lips twitched as if zapped by static electricity. "Oh." The bike's metal parts rattled as he gripped the handlebars. "The lying son of a bitch deserved to die." He thumped the front tire on the sidewalk.

Mark's anger frightened her, and his satisfaction with the news of a man's death was too much. Packi turned and hurried toward her car.

"Wait! Don't go." He swung his leg over the bike seat. "You need to understand what happened."

The intensity in his voice set off alarm bells. She broke into a run with her hand in her purse, fumbling for the key fob. *Where is that thing?* She reached the driver's door and darted a look from over her car at her pursuer. He'd stopped at a safe distance.

"Let me explain," he pleaded from the sidewalk where he straddled his bike.

Packi dumped her purse on the hood of her car and searched through her junk. *Dang.*

"Please, Packi—Mrs. Walsh, let me tell you my story." He rolled his bicycle forward.

"Stay where you are!" Fear sharpened her words.

Mark held out the palms of his hands. "Okay. I'll stay here, but don't leave this way. I want you to know what happened." Worry and the hint of a dimple, replaced his angry scowl. He became the Mark she'd met at the food pantry.

Packi swept her stuff into her purse. *Is he going to confess to killing Danny Golden by accident? Maybe in anger?* Curiosity dampened her fear, but she kept the car between herself and Mark.

"Go on." Her heart pounded against her ribs as if demanding to get out. She leaned on the roof of the Audi for support.

"I'm broke," he said, "bankrupt because of that fast-talking bastard. Danny Golden." He spat out the dead man's name as if it was an obscenity. "What a con man. His face plastered on commercials all over TV."

Packi raised her eyebrows at Mark's resurrected anger. He pursed his lips and calmed himself.

"I invested in a high rise." Mark motioned toward the waterfront, to a line of condo complexes towering above live oaks and palms. "Golden had to know that his Skyview project was dead, but he insisted I'd get a good return. He claimed he had investors and banks to back him. He believed all his own bull…" Mark clamped his mouth shut. "Sorry."

He got a hold of his rant and took a deep breath. "They showed me bank statements. All good, I thought, but the documents were fakes. Golden knew his little empire was collapsing. He needed my money—and everyone else's to pay off the Jersey boys."

"Who?"

"The mob. They invested union funds in Florida," he said. "Everybody got caught up in the growth and promise of quick returns. I was guilty, too." Shame aged Mark's face. "I never thought our economy would collapse. We'd always need housing. For twenty-seven years, I gambled and won. Then I bet everything I owned and lost."

"You must have had savings." Packi tried to sympathize, but remembered how Ron squirreled away ten percent of every paycheck, how he hated risk.

"The business owners I know put every dollar back into their companies. I did." Mark held up both hands as if in defeat and helpless disbelief. "I borrowed millions for land for future subdivisions east of here. The value fell by 70% in one year." He snorted in disgust and looked for answers in the Spanish moss hanging above their heads. "I never imagined the collapse. I tried to hold on, and ran up my credit cards to pay my vendors and employees, but the bank took the land and all my collateral."

Packi made a second assessment of the proud man astride the battered bike, his clean shirt, worn gym shoes, and beaten eyes. She pitied Mark, but felt compelled to point out the flaw in his anger at the dead man. "Maybe the same thing happened to Danny Golden."

Mark's cheek twitched, but he then conceded. "Rumors say he leveraged too many projects with banks all over the state: Miami, Naples, Captiva. When one bank called his loan on the Fisherman's Wharf subdivision, his other projects fell like dominoes. His investors from New Jersey took a beating."

So that's why he's dead, Packi thought. She pictured guys with broken noses and black suits dumping his body in Big Joe's pond.

"The building industry collapsed in Indiana, too," Mark continued. "I laid off my employees, mortgaged my home, but it wasn't enough. I lost my business."

Mark's anger dissolved into sadness. He lowered his gaze and picked at the peeled paint on the bicycle frame. "When the money disappeared, so did my wife. Stress wore her away. I tried to protect the house, but she lost that, too. My daughter dropped out of college. They both hate me for ruining their lives." Mark dragged his shoe along the crack in the sidewalk. "They don't believe I can put our lives back together."

A surge of anger shot through Packi at the woman who had been this man's wife. His story rang true. In spite of her apprehension, she cared. "Do *you* believe you can make it right?"

He raised his face to her with a spark in his eye.

"I lost a $200,000 deposit on a condo in Skyview Towers." Mark pointed upward at a high-rise building on the riverfront. "Someday I'll own that penthouse."

Packi smiled at his renewed energy. "How's that going to happen?"

"Madam, I have my ways!" Mark's shoulders relaxed. "I'm saving every penny I earn. The Victoria House on Hendry Street hired me as maître d' and I'm good at it. That money goes for materials and interest on a house in bad shape on Poinsettia Street." He held up his carpenter hands for proof. "I convinced the bank to give me the house cheap, interest only, rather than let it fall apart. After I repair the place and flip it, I'll buy another and another."

Packi crossed her arms over her chest and marveled at his determination. "So that's where you stay?"

"Not yet, too much mold." Mark looked at her out of the corner of one eye. "I'm sort of the caretaker at another place."

Okay, Packi thought, respect his privacy. There was something he was hiding, but she admired his tenacity and work ethic. She stepped out from behind her car and stood at the curb facing him with no barrier. Packi let her arms fall to her sides in a helpless gesture and found the car keys in her skirt pocket. She jangled the keys and laughed at how foolish she'd acted.

"Thank you for the tour, Mark." She wished they could return to the easy banter they shared at the food pantry, but a gulf had widened between them. It's not to be, Packi thought, and offered her hand for a formal good-bye.

"It's been a pleasure to meet you, Mrs. Walsh." He bowed like a French nobleman, took her hand, and kissed the back of her fingers.

"Good luck to you, Mark."

Her fear of him had gone, but so had her schoolgirl attraction. She settled into the Audi's front seat and started the ignition, but her eyes went to the rearview mirror. Packi watched until Mark peddled around a corner and out of her sight. As she drove back to her own world in Paradise Palms, she imagined him salvaging one abandoned house after another and making them beautiful.

21

Packi kept her thoughts about Mark Hebron to herself as she inched her way through traffic along Summerlin, looking for the funeral home. She was certain that Lyla Golden didn't want Packi at her husband's wake, but Carla insisted that the club's tennis teams attend to represent Paradise Palms. Kay had knuckled under to Carla's dramatic pleading and organized the outing for the 3.5 team. Packi planned to stay in the background, maybe outside, and out of Lyla's sight.

"On your left," said Kay from the passenger seat, pointing with her GPS unit. "Turn at the light."

Cars lined up in the road, waiting to enter the funeral home's packed parking lot. A traffic cop waved the Audi away and into a nearby shopping mall. "I guess we should have expected this," she said. "His TV ads made him famous around here."

"Or infamous," Kay said. "His murder and all the publicity about Big Joe has people talking. They all came to get a look. Maybe your protesters are here."

"No way." Packi gasped at the thought of creating such a spectacle. "They'd never desecrate a funeral."

"Relax. I'm kidding."

Kay's toothy grin took the edge off of Packi's nerves, but by the time they walked to the funeral home's door, her apprehension over confronting Lyla again was back in full bloom. The sight of her teammates waiting outside the front door bolstered her.

"I had nothing to wear," Marilyn said as a greeting. "Is this okay? I went shopping."

The understated dress fit her well. "You look great," Packi said. Unused to seeing the team in dresses and make-up and with their hair styled, she had to look twice to identify a few of the women. She decided she preferred them all in tennis clothes, barefaced and sweaty. Here, they seemed uptight, especially Beth, who had dabbed make-up over her fat lip, but still seemed self-conscious about it. She hadn't said a word while the others gossiped and twittered—stalling the visit to Danny Golden's casket.

"Are you okay?" Packi asked.

"I'm fine," Beth said. "I shouldn't have come."

Marilyn filled in the blanks. "Suncoast Realty fired her from her job."

"No," Packi said. "But why?"

"They say they're downsizing in the aftermath of Danny's death." Beth shrugged. "They've been treating me like a pariah all week." She sighed and ran her fingers through her no-nonsense haircut. "I really needed the health benefits. Insurance is so expensive."

The tennis team offered encouraging words, but Helen interrupted, pushing herself into the group. "It's too hot. Why are we standing out here?" she asked in her nasal whine. "Let's get this over with."

The woman's gruffness irritated Packi, and Kay arched her eyebrow, but Helen was right. They had come to pay their respects. Packi figured she could hide from Lyla in the crowd. Besides, she needed the air conditioning, so when Helen yanked open the heavy wooden door, she followed.

Inside, the line of visitors crowded the lobby and snaked from room to room.

"This is ridiculous," Helen hissed. "I'm not staying. Let's get out of here." She waited a moment, expecting support from the team, but the women ignored her complaints. They talked among themselves and settled in at the end of the line. Helen stalked off toward the ladies' room.

"There's Art Maddox," Marilyn said, nudging Packi's elbow. She pointed through the lines of mourners to a man standing against the wall, off to the side.

Packi peered through the mass of bodies. Taller than most, Maddox stood out over the crowd. He looked the same as when she'd seen him at Lyla's, but less stressed, like a man uninvolved with the surrounding chaos. As Danny Golden's business partner, Arthur Maddox was on her list of suspects. She maneuvered herself to get a better view. Steam rose off the coffee mug in his hand.

Maddox spotted the women staring at him. He raised his mug in acknowledgement, but then smiled, as if he'd been welcomed, put the mug on a side table, and came toward them.

"I'm outta here," said Beth. "I don't want to see that son of..." She held up her hands to stop herself. "Come get me when you get near the front of the line. I'm going to find Helen."

"Let her go," said Kay as she watched Beth disappear into a side room. "I don't blame her for being upset, but a layoff after the owner's death seems expected. I'm sure her boss was just doing his job."

Packi agreed. "He seemed pleasant enough, concerned about Lyla." Maybe too concerned, she thought.

The man sidestepped the last of the crowd. "Thank you for coming," he said, bending down to shake hands with Marilyn. "You're part of Lyla's tennis team, aren't you?"

"We're on different teams," said Kay as he grasped her hand. "From Paradise Palms. Competitors."

"Ah, but I remember *you*," Art Maddox said, taking Packi's hand into his cool fingers.

An accountant's soft hands, she thought, unimpressed. He could have been handsome in his younger years, but now appeared too serious and pasty white. She wondered when he'd last visited the beach or played tennis in the sun. Packi gave him a polite smile, trying to read his eyes.

"Thank you so much for visiting Lyla's home in her time of need," Maddox said. "She truly appreciated your thoughtfulness."

"Lyla threw us out," Packi reminded him.

Marilyn poked her with an elbow.

"She felt so bad about her outburst," he said. "She was in shock. Please forgive her."

Shock, thought Packi. Could shock have caused Lyla to show up screaming in court on the day of her husband's wake? Maybe that's the woman's natural state.

Maddox put on a pleasant smile, and turned to Kay and Marilyn. "You know, I played tennis in my youth."

It could be true, thought Packi, sizing up Danny Golden's business partner. A strong man with long arms would be great on the net. Could those arms also carry a body to Big Joe's pond?

"Let me thank you for your kindness to Lyla," he said. "I'll arrange for a tennis court for you and your friends at White Egret Marina, followed by lunch in the club house. What do you think?"

The line had moved along, bringing them into the main viewing room. Kay bent over the registration book with pen in hand, but looked up with a nod to urge Packi to accept the invitation.

"Really, Mr. Maddox, that's not necessary." Packi ignored Kay and earned another poke from Marilyn. "We came today to support our friend, Carla Baker. She's here with her husband, Vern, who was a close friend to Mr. Golden."

"Yes, of course. I know Vern. That's very good of you, too." Maddox's smile faltered for a second. "Well, the invitation is open, Mrs. Walsh. I hope to see you again."

Packi turned away from him to take a memorial card from the desk. She wrote a note of sympathy in the book, but omitted her name and left the address line blank. *No need to tell the flirtatious Mr. Maddox where to find me.* When she straightened up, he was gone.

"Why did you blow him off like that?" Kay whispered. "He wants to see you again—as in a date."

"Number one, dating is not for me," said Packi, nudging her friends away from the nearest mourners. "Number two, he's on my list of murder suspects. Don't forget, he might have had something to gain by Danny's death."

"Like what?" Marilyn said. "I thought the company went under."

"When this is all over," said Kay, "you should give him a chance. He appears professional, stable, *and* has a full head of hair."

"He plays tennis," Marilyn said.

"He *used* to play tennis," Packi reminded her, "and I suspect he uses that dye stuff for men."

As they argued in a whisper, Carla waved to them from the folding chairs lined up in the center of the room. "I'm going to sit with Carla," Packi said, "I doubt Lyla will take comfort from seeing me in the receiving line."

"We're supposed to view the body," Marilyn said.

"I already viewed the body—at the morgue."

"Oh." Marilyn blanched. "I'll sit with you."

Kay and Marilyn gave Carla pecks on the cheek. Packi followed suit, but braced herself for another rebuke from her for advocating for Big Joe. None came.

"Thank you for coming," Carla whispered, twisting a handkerchief in her lap. "Lyla has so few relatives. I have no idea who all these people are. None of her team is here that I can see."

Beth slid into the chair behind Carla's and squeezed the woman's shoulder. "Yeah, I thought her team captain at least would come," Beth said. "I tell ya, those trophy wives are a different breed."

Carla wagged her head as if the nature of trophy wives was as imponderable as the national debt. She suddenly sat up straight and strained to scan the room. Packi noticed Carla's eyes light upon a man across the room.

Vern Baker. Packi recognized Carla's husband, the pharmacist to whom Packi had poured out her worries over Ron's disease, but this Vern seemed too edgy and dark to be the friendly man behind the prescription counter. He looks guilty, she thought, but dismissed the notion. He's grieving for his friend, she reminded herself. Don't get carried away.

While the women commented on the flower arrangements and memorial video, Packi studied Vern as he spoke to a group of men in golf shirts and khaki pants. *Guilty men shift around like that.* She pictured Vern taking revenge on Golden for losing his life's savings. *Did he kill him by slipping in extra-strength oxycodone or some other lethal drug? Could he drag Danny's body to Joe's pond? Maybe they walked in, and only the pharmacist walked out.*

Packi suddenly realized that her stare had caught attention. Vern squinted back at her, deepening the crease between his eyebrows. She gasped and ducked behind Beth's shoulder.

"What's with you?" Beth said.

"Nothing. Nothing," she said. "Come over here I want to show you these roses."

"What?" Beth clucked her tongue, but followed Packi to the side of the room where their voices would be lost amid the hum of other conversations.

Packi positioned Beth between herself and Vern. "I'm thinking that Danny's murderer is in this room," she said in a whisper. "My current top pick is Vern Baker, but the others…"

"Vern?" said Beth. "No way. They've been friends for years."

"Maybe, but Danny lost his *friend's* money. Vern's name was on the investor list, and *Vern* has access to the drug found in Danny's system."

"Possible." Beth gestured toward the receiving line where Collin Bainbridge offered his condolences to the new widow. "What about the lovely Lyla and lover boy?"

Packi stood on tiptoe to see just as Lyla wrapped her arms around Collin's chest. The tennis pro quickly disengaged himself from the hug and held Lyla away from him by grasping both of her shoulders. He spoke to her bowed head. With the petulance of a child, she seemed to agree with whatever he had said. She lifted her chin and greeted the next person in line.

"That's *my* top pick," said Beth. "Mary turned up documents showing that, when they got married, Danny added Lyla's name to the titles for their beach condo and yacht. Last month he sold them at a huge loss. Their house in White Egret Marina is also for sale."

Packi felt a sudden surge of compassion for Lyla. No wonder she's been acting crazy. "Where's she going to live?"

Beth shrugged. "Don't know."

Packi watched Collin move through the crowd and duck out the exit. Scenarios built in her imagination. "So Danny found out about Lyla's affair with Collin, threatened to divorce her, and cashed in her assets," she said. "Are they stupid enough to kill her husband for the insurance money?"

"It's the first thing the cops look for. Follow the money." The team captain sniffed.

"What'd you see?" asked Packi.

"My other top pick—if I thought he had the guts." Beth pointed with her chin toward the entrance where Art Maddox watched the crowd from his post against the wall.

"Why? Because he fired you?"

"That's enough evidence for me."

Packi spotted defeat hidden behind her team captain's wry humor. She wanted to reach out to give reassurance, but felt they hadn't known each other long enough. "Don't worry," she said instead. "You'll find another job."

"When?" A touch of panic sharpened the question. "Health insurance costs more than ever, and Medicare doesn't kick in for eight years."

Packi moved closer and said in a low voice, "I can help. I have more money than I need."

"God, no!" Beth stepped back as if offended. "I'm sorry I said anything. We—Rex and I—will make do." She crossed her arms and stared out over the roomful of people.

Surprised by her reaction, Packi feared she'd hurt her feelings. When Beth's shoulders relaxed, Packi searched for a way to change the subject. "So, were you joking at practice when you said Lyla hates you?"

"Not really, but it's old news." Beth turned away from the crowd and smirked. "She used to tend bar at the club, but her goal was to hook a rich husband. Played tennis with us, too."

"Lyla? At Paradise Palms?"

"Yup," Beth said. "Anyone could play when the league was new. When the club grew, rules changed, and I had to exclude her from the team."

Packi took a second to digest the information. "I can't picture her on this team."

"She was, and has hated me ever since. Claims I kicked her off the team because my Rex flirted with her at the bar. Ha." Beth clamped her hand over her mouth and cringed as several people turned toward her laugh. "He no more wants a kewpie doll than he wants a stick in the eye."

"But then why are you here, and how can you play tennis against her?"

Beth glanced across the room and stared daggers at the receiving line. "If I held a grudge, the lovely Lyla would think I took her seriously."

Yikes, thought Packi, uncomfortable with touching that nerve. "You know," she said to change the subject, "Kay thinks Maddox wants to ask me for a date. What do you think?"

"Eeww! He's about as exciting as dry toast. You're not going?"

"I might."

"Oh, my God." Beth gripped Packi's arm.

"I'm kidding." Packi muffled her laugh in respect for the solemn mood of the funeral parlor. "Though it might be a good way to worm more information out of him. I want to get the names of people who lost their money on Danny's investments. His accountant would know."

"True. He could even..." Beth's eyes went wide. "He's coming this way," she said. "Listen, I might pop him if he gets too close, so you're on your own." She retreated into the crowd, cutting through several lines to escape.

Packi sized up Arthur Maddox as he waded through the people waiting to greet the widow and Danny's family. Well-fitted suit, she thought. Power tie. Clean handkerchief in the breast pocket. No wedding ring.

"She's mad at me, isn't she?" asked Maddox as he arrived at Packi's side. With a sad shake of his head, he watched Beth disappear down the hallway.

"Yes, she is." Packi fixed him with an accusatory look. A fine scent distracted her. How did I miss the cologne earlier, she wondered. Did he just spritz himself?

"It was a business decision." He mimicked defeat with his hands in the air. "There will be more layoffs this week. Danny was the engine that made our company run. Without him, sales will go down dramatically, banks will call our loans." His shoulders slumped as if the weight of Suncoast Realty and Danny's other projects were upon them. "All of our people will be out of a job. Myself included."

The responsibility of cleaning up the financial mess probably did fall to Maddox, Packi thought. She cut a look up at him. "The Gazette reported that lenders have already foreclosed on Skyview Towers."

Maddox's left eyebrow twitched. "We were negotiating that. Perhaps the bankers will give us a grace period after this tragedy." He put his hand over his red power tie. "Poor Daniel. He couldn't stand the stress. I'm afraid he took the easy way out."

Packi sucked in her breath. "You think he killed *himself?*" She listened hard for phoniness, but heard only concern and grief in his reasoning. She tried to reconcile his opinion with the coroner's assertion of murder.

He leaned close to Packi's ear. "Danny took a hard hit from this economy. He got depressed. Drugs addled his brain."

Packi nodded in sympathy. "I knew he was on oxycodone."

Maddox pulled back, surprised. "That's not public knowledge." He looked down his long, thin nose. "You seem to have an unusual interest in this tragic event, Mrs. Walsh. More so than Lyla's other friends."

This man is better than dry toast, she thought. About as warm as a tax auditor. Still, he seemed concerned about the new widow. Maybe a lunch meeting to gather information wouldn't be so bad.

"I'm afraid I can't describe myself as Lyla's friend. We first met three days ago," Packi said. "I wanted only to prove that Mr. Golden was dead before Big Joe..."

Maddox frowned in confusion.

"The alligator," she explained, "before the alligator found the body. I've been trying to prove Big Joe's innocence, searching around for whoever dumped Danny's body in the pond. Yesterday morning the judge was this close to saving him." She held her fingers an inch apart.

"Then Lyla showed up in court."

"Exactly."

Maddox's pale face, which stood out beneath his dark shock of hair, showed no emotion. He stroked his chin with long, clean fingers. "The police don't mind you interfering with their investigation?"

"They've warned me away, but one deputy is partial to cookies and cupcakes." Packi smiled in spite of herself. "Besides, I've given them valuable information."

Maddox stared across the room at his business partner in the satin-lined casket. "I can help." He clapped his hands together once. "You'll understand Danny better if you see his beautiful work. I'll give you a tour of Skyview Towers, and you'll see why he was in such agony over losing the project to the bank."

The sadness of the realtor's death gave Packi pause. Yet, the prospect of seeing the elegant building intrigued her, and she wanted more information out of Arthur Maddox.

He reached for her hand and held it between his own. "Mrs. Walsh, I realize this is not an appropriate place, but would you also do me the honor of having dinner with me?"

"What?" Dumbfounded by his abrupt advance, she tried tugging her hand away.

Maddox held firm and rushed on. "I may not get another opportunity to approach such an attractive woman of quality." A smile slid across his face. "At our ages, we can't waste a moment."

Our ages? Dinner? Embarrassment heated her cheeks and hobbled her speech. *He thinks he's romantic.*

Oblivious to his off-putting remarks, Maddox laid out his impromptu plan. "I'll show you the penthouse, and then we'll walk to the newest restaurant downtown…"

Her hand went limp in his, and she stared up at the man. "Not Victoria House?" Her heart did a little flip-flop at the mention of Mark Hebron's place of employment.

She didn't mean to imply that she'd accept his invitation, but Maddox seemed to take her reaction that way. While he extolled the virtues of the fashionable restaurant, Packi pictured Mark as Victoria House's maitre d', all sophisticated and proper, showing them to their table. *I won't do that to Mark.*

"I can't." She tried to let Maddox down gently. "I'm a vegetarian."

When his grip faltered, she extracted her hand and wiped the moisture onto her skirt. But Art Maddox was a determined suitor.

"Then we'll go to Twisted Vine," he said. "Their chef does an excellent job with vegetable dishes. Their outdoor patio will be perfect for us to get to know each other."

His earnest face reminded Packi of her husband's. Ron had always needed to be in control, too. Dinner might not be so bad, she thought. It'll be my chance to question Maddox about Danny Golden's investors, and I want to see the decorating in that building. Still surprised by her sudden conversion to vegetarianism, she agreed to the date.

"Wonderful." Maddox pulled a notebook and pen from his pocket. "Here's the address to Skyview Towers. Meet me there tomorrow evening at, say, seven o'clock? We'll watch a fabulous sunset from the penthouse." He pressed the note into her hand and walked off before she could change her mind.

Packi watched him sidestep through the milling crowd with a youthful, eager bounce. She regretted she'd have to squash his romantic notions, but it couldn't be helped.

Worn out by the whirlwind of events, she patted her hair and adjusted her collar before wandering back to her seat in the center of the room. Carla sat as straight as a post, looking beyond her teammates as if doing a radar search for her husband.

"What an impressive turn out," said Packi, sliding onto the folding chair.

Carla acknowledged her, but kept her vigil until she zeroed in on her intended target. Packi glanced over her shoulder to follow the woman's stare. In the back of the room Vern conversed with two men in business suits, his hands stuffed deep in his pockets.

She's worried about him, Packi thought. About the cause of his friend's death? What could she know? "So, Carla," she began as if making polite conversation. "How well did you know Danny and Lyla Golden?"

"Vern and Danny were friends for two decades." Carla bit at a fingernail and kept her stare riveted on her husband. "Then he married her." Her eyes slid to Lyla holding court in the crowded receiving line. "We all had dinner from time to time."

"So, you must have known the first wife, too," Packi said. She had forgotten about Catherine as a suspect.

"I did," Carla said, looking at Packi. "Catherine took the divorce hard and moved to Long Boat Key. Her last Christmas card said she's getting remarried. I'm glad for her."

"Do you know Art Maddox, the business partner, too?" Packi tried to control the hot color creeping to her cheeks.

"Oh, him. What a wet blanket." Carla dismissed Maddox with a sniff. "Excuse me. The line's getting bunched up. Lyla doesn't have a clue about etiquette, so I'd better help her."

Carla brushed imaginary lint off her black pants and bustled off to take a spot beside the widow, to greet visitors and move them along. Busybody or friend, thought Packi. Either way, Carla would help Lyla get through the funeral ordeal.

* * *

Fanning her face, Packi worked her way into the second viewing room to find Beth or Kay. She wanted to get their reaction to her 'date' with Art Maddox before it was too late to back out. As she strained to see over shoulders and through the crowd, she again spotted Carla's Vern. From behind a row of mourners, she studied him as he spoke to a visitor.

His haggard, gray face bore little similarity to the pharmacist she knew years ago. Tight crow's feet tracked across his temples and more than age worked to erode the once hearty man. Still, she saw a resemblance to Danny Golden—like a brother, or maybe a cousin. Not the Danny Golden in the morgue nor the man in the casket, but the TV spokesman for Suncoast Realty. The same mannerisms and expressions, but tired and muted now. No toupee, but the same cheekbones, long nose, jaw. Is it possible, Packi wondered, that the murderer got the wrong man? Why had Vern gone missing? Was he also a target?

That's crazy, she thought, but no wonder his wife is a nervous wreck. After the morgue scare the other day, of course, Carla keeps an eye on him.

When the man in the polo shirt drifted away from Vern, Packi approached. "Hello, Mr. Baker."

He flinched and stepped back.

"Remember me? I'm Packi Walsh. You used to fill my husband's prescriptions, and we talked."

The pharmacist pinched the bridge of his nose as if to quiet turbulent thoughts swirling behind his bushy eyebrows. "Oh, yes. Mrs. Walsh," he said. "Carla told me how kind you were going to the morgue when they thought it was me." He sighed as if he bore a great weight and glanced into the other room toward the casket adorned with sprays of flowers. "Poor Danny."

"Thank goodness, it wasn't you." She lowered her voice and leaned in, catching the slight scent of smoke lingering in the fibers of his suit. "He looked similar to you," she whispered, "but I knew you didn't wear glasses." She winced at her inept attempt to steer the conversation. *How else will I get information out of the man? How else would he tell me how Danny ended up in the pond?* She decided to barge right in. "Carla thought you were on a business trip to Miami the night Danny was killed."

Vern hushed her. He grasped her wrist and guided her into a quiet room set aside for the grieving family. He glanced down the hallway before easing the door closed, his long fingers pressed along the door jamb. She remembered watching his long, clean fingers years ago as he prepared prescriptions for Ron. His hands hadn't trembled then.

"Listen, Mrs. Walsh. If something happens to me, you've got to watch over my wife. She'll need friends—you, the others on that tennis team of hers. She's not a strong woman."

"Why would anything happen to you?"

"Please promise you'll take care of Carla."

"I'll need to know what's going on," Packi said. She refused to make promises to a person who might have used his medical expertise to kill a man. "Did your trip have anything to do with providing Danny with oxycodone?"

"Mrs. Walsh, please!" Color drained from his face, and he gripped the back of a chair. "Who told you about that?"

"It was on the coroner's report."

Vern hung his head and groaned. "The police questioned me about the drugs. I could lose my license." He bounced his fist on the padded chair with each measured word. "Of course, it's wrong to enable an addict, but Danny was in such pain. He broke his back ten years ago in a boating accident." Vern twisted his own spine and grimaced as if Danny's pain lived on in him. "Oxycodone helped. Over the years, he needed more of the drug than his doctors would give him."

Packi hated witnessing Vern's misery. *I'm doing this all wrong.* To give herself a moment to think of a better tack, she turned toward the refrigerator and fished through the assorted refreshments. She found two bottles of water and offered one to him. He refused it with a tired wave.

"Carla mentioned that you invested in the Fisherman's Wharf project," Packi said. "Were you angry when you lost all your money?"

"I know where you're going with that question, Mrs. Walsh. I'm carrying enough guilt about giving Danny unprescribed medication." He rubbed pale, sanitized hands over his face and kneaded his forehead. "No. I didn't kill Danny over my investment losses. I'd have given him more money, if I had it, to get him out of his troubles. I owed him."

The pharmacist faced the window and looked across the parking lot to a pond surrounded by hibiscus and live oaks. "When my daughter needed heart surgery five years ago, he paid the bill. Every penny. Flew us all to Mayo Clinic in his plane, got the best surgeons." Vern turned back to her with a doleful smile. "My daughter named our grandson after Danny."

So the deceased had been a generous man, Packi thought. She wanted to believe Vern, to believe that he—and Danny Golden—were *both* good men, but the pharmacist seemed scared to death. "Are the police trying to convict you of something?" she asked.

"It's not the police I'm afraid of."

"Who then?"

He didn't answer and slumped into a Queen Ann chair meant to provide comfort to bereaved families. He looked far older than his fifty-some years.

"Vern," Packi prodded, but softened her words. "Who else knew he took the oxycodone?"

"His wife probably," he said as if giving up the fight. "It's not something that you announce to the world. We tried to keep it quiet."

She slid into a chair next to Vern and leaned toward him like an old friend. "People say he stole their investment money," she whispered. "They're very angry. Who do you think did this thing to him?"

"I thought Danny had paid enough." Vern jumped up and paced the small room. "He paid them off—everything he had. I know, I delivered the cash—and on time." He turned a fierce glare toward Packi and pointed his clean, pharmacist finger as if teaching her a lesson. "Real estate all over the state fell forty percent, but they want it all back. He couldn't do it."

"Vern." She touched his arm to get a connection, to stop his rant. "Please explain. Tell me who could have killed Danny."

The man rushed to the door, cracked it open, and peeked down the hallway. He pressed the door closed and leaned his back against it. "Don't repeat this, Mrs. Walsh. You wouldn't be safe, but I must tell someone. Carla will need someone, if…"

"Who, Vern?"

Bristling with kinetic energy, he returned to the upholstered chair. "There is a consortium of investors from New Jersey," he said in a hushed tone. "They think Danny swindled them, but I swear he didn't."

"Do you mean the mob?" she asked, remembering Mark's words.

"Shh." He looked over his shoulder and around the room as if listening devices had been installed in the flower vases. "A consortium."

"What is your part in this?"

"I'd do anything for Danny," the man said. "He was afraid to go in person—afraid he wouldn't come back. I flew each month to New Jersey to deliver the payments."

"Carla said you had business in Miami."

"That's what I told her. She'd worry herself sick."

"You must tell the police." Packi leaned forward to take the man's hand. "They can help."

Vern sent her a scornful look and fell back against the chair, shaking his head. "Just take care of Carla."

She realized he thought her naive, and it was true that big money and crime had never touched her world. The specter of their involvement with the realtor's death, and her impotence against such things, weighed on her mind. *Who would pay the boys from New Jersey now? Would they demand payment from Lyla? Who was next?* She decided not to burden Vern with the questions.

"The team and I will watch over Carla," she said. "I promise."

She offered to fetch a cup of coffee, but he waved away the suggestion. "Thank you, Mrs. Walsh. You were always good to talk to." Vern Baker forced a small smile and heaved himself out of the chair. "I'd better go find my wife."

He left the door open, allowing new air to swirl into the family room. Packi stayed seated in the winged-back chair, thinking. She found the over-decorated room disturbing, not at all comforting, as the designers intended for relatives and friends of the deceased. But then, she wasn't a direct mourner this time. In any case, the quiet room allowed her to sort through the new information Vern had supplied.

Who murdered Danny Golden? The Jersey boys as Mark called them? A picture flashed through her imagination—Mark's tan, dimpled face sweating in the tropical heat as he replaced drywall in his abandoned house, working to rebuild his future.

Packi allowed herself a small grin, but then banished those thoughts and got back to the problem at hand. The killer could have been any distraught investor, she thought, but her money was on the mob—professionals.

Still, she should consider *all* the investors and get the information to Deputy Teig. Art Maddox would help narrow that list, she thought. Which investor lost the most? Which had the greatest reason for revenge? The possibility of getting the information out of Maddox made her date with him more palatable.

"Knock. Knock." Kay poked her head into the doorway. "They said there's coffee in here."

Packi roused herself, relieved to see her friend and regain some sense of normalcy. "Hi, Kay. Over there." She pointed to the coffee urn on the counter. "There are also donut holes and brownies."

"Oh, no, not for me." Kay pointed at her stick figure. "I work too hard keeping off the pounds."

"You look great." Packi spoke the expected words.

Kay dismissed the compliment and filled a cardboard cup with black coffee. "What are you doing in here?"

"Thinking," said Packi, "and staying out of Lyla's way. The sight of me would send her into hysterics."

"Probably. She enjoys the dramatics." Kay slapped her hand over her mouth. "Sorry, that was mean. The woman is grieving for her husband, and this is her show." She raised her cup at Packi. "If you want to stay out of Lyla's way, you'd better slip out the back door now. Carla and she talked about getting coffee and were making their way through the crowd."

"Gather the troops," Packi said, glancing into the hallway. "I'll meet you at the car."

* * *

While Packi concentrated on her driving and stewed in her own thoughts, the others discussed the characters at the funeral home and then moved on to more mundane issues. Caught at the long light at the intersection of Daniels and Cleveland, she listened to the women chatter. In the backseat Marilyn and Kay gave their opinions of facials.

"I hate them," Kay stated.

Packi glanced in the rearview mirror to catch the joke. Beth twisted around in the front seat, her long legs confined by the dashboard. "What are you talking about?"

"At the spa," said Kay, "they pushed and shoved my face around, like they didn't know what to do with me." She kneaded her cheeks to demonstrate the assault. "The girl complained my wrinkles go horizontally, not vertically." She sniffed, feigning disgust. "I don't need some young thing telling me I got the wrong kind of wrinkles."

Laughter erupted in the backseat and Beth turned forward again shaking her head.

"And I paid for that!" Kay said.

When the amusement died down and a lull gave her the opportunity, Packi asked, "So, what do you think of my date with Art Maddox?"

"You didn't?" said Beth as if tasting sour milk.

"Ooh la la," one of the two in the backseat murmured.

Kay leaned forward and hit Packi's shoulder. "He asked you for a date at a funeral home? How romantic. When?"

"Tomorrow night." Packi caught her eye in the rearview mirror. "He said we were getting too old to postpone opportunities."

"The silver-tongued devil!" With a laugh, Kay flopped back into her seat just as the light changed and Packi accelerated alongside several lanes of traffic.

"I'm not thinking so much of it as a date, but more like a reconnaissance mission." Packi gripped the steering wheel tighter. "I think I can get more information out of Mr. Maddox if he thinks of me as a romantic interest. I want to find out more about his business dealings and about the investors who lost the most money." She stopped at a red light and turned to her passengers. "Who lost so much that they'd kill Danny Golden?"

Beth stroked her chin. "Now your date makes sense."

"Like Mata Hari." Kay pulled herself forward by grabbing Packi's seat back. "You'll be a femme-fatale. We'll get you all dressed up. I've got this sexy little black dress that'll fit you. It's down to here." She tapped her finger on the bone between her breasts. "Does nothing for me, but on you..."

"I'll lend you some bling." Marilyn wiggled her fingers as if they were laden with jewelry. "For Valerie's celebrity sleaze party, I bought three huge rings, cubic zirconia, of course, and ankle bracelets."

"What..." Packi's question was drowned out by an interruption from the front seat.

"You gonna put a tramp stamp on her too?" Beth clucked her tongue. "At least get the man to treat you to some place expensive, like that new Victoria House."

"Anywhere, but there," Packi said. "He mentioned Twisted Vine."

"Oooh, yum. I ordered their tiramisu." Kay smacked her lips. "Get a table out on the patio if it's not too hot."

Packi's mouth watered. Maybe the dinner date would have a few advantages, she thought. The light turned green, but she kept her foot on the brake, waiting for the red light jumpers. She clucked her tongue as a black pickup truck sped through the intersection. A battered, red compact followed right behind.

"What's a sleaze party?"

22

Yachts and sailboats of all sizes and degree of luxury lined the river side of Edwards Street. The wide Caloosahatchee River lay beyond, gold spangled as if a billion sequins had been cast upon the warm waters by the sun which hung low in the sultry, peach sky. The boats bumped and bobbed, straining against their mooring ropes. Packi imagined couples on deck chairs toasting to their romance with a clink of fluted stemware. She wondered where they were. In nearby condominiums, no doubt—though most of the high rise buildings seemed deserted, with lighted balconies only here and there.

Skyview Towers stood among a dozen grandiose properties dominating the marina, but not one light above the ground floor gave the building life. Packi stopped the car in the street to check the address and looked skyward at the darkened behemoth. *What a view they must have from the top floors.* She relished the promised tour of the penthouse.

Light spilled from the elegant building's ground floor lobby and seemed to welcome Packi through its grand entrance. She parked her Audi in the vacant lot, noting the well-tended flowering shrubs and small patches of manicured grass. The bank is maintaining this property, she thought. Protecting its investment.

Where is he? Maddox had been so awkward when she phoned to accept his invitation, she expected him to be pacing at the door with a bouquet of wilted violets in his fist. She glanced at the dashboard clock. *Shoot. I'm fifteen minutes early. Still, he should be here waiting. Maybe he parked in the building's garage.*

She checked herself in the rearview mirror. Her teammates had offered bling, as they called it, but she opted for her own understated earrings and silver tennis necklace. Kay's little black dress may have been a mistake. Packi had pinned the neckline to hide her small cleavage, but she still felt wanton. Too late now, she thought. She climbed out of the bucket seat, slammed the door, and held onto the roof of the car to steady herself on the borrowed heels.

A warm, moist breeze tickled her inner thigh and made her glance down. The hem of the dress had ridden up, exposing far too much flesh. *Oh, good God!* She yanked at the hem and scanned the quiet parking lot. Apparently, no one had seen the display.

Relieved, she inventoried her outfit for other faux pas. She picked off a thread and smoothed wrinkles from the skirt, but stopped in mid-motion. Eyes were upon her. She knew it and stopped breathing to listen. Cars on the street. Gulls screaming low over the river. A siren somewhere among the downtown buildings. Nothing odd. *Relax,* she told herself. *You have to get used to going out alone.*

She breathed again and brushed at the dampness at the nape of her neck. *Maybe it's just Art checking me out from one of the windows.* A ridiculous thought, but she sucked in her little pooch of a stomach and lifted her chin. She posed as a Hollywood seductress might and locked the car. *Well, why not? My feminine wiles may come in handy to pry information out of him.*

Packi shoved the ignition key into her beaded evening purse and strolled toward Skyview's lobby doors. A snap sounded behind her. The smile fell from her face. *A twig? A stone?* She whirled around to scan the empty lot and the tangle of tropical vegetation around its borders. Nothing. She blew out short, silent breaths, and widened her peripheral vision. *Something isn't right.* She focused on a palmetto on the far side. A shadow filtered through the long, thin fronds—darker than the greenery. The shadow began to take shape. She squinted as if reading fine print and stared until the outline made sense. *A man.* She gasped and stepped backward, falling off one silver heel. The shadow stared back, but didn't move. She recognized the homeless man. *Jake.* He had hidden within the banana palm in the park. *Harmless,* Mark had said, but she wasn't so sure, and this time she didn't have Mark to protect her.

Get to the car. She calculated the distance back to her Audi with its canvas top, easily knifed. She then glanced at the welcoming lobby. She scooped up her lost shoe and rushed toward the lights.

Packi rapped on the locked door with the heel of the silver pump. "Art! Where are you?" She checked over her shoulder for Jake, but he hadn't come after her. The saw palmetto quivered in the tropical breeze, just like any other foliage. The parking lot was quiet, peaceful even. *Maybe bright lights scare him away,* she thought. *Still, Art should be here.* A sharp stone bit into her heel as she stomped her foot. She winced in pain and leaned against the building to massage her heel. Disgusted, she hit the glass door again before slipping her toes into the shoe.

Afraid to venture back to her car, Packi cupped her hands around her eyes to peer further into the lobby. She was miffed that he'd left her outside, prey to homeless people and muggers. *He should be watching for me, for goodness sakes. For all he knows, this is a real date.* In a fit of pique, she yanked the handle of the second door. To her surprise, the door cracked open.

Well, good. At least he left it unlocked for me. Packi leveraged her weight, pulled the heavy door, and stepped inside. "Art?" She listened. "I'm here. Art?" She peered back through the window to see if Jake lurked outside and pulled the door handle until she heard the lock click.

Feeling safe, Packi gazed around the room. The spacious, marble-lined lobby could have been featured in an architectural magazine. *What a shame such a beautiful building is abandoned. Elegant people should sit in those leather chairs, perhaps talking about last Friday's art show or the play down at the old Arcade.* She envisioned herself living such a cultured life and understood how Mark and the other investors had become irate. *Enough to kill Danny Golden? That's far-fetched.*

Her silver heels clicked along a short hallway on shiny marble floors, sounding ridiculously like the spikes they were. *How did I let Kay talk me into these stupid shoes? They've been nothing but trouble.* The clicking echoed through the high-ceiling room until she stepped onto the plush carpet.

A far-off sound caught her ear. She stopped to listen. *Whistling?* Coming from beyond a set of double doors. This isn't right, she thought. She sat on the edge of a leather sofa in a corner seating arrangement, but then stood up again and looked back toward the front entrance. The quiet disconcerted her.

Suddenly, "In-a-Gadda-da-Vida, baby" blared, announcing an incoming message. Hair stood up on her arms, and perspiration stung her armpits. *What possessed me to buy that ringtone?* She shoved her hand into her little beaded purse and pulled out her phone, crumpled tissues, and a five dollar bill. She swiped away the low-battery icon and brought up the message:

I hope you get this before you arrive at Skyview. I can't meet you tonight. An emergency came up at the office. Please forgive me. Art

Disgusted, Packi pursed her lips. *A text message? The coward.* She slumped back onto the sofa, angry and worn out. *I won't give him the satisfaction.* Packi tapped out her own message: *Works for me. I'm having cocktails with friends downtown. Next time. P*

The phone lost power and flickered to black. *Dang. Did that send?* Packi put her head in her hands and fought the feeling of rejection. *I'm such a fool. Sure, I only wanted to question him about Danny Golden's business dealings, but Art didn't know this wasn't a date. Who does he think...*

A new thought raked at her heart. She swallowed hard. *Then who is in this building? Did Jake find a way in?* The aura of security given off by the luxurious building evaporated. She sat up straight and listened for the whistling, but heard nothing. She suddenly felt like a deer caught in an open field. Warnings flashed through her mind. *Get out of here.* Without a sound, she slid off the couch, but then sat again to remove the dang shoes. She made a beeline for the exit door with her bare feet slapping against the marble floors. Stoney cold shot through her leg bones and up her spine.

Packi focused on the glass door and beyond to her car. The Audi beckoned to her from the end of the walkway. She slowed only a fraction before shoving against the door's metal crash bar. Her shoulder slammed against the glass. Her elbows buckled. The unyielding door jolted her backwards. She crumbled against the arm of a nearby sofa and fell to her knees, dropping her shoes and purse. Too stunned to move, she clung to the sofa for a moment before gathering her wits. *Locked? That's against the law!* She stumbled back to the door and rattled the metal bar in frustration. *Definitely locked. But how?* Packi ran her fingers along the bar and the door jamb, searching for a key or a button. *Nothing. Who'd have a key? Surely they saw me in the lobby. Or heard In-a-Gadda-da-Vida.*

"Hello! You locked me in. Please come and unlock the door."

Maybe a caretaker stopped by and is still in the parking lot. She ran to the next set of windows and squinted into the night. Her Audi now looked small, alone in the empty lot beneath leering palms, lit only by light pouring from the lobby. She left handprints on a large pane of glass as she hoped for a car to roll down the road. Through an opening in the hedge, the street resembled a dystopian movie scene in which zombies come out after dark. At the marina, yachts lurched and bucked in ominous hulking shadows.

Maybe this isn't the caretaker's mistake. The thought hit Packi like an electric shock. *Did someone lock me in on purpose?* She darted to the side with her back to the wall, breathing heavily, not knowing whether the danger was in or outside the building.

Don't over react, Patricia. Think it through. She gripped the thin chain of her evening purse for security and assured herself it was all a mistake. *Why would anyone want to trap me? I probably locked the door myself when I pushed it closed. Yes, that's it.* Deciding there was no real danger, she ventured a step away from the wall.

Then the lights went out.

Stunned by the thickness of the dark, Packi froze in place and refused to breathe. From somewhere in a distant room, she heard the distinct thud of footsteps, slow, unhurried, heavy—not a woman's four-inch heels. She ducked as if bullets would whiz over her head. Instinct told her to hide. She felt for the damask drapery that framed the windows and stepped behind the floor-length fabric. She pulled the edges around her like a shroud and stood dead still.

Packi clutched her phone. *Should I turn it on? Will he hear the tone?* She listened, trying to pull sound and meaning from the darkness. A distant door's lock mechanism clanked, hinges creaked and echoed. *Is that on this floor?*

Get a hold of yourself, Patricia. The janitor is doing his rounds, she reasoned, but didn't want to bet her life on it. *Just get out.*

She peeked from behind the curtain, searching for movement, for a shadow. Red light pierced the blackness. The exit sign above the door to the parking lot taunted her, signaling a path to the locked door. She let out a frustrated sigh. Another red glow emanated from around a corner at the far side of the room and gave her hope.

Packi left her concealment, feeling along the wall, and padded across thick carpet, but intermittently had to brave the cold marble. A cocktail table caught her shin and screeched as it scraped the floor. Nasty, four-letter words came to her mind. She gritted her teeth and clamped her lips closed to keep from crying out. She breathed out the pain and calmed herself, listening.

No sound came from behind the double doors at the far end of the lobby. The whistling had stopped. Packi tiptoed closer to the second exit door, but anxiety made her impatient, and she ran the last thirty feet to push against the door's crash bar. The door stood firm.

Whoever's here had to hear that. She looked over her shoulder and saw nothing, but heard quickened footsteps. She glanced around in panic for an escape route. She rushed toward the only other source of light. Green and red pinpoints. Buttons. She stopped short when she recognized them as elevator buttons. Her sweaty forehead and neck turned clammy and cold. *No way!*

The footsteps sounded more hurried, closer.

You can do this.

Packi curled herself around the elevator door's opening and hung on the railing inside. She jabbed at red-LED buttons. Nothing happened. She stole a glance outside the elevator and spotted a shadow near the exit door, where she had dropped her shoes.

Oh God. He knows I'm here. She hit more buttons in a quick staccato and heard the screech of furniture and curse words in a deep male voice. She pounded the LED lights with both fists. Finally, the one green LED at the top of the panel blinked. The doors slid shut. The car shuddered and rose. Packi sank to her knees, grasping the rail with both hands.

Panic brewed in her chest. She clawed at her throat to catch a breath and fell into a fetal position on the tile floor. She squeezed her eyes shut, gasping for oxygen. Beneath her cheek, the floor vibrated as gears and motors meshed and whirred. She sucked in air and prayed the nightmare would end.

Drunken visions swirled in her mind until, finally, the mechanical whirring ended in a wheeze and the elevator bumped to a gentle stop. Packi forced her eyes open as the doors pulled back and offered her freedom. With a shot of adrenaline, she scrambled out as if a monster spat her from its maw. Spread-eagle on the cold stone floor, she thanked the powers that be for her release.

More marble, she thought. It cooled her heated skin and revived her enough to notice she lay in a long, dark area. She inched her way up a wall to a standing position, pulled down the hem of Kay's dress, and pushed hair out of her face. *Some femme fatale I am.*

With a start, she realized that if the elevator descended, the man in the lobby could follow her up. Just as she lunged for the open elevator, the door began to slide shut. She threw her back against the rubber edge and braced herself, thinking she'd be crushed. The door bounced open instead. Half in and half out of the elevator, she fought down another claustrophobic panic. Stuck. *Prop open the door. A table or chair, anything. A rock would do, a book.*

At the end of the hallway, moonlight shone through a window. The eerie glow silhouetted a squat shape in the otherwise empty room. It looked like a stool or a large bucket. One of those five-gallon painter's buckets, she decided. That would do, but how to get to it and back before the doors closed?

I'm fast, she told herself—at least at tennis. *I could run over there,* grab the bucket, and dash back. She put her hand over the door's sensor and leaned into the hall. *I can do this.* She filled her lungs and ran. A moment later she swooped down on the bucket, grabbed the handle and turned to run back. Her arm nearly popped from its socket.

Packi grabbed the handle again, hefted the paint, and then dropped it. She yanked and shoved the thing halfway back to the elevator when she heard a ping. The doors slid shut. "No. Oh, no." Packi abandoned the bucket, ran to the elevator, and pried at the doors with her fingers. She then pounded on the button to summons the car back.

Dang! How long would it take for the elevator to go down and back? A few minutes at best. Whether the man was the janitor or someone who had locked her in on purpose, didn't matter. She didn't want to meet him and needed to get out, back to her car, back to Paradise Palm.

Packi got a grip on her emotions and focused on her situation. *Call somebody.* She pulled her phone out and poked at the black screen. *Who? Beth? No. 911.* She pressed the On button and waited. The battery warning flashed. She thumped the electronic headache against her palm. Lights flickered. She jabbed at the nine and one before the screen went black again. She mouthed an unladylike word and jammed the useless device into her purse.

There must be stairs. Don't building codes require two escape routes? Determined to find a stairwell, she felt along the hallway into a large, open area. Before her was a bank of picture windows from floor to ceiling. Beyond, in the radiance of a low, full moon, lay the Caloosahatchee River and a bird's-eye view of the City of Palms.

The awesome vista registered in her mind for an instant, but fear drove her from room to room in search of escape. Away from the windows, in the interior darkness, she found the kitchen. A likely place for a backdoor, she thought. Precious seconds ticked away as she opened doors to pantries, closets, and a bathroom.

She could hear her bare feet on the floor and the hiss of her breath, but nothing else. She then felt, more than heard, the hum of a motor, like a large refrigerator had just clicked on. *The elevator.* She let out a little cry. *Why is this happening? Help me, Ron.*

She darted into the darker recesses of the condo. Her hopes rose as she felt her way into a windowless, narrow space. She sensed its size and its purpose—a laundry or mud room. Surely, a good place for an exit. Using the wall as a guide, she rushed to the far end. A metal door. She grabbed the knob, twisted, and yanked, but it didn't yield. She skimmed the smooth surface, found a deadbolt, and bruised her fingers trying to twist it open.

She pressed her forehead against the cool metal. *Please, God, help!*

Her evening purse fell to her feet with a clunk. The phone inside chirped in protest. *Try it again. Text uses less power.* She swept up the beaded bag, forced open the clasp, and depressed the On button. When the screen flickered, she poked at the message icon, spotted Beth's name, and typed *H, E.* The battery warning leered at her and went black. *Help,* Packi thought and jabbed at the screen, but the phone had given its last watt of power.

A ping from the elevator added to her desperation. *He's here.* The atmosphere in the condo changed as if the air had been sucked down the elevator shaft. Her chest constricted, but she refused a panic attack.

The bathroom! Lock him out.

Packi tiptoed through the laundry room and peeked around the door jamb. A bright light bounced off the white walls on the far side of the condo. She gasped and ducked into the shadows with her back to the wall. The light swung her way. Instinct told her to hold her position, like a fawn in tall grass.

When he didn't run toward her hiding spot, she peered around the corner again. His light shone from inside a room forty feet away. Packi crept into the hallway and retraced her steps toward a small bathroom off the kitchen and slipped inside. The push button lock sounded like gunfire and echoed through the empty rooms.

Who am I kidding? He'll find me here eventually and just kick in the door. Determined to give him a fight, she searched under the cabinet for a makeshift weapon, a forgotten tool, towel bar, unused tile maybe. Nothing. She yanked open the linen closet and began to wrestle with the lowest shelf, but then had a better idea. The toilet tank cover.

Packi eased the heavy porcelain cover from its position and winced when it screeched, glass on glass. She tested her grip on the weight and swung it left to right. *This could do some damage.* She pictured him barging through the door and hitting him only in the shoulder or chest, just enough to enrage him. *You get one chance.*

To ambush him from above, she clambered onto the counter top with her back to the mirror. As she squatted to retrieve the porcelain, pain shot through her knee. She clenched her teeth until the pain subsided, then balanced the lid on its edge to use it to push herself upright.

A moment later a soft glow came from under the door. The light mesmerized her, left her transfixed and unable to move. *Dear God, make him go away.*

The rattling of the doorknob interrupted the prayer. Packi swung the porcelain lid into position above her head and took one long breath. The door crashed open and light filled the room, bouncing from mirror to mirror. She brought the tank lid down on the densest part of the shadow. With a fleshy thud, her weapon connected. The man bellowed in anger, and his arm shot up to grab the lid. His curse reverberated in the small room. He clamped a hand on her wrist and yanked her from her perch.

As she fell, Packi twisted away, and he lost his grip on her. She scrambled to her feet and threw her body into the hallway. A jolt caught her between the shoulder blades and knocked her to the floor. She faltered and collapsed. Unable to breathe, she curled into a ball, gasping for air. She pulled her knees to her chest and protected her head with her arms.

He breathed in angry grunts. In her defensive position, she snuck a glance at him from behind the crook of her arm. The flashlight on the bathroom floor silhouetted a bulky, distorted body looming over her. He paused with a rectangle shape held over his head. *The tank cover.* Packi cringed and waited for the crushing blow. Instead, the man smashed the lid on the tile floor next to her head. The shock forced her to cry out. Bits of porcelain stung the tender skin of her forehead and neck.

"That isn't my plan for you." His voice was thick and wet as if he spoke through a muffler.

With fists and feet churning, she struck out toward the voice, hoping to connect with vulnerable flesh. He knocked her limbs aside. She rolled away onto her hands and knees and crouched to run. He caught her by the nape of her neck and pushed her chest into the floor.

Determined not to be taken without a fight, she kept her arms moving, swimming against the tile floor. Broken porcelain bit into her forearms. *Cut him,* she thought. She felt for a chunk of the shattered tank lid and slashed out with it until he caught her hands. He pulled her arms tight behind her, pried the porcelain from her fist, and tossed it away. Rope or strips of fabric cut into her wrists. She tried to expand the muscles of her hands and wrists, so the restraints would loosen later. The effort exhausted her as he fussed with the knots, tying and retying. She lay quiet, breathing hard, thinking. *What am I supposed to do?* She tried to recall articles about kidnap victims—about rape. Hope sickened and died within her.

Desperate to connect to his humanity, she twisted around to look at his dark shape. "Who are you?"

He pushed her face away and held her head against the floor. His long fingers gripped her skull like an electrocutioner's headpiece.

"Curiosity killed the cat," he whispered next to her ear. He flipped her onto her back and grabbed her legs. He crossed her feet at the ankles and looped them with a strip of fabric, winding it around and around.

Trussed up like a calf, she stopped kicking. "Don't kill me."

"I don't intend to." He laughed through his mask. "But if they find you months from now, all shriveled up in this lousy condo, it won't be my fault. Maybe you'll have a heart attack." He chuckled like a ghoul. "Think of this as your tomb, little kitten. They'll figure your snooping lured you here."

Snooping? What's this all about? She felt her seconds ticking down, her chances to save herself slipping away. "I don't know anything. I can't hurt you. Who are you?"

Packi contorted her body to face her tormentor, but a cruel grip on her shoulder rolled her back. Her pulse pounded in her ears. *He's in control. Okay, I get that.* "Please let me go."

He grasped her jaw, forced open her mouth, and shoved a rough cloth between her teeth. She fought the rag with her tongue, blocking it from her throat. She heard duct tape ripped from its roll. When he slapped tape across her face, she abandoned the effort to dislodge the cloth. She wanted only to breathe.

He smoothed wrinkles from the strip on her cheek and then stood as if to admire his handiwork. "Sleep tight." He sniggered at his joke, retrieved his flashlight, and disappeared down the hallway. The elevator pinged.

She listened to the hum of the descending elevator until silence enveloped her, the room, and her entire world. This *is* my tomb, she thought. *Ron, help me.* Tears brimmed in the corners of her eyes and slid into her ears. Her thoughts wandered to the pleasant life she and her husband shared. *Why had it ended so badly?* She sniffed. *Ron wanted* me *to be strong. Now look at me.* Packi gritted her teeth, as well as the gag allowed, and began to save herself.

The cloth in her mouth smelled faintly of turpentine, a painter's rag. She fought off nausea. The cloth absorbed all moisture her mouth produced. She worked her lips and tongue, pushing against the duct tape until her jaws ached. She wiped the tape against her shoulder again and again, but to no avail. She then put her face flat to the floor and rubbed against the tile, trying to catch a corner of tape. Finally, she lay still, concentrating only on breathing in and out through her nose, hating the darkness, and wondering what had brought her to this end.

* * *

Packi awoke disoriented in complete darkness, unsure whether she'd slept or passed out. Her spine and neck ached. Her shoulders screamed for relief. The back of her throat stuck to her tonsils as she sucked air.

Help, she cried when her memory clarified the attack. She lurched into a less painful position and tried to ignore the odor of turpentine beneath her nose. She attempted to concentrate instead on a hint of a spicier smell, but paint fumes went deep into her lungs.

For thirty minutes or more, she worked the duct tape against the ceramic tile until abrasions burned her cheek. *Who am I kidding? He said no one would find me for months. Even if I get this dang cloth out of my mouth, who will hear me scream?*

I've got to get back to the elevator. The idea of those doors closing, trapping her inside again, sent a wave of panic through her stomach. *You must,* she told herself. *It's the only way out. Get up and hop.*

But gravity fought her willpower, and she could not stand. Trussed hands and feet were useless weight. Every possible maneuver seemed momentous and beyond her ability.

Now what? Packi thought of her husband for inspiration. Ron had run marathons to beat back his cancer. He'd struggled with his pain and pushed himself to finish every race. This was her marathon. Moonlight would be her reward. Determined to face her challenge, she writhed and squirmed like a worm on a wet sidewalk, moving inch by inch along the tiled hallway. Endless time crawled with her.

Kay's little black dress bunched itself around Packi's hips. Perspiration drenched her hair. The adhesive across her face irritated her skin. She knew it would leave an angry, red mark. *Like a chemical peel some of the women swear by,* she thought as she grunted and lurched across the tiles. *What if Art had shown up for our date and saw me like this?* She amused herself with the little joke. *He'd run the other way, cured of his romance.*

After what seemed like an hour, Packi rested and searched the darkness around her. A glow seeped in from around the corner. *Almost there,* she thought. She doubled her effort, and reached the end of the hallway. With one last push, Packi squirmed into the condo's main room. She lay on her back, basking in the moonlight that streamed through the floor-to-ceiling windows.

Packi's smile tugged at the duct tape across her cheek. She knew she'd be all right. The twinkling stars told her so. She was never so happy to see blinking, red lights on a passing airplane and the fluorescent glow emanating from other tall buildings. When the airplane, carrying tourists into Fort Myers International Airport, descended out of her view, she surveyed the condo's main room. Her good humor withered when she calculated the distance to the elevator, but she resigned herself to the task. *Better get started.*

No longer confined in the narrow hallway, she abandoned her inchworm technique and stretched to her full length. She rolled, flopping front to back like a lopsided log, toward her escape route.

Every rotation hurt. She used her chin to push off. Her shoulders and hips complained, and restraints cut into her wrists and ankles. After a half dozen flops, she quit. Dizziness left her nauseous. She closed her eyes to stop the room from spinning.

She could almost hear her husband's voice, nagging at her. *Keep moving. Go.* She gritted her teeth, squeezed her eyes shut, and rolled, stopping only to reorient herself and adjust her direction.

When she banged into the five-gallon bucket of paint, she stopped. She opened her eyes and rested. The elevator's red button glowed three feet above her head. She twisted her body around and slid her feet up the wall and kicked at the button. She missed by four inches. She hitched her butt up two inches higher. The button might as well have been on the ceiling. Words, to which she was unaccustomed, fought to escape the gag in her mouth. She let her legs fall to the side and curled up into a fetal position to feel sorry for herself.

Two minutes later, she groaned. *Stop it, Patricia Walsh. No one else is coming to the rescue. Get at it.* With the little strength she had left, she twisted into a sitting position and propped her back against the wall. She planted her feet, pushed with her legs, and slid her spine up the smooth painted surface. She butted the elevator button with her shoulder and waited for the doors to slide open. She butted again. Nothing happened. She raised her trussed arms to an unnatural angle, aimed her elbow at the glowing red light, and pushed. The doors remained closed.

He jammed the doors downstairs. She moaned in disbelief. For the first time, Packi hated the man in the dark with his paint rag, confusing smells, and wet voice. He had thought of everything. *He really means for me to die. This condo is my tomb.*

Exhaustion invited doubt and defeat. I'm done, Packi thought. This tape isn't coming off. No one will find me. She slumped further into herself, sighed, and resigned herself to being a quitter, with dying. With that realization, relief flooded her body. Tension drained from her shoulders. Pain eased from her neck and spine. She struggled less to breathe. Packi rested her head on the tile floor in the light of the moon and gave up the fight.

23

"Good morning, Kay," Marilyn called across the parking lot. She waited as Kay secured her bike in the metal frame next to the pro shop. "What did Packi have to say about her date with Art?"

"Don't know." Kay adjusted the shoulder straps of her tennis bag and fell into step with Marilyn. She glanced down at the tennis courts and bleachers. "She should be here. I stopped by her house. No answer."

Marilyn stopped short and faced Kay. "You don't suppose she stayed…"

"Absolutely not. Not on a first date." Kay hesitated. "You think?"

"Good morning, ladies," Collin yelled from the far side of the court. He stood next to a wire basket filled with hundreds of tennis balls which he hit in quick succession at the rest of the team on the near court. "Glad you could join us." He hit a hard shot to Grace's backhand making her swing at empty space. "Is Packi not showing up?" Collin smirked. "Did I scare her away?"

Marilyn and Kay ignored the rhetorical taunt, dropped their gear bags on the bleachers, and trotted onto the court to take their places in line. Mary greeted them, but focused on Collin, ready for her chance to volley. The four other women in line had already worked up a sweat. In a burst of speed, Beth hit her powerful forehand directly at Collin. The ball struck him in the left shoulder and spun him around. He winced in pain, dropped his racquet, and grasped the injured arm.

Shocked that he hadn't deflected the shot, Beth ran toward the tennis pro while the rest of the team stared. "I'm so sorry. Are you hurt?"

Collin glared at her and pulled his sleeve over a badly bruised bicep. "You'll have to do better than that." He picked up his racquet and grabbed five balls from the basket. "Now put some pace on it." He fed her another back line shot just beyond her reach, and she lobbed it out of bounds.

Disgusted, Beth trotted off the court and rolled her eyes. "Why do we pay him?" she asked no one in particular as she joined the end of the line. "What a jerk."

"You got him good," said Kay. "I'm impressed."

"Somebody got him before I did," said Beth. "He's already bruised. Our man, Collin, must be slipping." She wiped sweat from her forehead with her wristband and readjusted her visor. "Where *is* Packi anyway?"

"Haven't heard from her," Kay said. "I'm beginning to worry."

"Maybe she went downtown," Mary suggested. "To the county office to work on her petition to save the alligator."

"Probably. We shouldn't worry. She's a big girl." Beth shrugged, but frowned as she pounded her racquet strings against the palm of her hand. "If she doesn't show up, we'll track her down right after practice."

After an hour of drills, the team took a water break. Hot and sweaty, they slumped onto the benches and mopped their faces with towels. Beth guzzled several ounces of water, wiped her mouth on her wristband, and then paused in mid-thought. "My phone's in airplane mode. Maybe I missed a message from Packi." She fished her cell phone out of her tennis bag and switched it on.

"Leave your phones at home, ladies," Collin called from his spot in the shade. "It rings during a match, and you lose that game. League rules."

"Somebody stuff a tennis ball down that man's throat," Beth said half to herself, but earned a few snickers from her teammates. She turned her back to Collin. "Hey. She sent me a text."

The team crowded in closer under the canopy to hear the message.

"Uh." Beth screwed up her face in serious thought. "All it says is *He.*"

"He who?" asked Kay.

"That's it. Just *He.*" Beth shrugged as she punched in Packi's cell number. "Has to mean Maddox. I wonder what Romeo did."

"When she send it?" asked Marilyn. "This morning?"

"Last night," answered Beth, but then spoke into her phone. "Packi. How'd your date go? Gimme a call." She frowned, disconnected the call, and slipped the device back into her bag. "We'll keep checking. That's too weird."

"Yeah," said Kay. "Why wouldn't she finish her text?"

"Something's up," said Beth. "I'm going to Packi's house to see what's going on."

Kay and Marilyn nudged each other. "We're coming with you," Kay said.

Mary had been listening. "Grace and I are going for a walk at the slough after practice. We'll see if she's been there."

"Call me if she is." Beth zipped her gear into her bag and slung the strap over her shoulder.

"We got another half hour, ladies," Collin yelled as he took his place next to his basket of ammunition.

"We have important things to do." Marilyn waved to him and jogged after Kay and Beth.

24

Deputy Billy Teig's lunch, a Reuben sandwich with all the fixings from Jason's Deli, began to congeal as he pecked at his keyboard in the sheriff's headquarters. He had lost his appetite after the call he and Leland handled a few hours earlier. A bad one. The old lady did not have to die that way.

The report could have waited, but Teig needed to get off the street—needed the impartial, cold feel of the industrial-type desk, the weary paint, the mounds of dog-eared files—to put what he had seen into perspective. *With so many old people flocking to Florida's tropical paradise*, he thought, *some of them were bound to be victims.*

Teig clicked *Save* and stared at the hourglass blinking on the screen. The house on Estero Lane had been filthy and reeked of death. Lynette Sanders had lain on that ratty couch for so long that the cushions molded around her emaciated body. Her son had to point out the woman among the piles of junk. She'd been dead for several days, and he hadn't noticed.

Teig tried to cram the ugly images in a painless part of his brain. He scribbled his name on the crumpled paper bag and shoved his sandwich inside. *Maybe later*, he thought. The secretarial chair creaked as he heaved his body up. He threw the Jason's Deli bag into the fridge in the break room and almost ran into Tanya on his way into the hall.

"You got guests," the receptionist and part-time dispatcher said with a snigger.

Deputy Teig ignored Tanya's provocation and moved to the smoked glass panel to view his visitors. He groaned when he recognized Kay Chandler with two other women; one bigger, stronger, the other skinny and as nervous as a banty chicken. All wore some sort of sports outfits. *Tennis*, he remembered. *But in public?* He glanced around the small reception area for Mizz Walsh. She'd have her usual plate of sweets, trying to wreck his diet. No Mizz Walsh. No cookies.

Teig pushed open the heavy barrier door. "What can I do for you, ladies?"

Kay Chandler flinched, reminding him of a reprimanded child, but she then stepped forward. "We just don't know what to do." She opened her hands to him, as if begging, and picked up momentum, getting louder and more desperate. "She didn't show up for tennis. She's not home. We can't find her!"

"Whoa, Mizz Chandler." Teig softened his voice, hoping to appear less intimidating to the poor woman. "Tell me. Who are you looking for?"

"Packi!" She drilled him with a hard stare.

"Mizz Walsh?" A quiver of unease snaked up his spine as he looked down on Kay Chandler. "How long has she been missing?"

"Overnight at least," the biggest of the three women said. "We figured it out this morning."

Her voice filled the confines of the small reception area and reminded him of a quarterback calling audibles. *Caucasian female. Five-ten, 145. Puffy lower lip.* She stepped forward and put a hand on Kay's shoulder.

"Packi didn't show up for tennis practice," she told Teig. "I'm the captain, Beth Hogan. This is Marilyn Scott."

He nodded a greeting to them both. "When's the last time you saw Mizz Walsh?"

"She had a date last night." Marilyn crossed her skinny arms and seemed to shrink as if she'd rather blend into the wallpaper.

"A date?" Teig tried to wrap his arms around that. "She didn't come home?" He shut out the images that popped into his mind. "You checked her house? Cell phone?"

They bobbed their heads in unison, their faces tense, expecting answers from him.

Teig minimized his own dread, kept his voice professional, calm. "Where's her family? Who would she contact if she was in trouble?" Mizz Walsh's last drunken call to his home came to mind. He cringed at the thought of phoning hospitals, but itched to get at it.

"Sorry. Packi's new to the team." Guilt tinged Beth's husky voice. "She's from Illinois, but I don't know much else. She's quiet." The team captain glanced at her tennis partners for confirmation.

Kay Chandler agreed. "She never talked about family. You'll do an APB, right?" Her question was a plea and a demand.

The deputy put on a reassuring smile. "Let's start with a missing person report. Please come in." He held open the heavy door and ushered Mizz Walsh's friends into the station and past the receptionist, who raised her pencil-thin eyebrows, giving a disdainful once-over to their short skirts and tennis shoes. Teig shot Tanya a warning look and guided the women through a maze of file cabinets to the conference room.

"Please sit." Teig indicated two worn chairs at an equally battered conference table and pulled over an additional seat from the corner. "Coffee? Water?" He positioned himself in a more substantial chair and laid the missing-person report form in front of him, his pen ready.

The women ignored the offer of coffee and perched on the edge of the chairs, leaning toward him. "We're really worried."

"These things usually resolve themselves," he told them and wished he believed it in this case. "The paperwork is just a formality." He asked all the pertinent questions, writing quickly. Name, height, age, weight. "How long has Mizz Walsh been dating the gentleman?"

"They just met," Kay said as if it was cause for celebration, something to be proud of. "Yesterday at the funeral home."

"Funeral?" Teig asked in disbelief. *I guess in a retirement community, funerals are just another social event.* A suspicion then hit him and pressed him back in his chair. He crossed his arms over his bulletproof vest and eyed the women. "Whose funeral?"

"That real estate guy on TV," answered Beth. "The whole team went. Carla wanted our support."

She's snooping again. The deputy groaned, but stopped the long, low growl when Marilyn froze in place, like a possum caught in a flashlight beam. Teig clenched his teeth and regained his official demeanor. *Okay, maybe Mizz Walsh is just one of them goodhearted people who bake casseroles for grieving families.* "What's the man's name?"

"Art Maddox," said the team captain. The web of lines at the edge of her left eye tightened as she spoke the name.

He tried to picture the business partner, the uptight suit he and Detective Leland met at the Golden's house, romancing the lively Mizz Walsh. Couldn't do it. *Maybe she's lonely,* Teig thought. *More likely diggin' into Suncoast Realty's business. Not good—Leland uncovered ties between Suncoast and a crime syndicate in New Jersey.*

Wooden chair legs moaned in complaint as he shifted his weight. *Could the enforcers from New Jersey be after Maddox and caught Mizz Walsh, too?* He didn't want to alarm the women, who already looked as jumpy as cornered raccoons, and chose his words carefully. "Did she say where they'd go?"

"Twisted Vine downtown," Kay Chandler tapped his report as if she wanted him to write it down. "The car's not in the garage. I don't think she came home." She stopped then as a blush rose on her cheeks. "She wouldn't have stayed with him. She just wouldn't."

That would be the best outcome, the deputy thought. "Tanya! Get me a phone number for an Arthur Maddox, Suncoast Realty," he yelled into the next room. "Let's just call the man and ask him."

The air conditioner faithfully spewed chilled air, but confronted by three agitated women, Teig sweated through his cotton shirt. "Tanya!" He smiled at his visitors to cover for his coworker's lack of response.

"How about one of those Silver Alerts," suggested Beth Hogan.

Surprised, the deputy considered that option. "You think Mizz Walsh has a mental impairment? Some physical issue?"

"No, of course, not," Marilyn interjected from the chair furthest from him. She shrank back into her seat when he raised his eyebrows. "I'm a nurse." Her voice trailed off. "I haven't seen any signs." She looked to Mizz Chandler for help or confirmation.

"No way," Kay said, casting a stern glance at Teig as if he'd offended her. "Packi's sharp physically and mentally."

"Okay," said Teig, "but we post Silver Alerts on highway billboards to locate impaired individuals who may have wandered off. That probably ain't what happened here." The worry in their eyes added to his own unease. He shouted over his shoulder to the dispatcher. "Tanya!"

What a... He glanced at the proper ladies across from him and forced a polite smile. "I'll find that number myself." Eager to get away from their expectant faces, the deputy heaved himself over to another chair in front of a computer screen. For the first time, he noticed the keyboard was blackened with years of grime. He positioned himself between the familiar equipment and the tennis players from Paradise Palms.

* * *

Billy Teig knew the land, the fishing spots, hunting ground, best shrimp joints. He'd been born in southern Lee County, but it no longer resembled the land of his youth. There had been orange groves, cattle pastures, and scrub dotted with ponds and sloughs and crisscrossed with creeks and canals. To the east, up river, tiny towns struggled to survive and the Babcock lumber and cattle ranch spread over 156,000 acres. Air conditioning and the Baby Boomers changed all that. Now terra cotta roofs sprouted everywhere, and manicured golf courses civilized open spaces.

Paradise Palm Golf and Tennis Club was on Deputy Teig's regular route. His phone calls to the Walsh home and to her "date" had gone unanswered, so a home visit was the next step. He had assured the busybodies that he'd locate their missing friend, and then sent them on their way.

He was familiar with the townhome and condo sections of the subdivision, but had few calls from the single-family units—the executive homes, as the developer named the cookie-cutter houses. He turned onto Hibiscus Way and cruised past a long row of homes, looking at mailbox numbers for 1135. The uniformity annoyed him. Only the choices of plants and hanging doodads made each house unique.

The Walsh house had the same manicured shrubs, thick Bermuda grass, and brick-paved driveway as all the others. She also had pots of flowers, two royal palms guarding the entry, and a sculptured art thing sitting next to the walkway.

Teig pulled into the driveway and surveyed the residence. A neighbor with a garden hose gawked at the cruiser and edged closer to the Walsh property. Teig didn't need a witness as he extricated his belly from behind the steering wheel. The effort made him hot and irritated.

"Good morning, officer," said the old gentleman. "What's going on?"

"Wellness check." Teig gave the citizen his obligatory friendly wave and slammed the car door.

"Patricia's not home," the man said, turning off the water hose and dropping it into the mulch.

Teig knew and dreaded the eager-to-help type. He kept walking. "Thanks, but I have to check."

"She gave me her key."

Good thinking, Mizz Walsh. He stopped and turned toward the neighbor. "Thank you. That'd be helpful." He continued to the front door while the old man hurried into his own house.

Teig rang the doorbell and knocked, and then peered into the windows at the sides of the door, but saw only a neat, sunlit room. He circled the house, testing locks and checking windows. He followed the sound of water and let himself into the caged lanai. A waterfall fed a small, kidney-shaped swimming pool. He scanned the bottom, but saw only clear blue water. Teig hadn't realized he'd been holding his breath and let it out slowly. Nothing appeared out of order.

The neighbor hustled to meet Teig at the corner of the house and handed him the key. The deputy stepped through the shrubbery, ignoring the gaggle of three women at the end of the driveway. They watched him, expecting him to find the answers.

"Ladies, go home," said Teig. "I'll take care of everything here."

The women in their tennis outfits nodded, but stood shoulder to shoulder at their car. He decided to let them be. He fitted the key into the lock, shooed the old gentleman back, and entered Mizz Walsh's house.

Big house for a single woman. He scanned the open living room area, the kitchen, laundry room, and small bedrooms to the left. He long ago gave up imagining such a house for himself and Mikey and didn't begrudge Mizz Walsh the classy layout.

The door to a larger bedroom on the other side of the entryway was open. The attached bathroom sparkled with clean tile, marble counter tops, and a glass walk-in shower.

"She's wearing my shoes."

Deputy Teig caught sight of Kay Chandler reflected in the mirrors and whirled around. "Go." He pointed to the door.

"I just wanted to tell you I was here last night," she said. "I could tell you if everything was in its proper place."

He sensed it took every ounce of the woman's gumption to offer her help, so he softened a bit. "I can see that there's been no trouble here. Now go on out."

"Okay, but I thought I should confirm…"

Gumption or not, this is police business. "Mizz Chandler, out." He had seen all he needed to see. Mizz Walsh had not had a break-in, hadn't gotten sick, nor had she been a victim of an accident—at least not in her home. He used his bulk to herd Kay back through the house and out the door. He turned the key in the lock. "What were you talking about? Your shoes?"

"Packi couldn't decide between my silver heels or her black pumps." Kay punctuated her words by poking a finger into the air. "I saw her black pair on the bedroom floor. She's wearing my silver shoes."

Everyone's a detective. Hidden behind his dark glasses, Teig rolled his eyes. *These women try my patience.* He opened their car doors and waited until the three of them loaded into the Prius.

"Thank you, ladies." He slammed the door. "Have Mizz Walsh call me when she comes home."

From the passenger side window, Beth Hogan handed Teig a business card with a tennis ball bouncing along the bottom edge. "Let me know if we can help," she called back as Kay Chandler pulled away from the curb.

Not a chance. The deputy watched the car drive down Hibiscus Way and turn toward the super-eights. He climbed into his cruiser and almost tossed the silly card out the window, but the neighbor still gawked from the edge of his property. *You'd complain to the sheriff about me littering your lawn, wouldn't you, buddy?* Teig gave the concerned citizen a curt nod and drove off.

* * *

Tanya claimed she couldn't locate addresses for Arthur Maddox or Suncoast Realty, so Teig pulled in a convenience store parking lot and fired up his laptop. *Man, did I dodge a bullet with that one.* He punched at the keyboard harder than necessary. The part-time dispatcher had made his life miserable in a hundred little ways since he rejected her come-on months ago. *Now she's affecting my work.* He groused under his breath and Googled Suncoast Realty. *What woman doesn't like kids? Me and Mikey are a team. Mizz Walsh could teach her a few lessons.* The sudden comparison bothered him. *Why am I thinking of...* He quickly dismissed the notion.

Teig jotted the realty office address on a pad and tucked the note in a clip on his dashboard. *Not too far out of my area,* he reasoned. *Do a drive-by. See what this Mr. Maddox is up to, and no need to inform Tanya of the detour.*

25

Beth drummed her nails on the dashboard. "Teig's never going to call us." She'd been thinking during most of the ride home. The prospect of sitting at home, waiting for news, didn't sit well.

Marilyn pulled herself forward from the backseat. "I agree, but what can we do?"

"We do our own search for Packi," said Beth. "I got a bad feeling we'd better be quick about it."

Kay stopped the car in the turn lane rather than pull into the clubhouse parking lot. "I'm in. Where to?" She gripped the steering wheel at the eleven and one positions and looked at her passengers.

"Suncoast Realty," said Beth.

"My thought exactly." Kay yanked her Prius into a tight U-turn, bumped over the curb, and earned a scowl from the driver of a golf cart. "Oops."

Marilyn gasped. "That was Ralph Clemson." She ducked into the shadows of the backseat. "He's a board member."

"He puts his pants on the same way we do," said Beth. "He'll get over it."

Kay waved her apology to the angry man and got the car into its own lane. "He'll publish an editorial in the newsletter—women drivers, blah, blah." She gave him another cheerful wave and headed for the exit.

The green lights were kind to them, though Kay challenged the tail end of two yellow lights. Traffic flowed well. During the twenty-minute drive north and east, the tennis partners convinced themselves that Packi's date with Art Maddox was the key to her whereabouts.

"Scenario number one." Beth held up one finger. "The date went well and the two of them are cozied up somewhere doin' a love-fest." She grimaced. "Or two, after the date, she drove…"

"Where?" Kay and Marilyn asked in unison.

"I don't know." Beth huffed in frustration. "But my ex-boss, the illustrious Mr. Maddox, will know something—time, direction." She thumped her hand on the dashboard. "Here, turn here."

Kay took a quick right into an unpaved parking lot. The Florida-style building had wide overhangs to protect the front porch from torrential rains. The porch and shutters wore white paint to set them off against slate-blue walls. Yet, the pleasant tropical setting looked abandoned. The grass along the sidewalk grew too tall, vines encroached on the railings, and wilted flowers hung from hanging baskets.

"Are they out of business?" Marilyn asked.

"No cars." Kay stopped and peered over the steering wheel as if reluctant to approach the unkempt building.

"Maybe he fired everyone," said Beth. "If he's here, he's parked in back." She eyed the far parking lot and felt a surge of fear, a reminder of the moment a man had jumped from those bushes to mug her. She touched her swollen lip. "Park on the side. We'll go in the employee entrance."

"Uh-oh." Marilyn twisted around in the backseat. "A squad car's pulling in."

Dust spun into the heated air as Billy Teig wheeled his cruiser into the side parking lot and came to an abrupt halt next to the Prius. The women scrambled out of their seats and stood behind their vehicle; Beth and Kay with their fists on their hips, and Marilyn, a step back. They waited for the deputy to extricate himself from the tight confines of his official vehicle. Red-faced from exertion and anger, he hitched up his pants and adjusted his shoulder holster and bulletproof vest. He brought himself to his full height and marched forward to confront the women.

Before the deputy could speak, Beth held up her hands in mock surrender. "I'm here to visit my coworkers and boss."

Teig's disbelief showed from behind dark sunglasses. "You work here?" He seemed to struggle to keep his face citizen-friendly.

Beth lifted her chin to bolster her case. "Until the day before yesterday."

Squint lines formed beneath the rims of his glasses as he scanned the three tennis players. "Didn't I make it clear you ladies are *not* to meddle in police business?"

"We're just..."

"I don't want to hear it." The deputy cut off Kay's explanation and pointed to the crushed shell driveway at their feet. "Stay," he said as if commanding a rambunctious dog. He then lumbered toward the front of the real estate office. The hum of distant traffic was drowned out by the crunch of coquina shells beneath the big man's boots. The sound died off as he rounded the corner.

"Geez," Kay muttered, when the deputy was out of sight.

Beth huffed in disgust and motioned the others to move out of the sun. From the shade of a live oak, they could watch the length of the building. Beth pointed to a car parked near the employee entrance. "Maddox," she said. The black Lincoln was almost hidden, its nose buried in a hedge of overgrown hibiscus.

Beth half expected her ex-boss to dart out the back exit as Teig rapped on the front door. The knocks, first on glass, then on wood, got louder and more impatient, then stopped. The women waited and watched.

Within seconds, Teig appeared from around the corner of the building. Sweat stains rimmed his underarms. He headed for his cruiser, but seemed to think better of it. He altered his route and veered toward the women. Ready for another rebuke, the tennis team members tensed.

The deputy stopped his advance when he noticed the rear parking lot. He pointed to the Lincoln half obscured by vegetation. "Whose car?"

Beth expected the question and replied in an instant. "Art Maddox," she said. "Come on. There's an employee entrance in back." She rushed toward the rear of the real estate office, not waiting for the deputy's response. His mouth turned in a downward arc, but he followed Beth. Kay and Marilyn gave him a head start and then hurried along behind.

While Teig knocked politely on the door, Beth knelt near a flower pot and found a key beneath a ceramic frog. She ducked under the deputy's elbow and fitted the key into the lock.

"You can't...," Teig said, but she already had. He grabbed for her arm a second too late. Beth burst into the building and knew her exact destination. The deputy entered more warily and shouted, "Lee County Sheriff's Department!"

Teig's booming voice startled Marilyn and reverberated against the walls of the small supply room. She backed into the exit door, but Kay took her by the arm and shadowed Teig into the hallway.

"Maddox?" Beth yelled, stomping past empty rooms toward the airy lobby. Teig followed, but paused to survey each office. Kay, barred by his bulk from advancing, glanced into the rooms as well. She sensed no danger or need for a police raid and took time to admire the upscale furnishing, nautical themes, and high-priced lighting.

"What a shame they're out of business," Marilyn said, motioning into one of the abandoned offices littered with Manila folders and half-packed, cardboard boxes.

Kay had no such sympathy and kept moving. Ahead, Beth stood in the doorway of a large, sunlit office.

"Hello!" a man's voice said as if surprised.

"Why didn't you answer?" Beth demanded. "Where is she?"

Teig maneuvered into the office and positioned himself in front of Beth. "Excuse our intrusion, Mr. Maddox. When I saw your car and you didn't respond to my knocking, I thought there was an emergency in here."

"I apologize, Deputy." Maddox stood behind his mahogany desk, his fingers spread like long-legged spiders on the polished surface. "I don't hear so well anymore." He pointed to his ear and shrugged. "As you can see, we no longer have a receptionist to attend to visitors or answer ..."

"Because you fired me!" Beth pushed past Deputy Teig, but he stopped her with a firm touch to her shoulder.

"I'm sorry, Mrs. Hogan." Maddox placed his spider-hand over the lapel of his suit. "A responsible businessman must do all he can to keep a company afloat."

Teig cleared his throat. "Mr. Maddox, these ladies are concerned about their friend, Mizz Patricia Walsh. Do you know her whereabouts?"

"Yeah!" Kay surprised herself with her outburst, but kept going. "What happened on your date with Packi last night? Where is she?"

Marilyn nodded in agreement as she clung to Kay's arm and glared at the man behind the desk.

"Mrs. Walsh?" Maddox tilted his head to the side and offered a sad smile to the trio. "Well, I don't know where she is. I had pressing business and had to cancel our date."

"Then where did she go, and where is she now?" Beth demanded.

"I don't know, Mrs. Hogan. The last I heard she was having drinks with friends."

"Who?" Beth sniffed and clucked her tongue. "I don't believe a word you say."

Deputy Teig stepped toward the perplexed man and gave the women a warning look. A small motion of his hand quieted them. "Mr. Maddox, the ladies are upset. Do you have any information to help us locate Mizz Walsh?"

Maddox seemed to relax as if pleased to talk man to man. "Now *I'm* concerned about Packi, too." He focused on the deputy's name tag. "Deputy Teig. I certainly hope the lady is okay, but all I can tell you is she said she was with friends last night." He picked up a cell phone from the desk, made three swipes to the screen, and offered the device to Teig.

The deputy read several messages and placed the phone on the desk. "Sorry to bother you, Mr. Maddox." He turned toward the door. "Let's go, ladies."

Beth protested. "What about the investor list Packi wanted?"

"Let's go, ladies," Teig commanded. He herded them out of the office to the front entrance.

"Tell Packi I'll phone her tonight," Maddox called after them.

Teig scowled as he ushered the women out of the building and let the door slam behind them. In the shade of the overhanging eaves, he said, "I can't overstep my bounds here, Mizz Hogan. Do you understand? First, we find Mizz Walsh. We don't worry about her damned alligator, and we let the detectives worry about the list and murder investigation."

Kay's head snapped up. "So, they think Danny Golden *was* murdered."

Teig stepped down from the porch into the hot sun, but turned back to the women. "I didn't say that, Mizz Chandler. I said they're *investigating.*"

"Packi was right," Marilyn said in a near whisper. "Now I'm really worried about her."

The tennis partners clustered together as they followed the deputy's bear-like body across the dusty parking lot. "We should have gotten more out of Maddox," Beth said. "Teig, wait up. What was in Maddox's text messages?"

Deputy Billy Teig paused at the door of his cruiser. "The text messages let Maddox off the hook. He sent one to cancel the date, and Mizz Walsh texted back that she was with friends." He opened the car door. "I'm going to check the overnight incident reports and, just as a precaution, the hospitals." He wedged his belly behind the steering wheel and slammed the door. The car window slid down as silent as a nylon zipper, and he propped his forearm on the window frame. "Now, if you ladies want to help, go home, check her house again, and call all of Mizz Walsh's friends." He poked his fingers into his shirt pocket and offered them each a business card. "Let me know what you find out."

The three women turned away and shielded their eyes as dust roiled and swirled around them in the wake of Teig's vehicle. He pulled onto the blacktop road and sped away at a speed that would get ordinary citizens ticketed.

In the ten minutes they'd been in the real estate office, the heat in the Toyota Prius rose by twenty degrees. Kay rolled down all the windows and turned the fans on full blast. From the passenger's seat, Beth eyed Maddox's office window. A shadowed hand adjusted the plantation shutters. "I don't trust that man," she said in disgust, "but I doubt we'll get anything more out of him."

Kay looked up from her cell phone with a frown. "Still no answer from Packi."

"Now what?" asked Marilyn. "Should we go back to Paradise Palms?"

"Try calling Grace," Beth suggested. "She and Mary were going to the slough. I don't know where else Packi would go. Did she ever mention friends other than the tennis team?"

"Not to me," said Kay as she tapped out Grace's cell phone number.

"Maybe." Marilyn held up her hand. "When we worked at the food pantry downtown, Packi met one of the volunteers, Mark. He helps out twice a week... and he's one of the patrons."

"You mean he's unemployed or homeless?" Beth turned around in the front seat to stare at Marilyn. "You didn't think to mention this?"

Marilyn bristled and pointed her finger at Beth. "There's nothing wrong with Mark. He's working hard to turn his life around."

Kay dropped her phone into her lap and looked back and forth between her friends. "When I dropped off the dress and shoes to her yesterday, Packi mentioned a volunteer. She wouldn't say much. Something happened, and he scared her."

Marilyn gasped and covered her mouth. Tears gathered as she shook her head in disbelief.

Beth shot her a brief glance of sympathy. "We're going downtown." She nudged Kay's arm, motioning to the road. "Turn left out of here, and we'll take 41 north."

26

Instinct wrestled her into consciousness, but Packi refused to open her eyes to the brightness. She rolled her head to the side to shield herself from blinding heat, and pain streaked through her neck. She groaned and tried again. Cartilage creaked in small increments at the base of her skull as she strained away from the sun. Awareness crept upon her. Dreams of cool pools of water drained away, replaced with the dry turpentine rag in her mouth. Numbness deadened her limbs. She squinted into the dimmer parts of her prison and wished again for the oblivion of sleep.

Cruel reality met her in the empty condo twenty floors above downtown Fort Myers. *I need water.* Her dress had sopped up her body's moisture and bunched like a wrung-out washrag around her waist. Dry sweat left a stiff film of salt on her skin. The expanse of windows that had brought the welcome company of stars and moon last night, now blasted her with tropical heat. She thought of mummies beneath desert sand.

Ron, why haven't you helped? Send water. Her dead husband didn't respond, and she figured she'd take the matter up with him soon. She resigned herself to their reunion until a cramp in her stomach reminded her that she was still very much alive. The angle of the sun told her breakfast time ended hours ago. She wondered if the tennis team was already at lunch after practice. *Do they realize I'm missing?*

Her bladder became uncomfortable and demanded attention, so she twisted toward the hallway. Shards of porcelain littered the floor. The journey to the bathroom would be painful, she thought, but then laughed through the duct tape. *You idiot. What would you do once you got there?* An image popped into her mind. Some real estate agent would eventually find her body. Packi dreaded the disgraceful scene, the smells, the decay, the dried puddle of urine.

This is ridiculous! She berated herself for being a pessimist and a quitter. *At least get out of the sun, so your face isn't all blistered when they find you.* She began to roll, banging her elbows and hips with each rotation, but not stopping until her skin contacted cool tile. She rested then, but only for a minute. She became determined to stretch her time on earth by another few hours, maybe a day, and to show that she tried by every means to escape. Ron would expect that of her. Her friends would expect it. She expected it.

Packi gnawed at the gag in her mouth and pushed it outward with her tongue. She grimaced and yawned to try to dislodge the duct tape. She rejoiced when the tape slipped a bit. Maybe the heat of the sun softened the glue, she thought, or her sweat loosened the adhesive. Maybe her attacker had bought the cheap stuff. *Thank goodness for penny-pinchers.*

She stretched and worked her face for an hour, stopping every now and then, to give her exhausted muscles a break. A dry sob escaped her then and wore away her resolve. Physically spent, she lay with her cheek rested against the floor. Her body argued against facial exercises or any other movement. *One more try,* she argued back, *and then I'll give up.* She groaned and shifted onto her back. Waiting to muster her strength, she studied the ceiling and then felt something dangling against her neck. She pulled in her chin to look downward. Doubting her eyesight and good fortune, she moved her head from side to side. A strip of duct tape trailed across the neckline of her little black dress.

Packi rolled to her knees, already imagining a fresh breath and saliva. She bent and contorted her spine to catch the dangling duct tape beneath her knee, and then tugged and pulled until the tape ripped from her face. With a violent head-shake, she expelled the gag from her mouth. Still on her knees, she scowled at the wad of cloth on the floor as if she had just vomited a tapeworm. A joyful shout was beyond her ability. Instead, she sucked in hot, dry air and fell to her side to enjoy the sensation.

With that major triumph behind her, Packi had new hope. "What's next?" She tested her voice and took pride in the spoken words, no matter how thin and raspy they sounded. Her throat burned too much for further discussion, so she went back to thinking.

Sometime during the night, her arms had gone numb. *Dead probably. Atrophied. If—no,* she corrected herself, when *I get out of here, they'll probably amputate my arms. I'll miss tennis, but I can still be useful. Maybe not. How do amputees manage?* She groaned out loud, hurting her throat. *Stop it! All this negative thinking will kill you.*

She tried to apply logic to her current situation and determined that getting her arms in front of her body, rather than behind, would be a vast improvement. *Why not? I'm spry.* While still on her side, she wiggled her hands under her butt and wished her hips hadn't widened over the years. She ignored the pain shooting across her shoulders and strained to pull her arms forward.

"Spry?" *I hate spry. Just another word to remind old people their bodies are falling apart.* She gave a mighty yank and screamed in pain as her elbows and wrists threatened to dislocate. With her hands still tied at her back, she sagged against the floor. Disgusted, she gave up the contortionist act.

Packi watched clouds sail by the great panes of glass and pictured speed boats, fishermen, and yachts below on the Caloosahatchee River. The square of sunlight advanced toward her, determined to catch her dozing; determined to broil her skin and pump the temperature in the condo up past a hundred degrees. She scooted a few feet further from the windows.

Keep moving. Blood flow. She rolled to her other side, stretched out straight, curled into a ball and then repeated the maneuvers. She rolled and stretched until it no longer made sense. *What's the use?* She watched the skin on her knees crinkle and flake off. *All those years of moisturizing, and they'll find me desiccated.* She groaned and closed her eyes. *It'll be a closed casket.*

"Stop it!" It was the first words she'd spoken in more than an hour. The noise awakened a bit of feistiness. *Keep this up and you'll die. Stay alert. Think of something else.*

But a review of her life and accomplishments only saddened her. *Why hadn't Ron wanted more children? Why hadn't she had them anyway? Who will mourn me?* Thoughts of the tennis team cheered her. They had rallied around Carla at Danny Golden's funeral, and she looked forward to being the center of attention at her own funeral.

Wait, she protested. *I'm not dead yet. Before I die, I want to know who did this to me.* She tried to recall the attacker's shape, his size, his voice, but clear thinking eluded her. She imagined Danny Golden was the man who stood over her last night, bound her up, and left her to die.

"Obviously not." The two words sounded odd in the naked room, but roused her. They grated against her throat and weren't worth the pain. She repositioned her stiff body and forced her mind through a review of possibilities.

Who could be so inhumane, so callous as to leave me to suffer like this? Jake, the homeless, possibly psychotic man in the parking lot, topped her list. Of all the suspects, only Lyla was vindicated. *Not so fast. Maybe she put her lover, Collin, up to it. Did the attacker seem like a tennis player? How tall was he?* Anywhere from five-ten to six-two, but Packi could only guess from the position of his flashlight. She closed her eyes to picture Collin. Though he'd taught her tennis for months, she couldn't recall anything about him.

I'm losing my mind. She worried then about dehydration or heat exhaustion and tried to remember the symptoms: *cold sweat, nausea, fever, racing pulse. All bad.*

To change the subject, Packi challenged her brain with more questions. *Who would have keys and know where to turn off lights and operate the elevator remotely? Art Maddox? He had been Danny Golden's partner. Did he turn in all the keys when the bank foreclosed? He never arrived last night,* Packi remembered. She couldn't imagine the bland, gentlemanly Maddox was the terrifying creature who tied her up. Jake seemed a more likely culprit. *How had he gotten into the building last night? Did he stash me here like Big Joe stored the body in his pond? What else did Jake have planned?*

Her gruesome imagination unsettled her, so Packi concentrated on another round of exercises to push blood into her extremities. She felt her pulse throbbing in her jugular vein and tried to ignore her racing heartbeat. *What does he want from me?* She groaned aloud and laid still. *Silence. Somebody's covering up Danny Golden's murder by killing me.* She pictured Danny Golden tying her wrists. *Why do I keep thinking it's him? Because somebody looks like Golden, or acts like him?*

Packi opened her eyes in surprise. *Vern? The pharmacist? Is that possible?* She pictured Vern's height, his weight and suddenly recalled a phrase the attacker had used. *Curiosity killed the cat.* She couldn't remember Vern ever quoting the old adage, but his wife had. At tennis practice Carla had warned her about curious cats.

Could Vern have done this to me? The thought sickened her. She preferred the attacker to be Collin or Jake or neither—just a hit man hired by the mob to clean up the mess she'd made. *Then why not finish the job? Why am I still alive? Someone wants a clean, guiltless murder—like expecting the gator to be the culprit. Now this condo tomb will kill me. It's someone who thinks of himself as good.*

Logic and questions hurt her brain, so Packi rolled her head to the side and welcomed a gray dimness that shut out even the hot Florida sun. A hazy doze took her. She dreamed of pain and the rap of knuckles on her skull. Her father morphed into Ron at the wheel of his 1957 T-bird. The old engine growled, and he drove until mosquitos engulfed the open car. She swatted at the insects, jerking herself awake.

Somewhere in the building, machines had sprung to life. Sound and memory connected, and Packi's eyes flew open. She squirmed around to see the numbers above the elevator door and flinched.

He's back. He's here to make sure I'm dead.

Adrenaline shot into her veins, urging her to run, to hide. Instinct pushed her by inches further from the elevator. *He'll kill me this time.* She rolled once, twice, but could not muster the strength for a third. The rooms down the hall blurred like a mirage in the desert. Their distance did her in. She lay exhausted with her jaw against the ceramic tiles. *I can't.* Dry tears stung her eyes. She willed herself to die of her own accord, but waited instead like an exposed slug in the shadow of a hungry crow.

27

Heat radiated off the white stucco wall as Mark propped his bike at the back door. His body ached for his dark, cool room, his cot. He thought only of sleep until rustling in the bushes caught his attention. *Oh, man. Not now.* He put the key back in his pocket. "Jake?" The homeless man emerged from the shadows thirty feet away. He twitched and jerked, as if bitten by fire ants, and disappeared around a corner.

Something's not right, thought Mark. He followed Jake to the front of the building and found him pounding his fist slowly against the glass door.

"It's okay, Jake." He approached one hesitant step at a time. "Nobody's in there. No one will hurt you." Even as he reassured the disturbed man, Mark became concerned about the darkened lobby, too. The lights should be on for security. The building should appear occupied.

Mark got to within fifteen feet of Jake and reached out his hand, but the troubled man squealed and lurched away. "I'm sorry, Jake." He dropped his arms to his side. "Come back. It's okay."

But Jake sped up and hobbled into the parking lot. He made a halting circle around a car and disappeared into the shrubbery.

He's getting worse. Mark shaded his eyes and watched the shadows swallow the man. He sighed at the hopelessness of Jake's plight and noted the car. *An Audi.* Dread snuffed out a brief flicker of joy.

What is she doing here? The Audi appeared neat and undamaged, but didn't allay his sudden fear. He called her name and scanned the sidewalks and streets and then looked upward. *Could she really be in the building? Is that what Jake tried to tell me?*

He ducked under hanging palm fronds and ran to the back entrance to let himself into the hallway. Hot, stale air hit him in the face. *What the hell.* Except for emergency exit lights, the entire building was dark. The AC was off. *Someone cut the power,* he thought. How did she, or anyone else, get in?

"Packi?" As he pushed against the door to the stairwell, the clank of the crash bar drowned his echo. "Where are you?" No answer. He descended cautiously, alert to movement and sound, but the basement was as noiseless as an abandoned mine. The electrical vault would be to his left, he knew, but in the dark he stumbled against boxes and paint buckets before he found the door. Inside, he felt the wall for the fuse box, but jerked back when metal sliced his cheek.

"Damn it." The corner of the electrical panel door had gouged his skin, just below the eye. He felt warm blood trickle from the gash. He pressed the heel of his hand to the wound and absorbed the pain before feeling for the main breaker. The lever was down, in the off position. No accident, he thought, pushing the handle up and then down and up again for good measure. One by one, he reset toggle switches to restore power to each zone. The overhead light blinked on. Machinery kicked into gear. Air conditioning units hummed.

He took the stairs two at a time and rushed to the bank of elevators off the lobby. The penthouse elevator doors stood open as if waiting for him. *That's where she is.* He pushed the green LED button and the doors slid halfway, bumped, and opened again. He punched every button on the panel, but the doors refused to close. He looked upward as if able to see through twenty floors.

"Packi!"

Get a grip, Hebron. Mark racked his brain for a cause of the malfunctioning doors. *Gotta be a blockage.* He ran his hands over the rubber edges. Nothing. He pushed the penthouse button again and watched the door slide eight inches and bump back. Mark knelt, examined the door's path, and found a yellow pencil jammed in the track. The stub had been broken flush with the floor. He picked at the obstruction with his fingernails and then his key.

"God, let her be okay."

Finally, he pried the bit of pencil from the track, jumped to his feet, and punched the button. *All systems go.* He ascended to the penthouse with just the hum of the elevator to announce his arrival.

28

Deputy Billy Teig cruised the city streets with the phone to his ear. At each intersection, he slowed and scanned the side streets for a charcoal gray Audi or a female Caucasian, blonde, sixty, five-two, 115.

"Thanks, buddy. When you get the results, give me a shout." He disconnected the call and tapped his pen against the steering wheel. *No relevant incident reports. Now what?* Bo Shaller, his Fort Myers connection, would watch for reports coming through the city PD today. Bo had also offered to triangulate Mizz Walsh's cell phone signals to narrow the search. He trusted Bo. They'd caught redfish and cracked a few beers back in the inter-coastal just last weekend.

Tanya finally did her job and called the area hospitals to review overnight admissions. She'd played the guilt card, but he wasn't taking any of her guff. Not now. Not when someone's life might be at stake. Neither Lee County nor Gulf Coast had a patient by the name of Patricia Walsh. *Good news, but what next?*

The Twisted Vine had been closed, but the manager and kitchen crew were busy preparing for the dinner crowd. None remembered seeing the couple Teig described, nor a reservation under the name of Maddox. The manager had offered the deputy a delicate looking pastry, but he had declined.

Should've taken it. Damn the diet. Teig's stomach growled in protest, and he wished he hadn't thrown the deli sandwich in the fridge hours ago.

A block away, he spotted a familiar car turn right onto Edwards Street. He slid in behind the slow moving Prius and ran the plate. When the report popped up, he flipped on his lights.

Kay Chandler pulled to the curb and waited for him to approach her vehicle. "I'm sorry, officer. We're looking for our friend and..." She shaded her eyes from the glare of the sun. "Deputy Teig?"

"Good afternoon, Mizz Chandler," he said. "Didn't I tell you to go home and stay out of this?" He leaned down to peer into the car.

"Sorry, Deputy," Beth said from the passenger seat. "We thought of an important detail and wanted to check up on it. Tell him, Marilyn."

"Yes." Marilyn, huddled in the back seat, pulled herself forward. "I, uh, work at the food pantry over on Edison." Her voice wavered and she avoided eye contact with the deputy. "Packi helped me with donations a few days ago and met a man. Mark. Mark Hebron."

"Another date?" he asked.

"No. I can't imagine." She glanced at her friends for reassurance before continuing. "But he's the only person we could think of here, downtown." Her words trailed off.

"And?" He kept his excitement hidden. Maybe the old ladies had something.

"And," Beth took up the explanation, "he's a homeless guy. He scared Packi last time she saw him, but he's the only one she'd know around here."

Not what I expected, Teig thought. Homeless. His mind flipped through the scenarios: mental issues, drug and alcohol problems. *This is going bad—fast. What was Mizz Walsh thinking?*

"What do you know about this Mark Hebron?" he asked.

The two women in the front turned in their seats to look at their friend in the back. Marilyn pulled the collar of her shirt closed and looked out the window at a palm tree silhouetted against a blue sky. "I don't know anything. Only that he's rehabbing a house somewhere near enough to ride his bicycle."

Mizz Chandler took over. "We already stopped at the food pantry. Now we're looking for houses being rehabbed. Found several, but he's not at any of them."

Teig pulled a description of Mark Hebron out of Marilyn and stepped away from the Prius to call Fort Myers PD. He gave a short update to his contact, Bo. "That's all I got, buddy. See if he's got priors or caused any trouble."

He ignored the women's gabbling and the slam of their car door until he felt a tug on his shirt sleeve.

"We have to go." Kay Chandler's anxious whisper irritated him like a gnat in his ear. "Marilyn saw a man who's a friend of Mark's. We're going to talk to him."

Teig glanced beyond the Prius, about one hundred yards away. *Black male, six foot, 190, about fifty years old—hard to tell with a street person—unshaven, tattered.* The man stood on the sidewalk as if in a trance under the shade of a live oak. Marilyn Scott walked toward the man with her hands outstretched, making hushing sounds.

"Get in the car," the deputy said. "Let me handle this."

"No," hissed Marilyn. "Stay back. You'll scare him away."

"Marilyn knows him from the food pantry," Mizz Chandler whispered. "But he hides all the time. His name is Jake."

Teig had seen the type before, barely able to function, maybe schizophrenic, should be in a hospital. He waited and watched Mizz Scott try to coax him toward her. She'd gotten within fifteen feet of him when he bolted. The man disappeared in a flash into the foliage, the overgrown hedge surrounding one of the high-rise condo buildings.

"Wait, Jake," Mizz Scott called. "Do you know where Mark is?" She flopped her arms to her sides and glanced back at her friends and the squad car. "He doesn't like cops. Stay there." She moved toward the hedge and turned into a parking lot, out of sight.

Teig waited five seconds and started after her with Mizz Hogan and Mizz Chandler behind him. He heard the scream and broke into a run. He ordered the women to stay back and advanced into the parking lot with his hand on the butt of his gun. From cover, behind a royal palm, he scanned the area.

Mizz Scott stood in the middle of the lot with her palms flat on the convertible roof of a charcoal gray Audi. "This is Packi's car," she said in awe as if she'd just found a holy relic. "I know it is."

Teig's heart thundered in his chest as he stepped into the sunlight and approached the vehicle. Fighting to breathe, he nodded to agree with Marilyn. The plate number belonged to Patricia Walsh.

But where is she? Teig paced around the car, tested the locks, and peered into the interior. Empty seats, front and back. He wondered about the trunk. *Too small*, he thought, but corrected himself. *For an average person, that is. Mizz Walsh is no average person.* He knocked on the trunk, listened, and then scrutinized the car, the ground, and the area for signs of a struggle. Nothing.

Mizz Scott must have read his thoughts. Her thin face turned skeletal, bloodless.

"Which way did Jake go?" he asked.

She opened her mouth, but couldn't speak.

"Mizz Walsh?" he called.

"Packi!" The other two women yelled in unison and then one at a time and in different directions.

He quieted them. "Stay here. I'll check inside the building." The tower of condominiums gave off an eerie, abandoned aura, like a ghost town. He rejected the image and tested the front doors. Locked. He walked around the side, checking in and behind the dumpster, and amid the shrubbery. A service door in back was also locked, so he continued around the other side of the building and back to the parking lot.

Marilyn stood at the far side of the asphalt, calling Jake's name. Beth Hogan poked around in waist-high foliage, searching for who knows what. Kay Chandler stood at the window next to the main entrance with her nose up to the glass and her hands cupped around her eyes. *They are such a pain in my...* Teig stopped himself. *Okay. Okay. Just trying to help their friend.*

"This place is locked up tight," he said loud enough so they'd all hear, and then clicked on his radio. "Tanya?" He waited for the dispatcher to respond. "I'm at the Skyview building on Edwards Street." He gritted his teeth, expecting her unwanted input. "Right. I took a detour on my way home. See if you can locate the owner and get me a key." He rolled his eyes. "Yeah, I know it's the city's jurisdiction. Please, Tanya. Thank you."

Teig reached for his cell phone to call Bo, but jerked back, interrupted by Mizz Chandler's high pitched scream.

"My shoes. Those are my shoes!"

She turned toward him with a smudge of dirt on the end of her nose and a potent mix of anger and fear in her eyes. He rushed to her side and looked inside the lobby where she pointed. A pair of shiny silver women's heels lay near the door. "Yours?" he asked.

"Yes!" Kay yanked on the handle and kicked at the door. "My shoes. I loaned them to Packi for her date. She's in there."

"Take it easy, Mizz Chandler. The owner will be here soon with a key." But Teig wasn't so sure, and if Mizz Walsh was locked inside with Jake... He didn't want to envision the scene. "I'm going to my cruiser for a crow bar." He double timed it back down Edwards Street and wedged himself behind the wheel of his vehicle. "Fort Myers. This is Lee County. Requesting assistance. Edwards Street. Skyview Towers. Missing woman possibly held captive inside."

"Ten-four, county."

He gunned the engine and wheeled into the Skyview parking lot with tires squealing. He popped the trunk and found a tire iron with a good flat edge and rushed to the door of the building. "Stop, ladies. Stop."

Kay and Marilyn stood back, flushed from bashing rocks against the windows. Beth raised a large chunk of coquina overhead and heaved the rock with a loud grunt. The coquina ricocheted off the safety glass, leaving a slight blemish in the smooth surface. Panting heavily, the women stood aside to let Teig pry open the door.

29

Play dead, she thought, though every cell in her body screamed to run. *Maybe he'll take one look and leave.* She turned her face away from the elevator and went limp, accepting her fate, and her last moment of peace.

In spite of her mental preparations, the elevator's ping startled her. Through the floor she felt the vibration of heavy footsteps. A man called her name. Her heart sank when she recognized the husky voice.

Is there no good left in this world? she moaned. She squeezed her eyes shut and waited for him to deliver the death blow.

"Packi? What happened here?" Mark dropped to his knees and gripped her shoulder. She shrank from his touch and shuddered beneath his anger.

"Who did this to you?"

Packi sank her teeth into his wrist and pushed off him with her knees. Wild to escape, she rolled and flopped away until she banged into a wall. In an instant, his knees were at her back. He grasped her shoulders and she jerked away. "No!"

"Packi—Mrs. Walsh, take it easy. Look at me." With a light touch he turned her toward him.

Face to face, she couldn't ignore him or play dead. She searched his eyes for one last shred of humanity. "Don't kill me," she begged. Her cotton-dry tongue mangled the plea.

"What!" He recoiled as if jolted by a hot wire. "Packi, it's me. Mark. Mark Hebron." He slumped back on his heels. "Marilyn, your friend, introduced us at the food pantry. Remember?"

Packi heard his anger turn to concern; his horror into gentle persuasion and wondered if she'd been wrong about him. She studied his stricken face and tried to separate her nightmares from the events of last night. She wanted him to be the man she'd met at the food pantry, not the angry man he'd become at the park. He had that faithful dog look again.

"Mark," she whispered. Speech was difficult with her teeth stuck to the lining of her mouth. "Water."

"Sorry. No water up here." His eyes darted to the elevator and back to her. "Outside spigot works. I'll go…"

"No!" The word rasped from her throat. "Don't leave me."

"Okay. Okay." He clenched his jaw and began to work his fingers into the knotted fabric around her wrists at her back. "I'll get you out of here."

Packi allowed her head to loll on the floor, to rest, to hope, until she heard Mark suck in his breath. She contorted her spine to face him. An unknown fear pricked her skin.

"Wait here." He straightened his back and used his knee to push himself to a standing position. He stepped over her bound feet and disappeared from her view.

He's leaving. The thought stole her remaining strength. *Just when I started to trust him.* Packi groaned and closed her eyes, mourning her last hope. She let numbness overwhelm her and did her best to slide into unconsciousness.

Mark's calloused hands prodded her into the light. "Drink this." He helped her into a sitting position. "It's from the toilet tank, but it's clean."

Cool water startled her cracked lips. She craned her neck to get at the liquid and lapped like a wolfhound at the few ounces. The paper container leaked and shredded. Water dribbled from the corners of her mouth and down her chin. She didn't care.

Mark squeezed the last few drops from the soggy paper onto her lips. "I'll make another cup. There are real estate brochures on the counter." He settled her head on the floor and began to rise.

"No," Packi barked from the depth of her raw throat. She would have clung to his ankle if she could, if her hands weren't tied. Her swollen tongue made words thick and cumbersome. "Please untie me."

Somehow Mark understood. While he struggled with the knots, she luxuriated in the feeling of a moist mouth. Hope revived her.

"How did you find me?" Each word grated against her throat, but she had to know.

"Jake." Mark picked at the bindings and swore beneath his breath. "He ambushed me outside. Something agitated him so bad, he couldn't speak. He showed me your car and banged on the lobby doors."

"Jake?" The man hidden in the banana palm in the park and last night in the shadows of the parking lot scared her. "He did this to me."

"No." Mark sat back on his heels and shook his head. "He's not capable." The deep furrows across Mark's forehead contradicted his statement. "No," he said, still trying to convince himself. "Jake couldn't have gotten in." He stared at her for a moment as if *she* was the crazy one and then yanked at the knots. "Did you see the man's face?"

She shook her head, but held to her assertion. "Jake followed me." A ragged cough accompanied the words. "Like he was spying."

Mark didn't respond. She twisted around to look over her shoulder and studied his grim face. Blood dripped from a small gash on this cheek. *Did a shard of porcelain cut him?* An impossible thought gripped her. *Mark and Jake are in it together. Did he return to be the hero? Why? To obligate me to him? Was he part of the real estate thing and wanted to scare me away from... from what? The investor list? Big Joe?* Every idea felt like a nail driven into her skull. She closed her eyes to shut out the headache and to better see the puzzle pieces. One question needed his answer.

"How did you get in?" *The doors were locked. He wasn't just a passerby.* Her hands pulled free from the fabric strips, but fell limp at her sides, useless in a fight. She pulled her wrists onto her stomach and winced as blood awakened painful nerve endings.

"Never mind that," Mark said, working on her ankle restraints. His face stiffened and his teeth ground together. "Do you have any clue who *else* could have done this to you? It wasn't Jake."

"Then I don't know." She veiled her eyes and watched for a reaction as she spoke in a low, painful whisper. "A man trapped me in the lobby and tracked me up here." She cringed at the memory of the dark figure's muffled voice. The smell of spice and turpentine. His large hands on her body. She suddenly remembered long, thin fingers. To be certain, she studied Mark's stubby fingers working at the fabric knots. *How did I ever suspect him?*

"The man said he'd leave me to shrivel up like a mummy in a tomb."

Mark grimaced, tore at the last knot, and freed her feet. "Let's get you out of here. You need a doctor." He hoisted her upright.

Packi cried out and her legs crumpled beneath her. She pitched forward as helpless as a rag doll, but he caught her in the crook of his arm. She sagged against his chest and breathed in the scent of fresh-cut lumber.

"Give me just a minute," she whispered into the cotton shirt beneath her cheek.

"Okay. Okay." Mark lowered her to the floor and propped her against the wall. "Take your time, but I'm taking you to a hospital."

In his capable, no-nonsense hands, Packi suddenly felt safer than she had for years. She rested her head against the wall as he knelt at her feet to massage her calves, slowly coaxing circulation to return. Packi became acutely aware of her bare feet, naked legs, and the dress that had crept up to her hips. She squirmed to pull at its hem.

Mark kept his eyes on her face. "Why were you here? In the building, I mean." His soft, low voice matched that faithful Doberman expression he had. "Were you looking for me?"

"What? Why would..." His question confused her. She lowered her chin to her chest. "I had a date."

Mark's face lost its youthful color. "A date?"

"I wanted to meet him here." Her voice dried up before she could explain her reasons for meeting with Art Maddox and how he'd canceled out. "Thank you for finding me." She slipped her fingers into his calloused palm and squeezed tight so he wouldn't pull back—so he'd forgive her for the date.

"The doors were locked." She still needed to know how he'd gotten in the building. The question wouldn't go away. "How did you get in?"

"I trespass," Mark said. "Last year, the bank took over the property and fired the janitor. Before he left, I talked him out of a key and have lived in the supply room ever since. Now I look after the building to protect my investment." He shrugged. "Can you stand yet?"

"Too hot." She wanted sleep, but fought to keep her eyelids open and to put sense to his words. Something about a midnight restaurant, drywall, dawn. She wanted to question his story, but heat stole her strength. *I'm dehydrated,* she warned herself. *Headache. Hot.* Her head wobbled on her shoulders, and she leaned against him.

Humming in her ears got louder. Wall vibrations transmitted an alert through her spine. Her eyes darted to the elevator. The doors were closed.

Mark heard it, too. "Nobody's supposed to be in the building."

"It's him," she cried. "He's coming back!" She grabbed at Mark's arm as if he could save them both.

"No. He wouldn't." Mark jumped up, ran to the elevator, and jabbed at the red button to recall the car. The numbers above the doors continued the count down.

Packi attempted to stand, but fell to her knees. An unnatural rhythm caught at her heart. Gray fog spun the room. She felt the tile for a handhold, but collapsed onto her shoulder.

Mark scooped Packi up and struggled with her dead weight into a back bedroom. He hid her in a closet, propped up against the wall. "Shh. This is only a precaution."

Sunlight left the room. Her ears buzzed. "I feel sick," she groaned. "So hot."

"I'll get help," Mark whispered, laying his hand on her clammy forehead. "Have to see who it is." His shadow stepped outside the bedroom door, and her vision went dark.

30

"Packi!" Their voices filled the spacious lobby and bounced off marble floors. Echoes mocked them. "Where are you?"

"Stay here," Teig ordered. "Watch for my back up."

The women nodded, but when the deputy disappeared behind a set of double doors, they ran through other hallways and into side rooms calling for their friend.

Teig tested every locked door in a long hallway, calling Packi's name. Finally, a door yielded, opening into stairwell to a lower level. He descended, listening and shining his flashlight into the dimly lit basement. All was quiet, until a scream came from the lobby. He hauled his body up the stairs, pulling himself along the handrail and cursing his weight and the steepness of the stairs. He heaved himself into the hallway and ran with loud, heavy footsteps to the lobby.

"Oh, my God!" Kay stood in the door of an elevator with one hand over her mouth and the other outstretched as if begging. "Oh, God. Oh, God."

The roar of his own heartbeat overwhelmed the woman's cries, but Teig read the anguish on her face. She held out a bit of jewelry to him. The silver chain and tiny tennis racquet all but disappeared into his fat palm. He stared down at the broken chain and remembered how delicate and vulnerable Mizz Walsh had seemed that first day at the alligator pond.

"That belongs to Packi," Kay insisted. "I found it in here. There's no way she got in this elevator voluntarily. She'd have a panic attack."

"Let's go," Beth said, rushing inside the elevator. "She's up there somewhere."

The deputy slipped Packi's chain into the pocket behind his badge. "Out, Mizz Chandler, Mizz Hogan." He jerked his head toward the front entrance. "Stay in the lobby. A city cruiser will be here in a minute. I'll go up and check each floor."

"Four can search faster than one." Beth held onto the car's railing in defiance. "Let's go." Her shout filled the crowded space.

Marilyn tapped the placard on the wall. "This car goes only to the penthouse."

Teig put his hand between the doors to stop them, to order the women out to safety, but Kay grabbed his arm and pulled it down. With the tenacity of a badger, she grasped his hand between her own. "Packi's up there. She needs help." Her eyes drilled into him. "All of us. Now."

Teig frowned down at the fierce, little woman and relented. "We're wasting time." He jerked his hand away from her. The door closed, and the car shuddered as it ascended.

"Now I gotta watch out for you three!" The sheriff would take his badge after this debacle, but it was Mizz Walsh that worried him. "Stay in this elevator," he ordered, "and take it back to the lobby the second I get out. I don't need you as liabilities."

In the face of the deputy's anger, the women bobbed their heads and backed into the walls of the car. They stared above the doors, as people do in every other elevator on earth, but this elevator had no numbers. Only the whir of the machinery and the pull of gravity indicated their ascent to the twentieth floor.

Deputy Teig drew his gun and held it pointed at the ceiling. The man's bulk comforted Kay, but that weapon meant trouble. Marilyn clasped Kay's elbow and Beth edged closer. The weird little tic in the team captain's cheek might have been a smile to reassure them, but didn't. In the deputy's shadow, the trio waited in silence until the car bumped to a stop. A ping sounded. Kay sucked in her breath as the door slid open and sunlight poured in.

Teig motioned for the women to stay behind. He pointed the gun into the open room and disappeared from view.

What if he needs to retreat, Kay thought. *What if Packi is here and needs help?* She stepped forward and put her hand over the door sensor to hold it open. She glanced back at her teammates for approval. Beth jerked her head *yes*. Marilyn hugged her arms to her chest with her knuckles pressed to her lips. She blinked once to agree.

31

"Lee County Sheriff's Department!" Teig had the man in his sights. *Caucasian male, sixty-ish, five-ten, 180. Not Jake.* "Out where I can see you." He motioned with the barrel of his Glock, and the man moved into the hallway, hands above his head.

"Don't shoot." The man raised his arms higher. "Don't shoot. We need water. Get some water."

Fat chance, fella. "Down on the floor." Teig glanced beyond the man down the hallway. *Are there others? Where's the vagrant?* His mind worked the scenarios. He scanned the spacious condo for ambush sites. He listened for movement. Nothing but the man's groan as Teig shoved him, face down on the floor. The deputy heard the expulsion of air as he pinned the man to the ceramic tile with a knee between his shoulder blades. He holstered his weapon and yanked the suspect's hands to the small of his back and with one practiced move, whipped out restraints and cuffed him. The man put up no resistance.

The deputy's hand covered the man's head and mashed his cheek against the tile. "Where is she?" Teig hissed into his ear.

"Water."

"You get nothin'." Teig pressed his knee further into the suspect's back. "Where is she?"

The man grunted and strained against added pressure to his head. "Closet."

"Closet?" He pushed himself off the prisoner.

"Back there." The man sucked in air. "Water."

"Forget it, pal." Teig loomed over the prostrate form with his fists balled. "If you hurt her…"

"Mark! Oh, my God!"

Marilyn Scott stood behind Teig with her knuckles pressed to her mouth and tears in her eyes. The other two looked like wolves on the attack. Their presence and their anger calmed him.

"You know this man?" he growled. The suspect's cheek oozed blood, and Teig wondered if he'd gone too far. Or did Mizz Walsh get a few licks in?

"Marilyn, I didn't do anything," Mark pleaded from the floor. "Honest, Marilyn! She needs water. Get her water! Downstairs, the outside spigot."

Mizz Scott covered her face and shrank back. Kay Chandler comforted her friend with an embrace and scowled at the man on the floor.

"Stay here," Teig ordered. He noted the hatred on Beth Hogan's face. "And don't hurt him."

"Dehydration," Mark yelled.

Teig worked his way down the long hallway. The muzzle of his firearm led the way into room after room. *This place is a furnace,* he thought. Sweat blurred his vision. He let down his guard for a moment to wipe his eyes on his sleeve. His Glock slipped in his hand. *I'm in deep shit if this is an ambush.* He gripped the weapon tighter and continued to search the empty rooms.

Teig nudged open the door to the last room on the hallway. No furniture, no hiding places. One closet. He stood to the side and opened the closet door. Her bare legs fell out and lay limp against the plush carpet.

"Mizz Walsh?" He fell to his knees and felt for the artery in her neck. He held his breath until he found a faint pulse beneath her burning skin. He clicked on his radio. "Get an ambulance to Skyview Towers. Penthouse. Edwards Street. Now, Tanya!"

Packi groaned as he hoisted her off the floor. He crashed into the door jamb on the way out of the bedroom. He protected her head as he careened down the hallway. The women in the great room jumped out of his way.

"There's a water spigot outside." Mark shouted from the floor. "Near the back door."

"Elevator," Teig yelled on his way past the prisoner.

"I got water!" Kay dug into her purse as the women ran into the elevator.

Beth removed the bucket which had held the door open and jabbed at buttons until one of them worked. The door's ping gave the rescuers hope.

Kay produced a bottle of water and dabbed a bit on the unconscious woman's lips. She poured water through Packi's hair and over her chest. "Good Lord. We have to get her temperature down."

Marilyn held her fingertips lightly against Packi's wrist and stared at her watch. "One twenty," she whispered. She and Kay exchanged glances.

"What does that mean?" demanded Beth.

Kay pulled a wad of tissues from her purse, soaked them with the remaining water, and swabbed Packi's forehead. "She needs an ambulance."

"On its way." Teig shifted the woman's light weight in his arms. He pursed his lips and stared above the door where the numbers should have been.

The elevator's occupants felt the gravity change beneath their feet as the car settled at ground level. The door pinged and slid open. Fort Myers PD greeted them with handguns drawn.

Teig rushed out into the midst of the adrenaline-hyped officers with Packi in his arms. "Water!" He had no time for explanation or jurisdictional protocol. The city cops holstered their guns, cleared a path for Teig, and waited until he shouted over his shoulder. "The suspect is cuffed up in the penthouse."

As the responding officers swarmed into the elevator, Teig followed Mizz Chandler to a couch away from the heat of the windows and settled his burden onto the cool leather seat. He knelt at the side of the sofa and took her limp hand into his big paw. She rewarded him with a sigh. Her eyelids fluttered open.

"Hey, Mizz Walsh," Teig said.

Packi frowned with the effort to focus. She squeezed his fingers, but had a foggy, startled look. "Billy."

He leaned forward to hear.

"I'll bake you cookies," she whispered.

"Stay still, Packi." Kay elbowed the deputy out of the way so that she could minister to her patient. Beth rushed to the outside water spigot while Marilyn ran to their car for tennis towels. Together they wet the towels and draped them over Packi's naked legs, bathing their friend in lifesaving coolness.

Deputy Teig, feeling useless and ham-fisted, excused himself from the action and stood at the door to wait for the ambulance. In the west, the sun began its downward arc into the Gulf of Mexico, bouncing long, golden rays off the ripples of his beloved Caloosahatchee River. A bit of dust irritated his eyes and he swiped it away.

32

"I don't know what to think." Sadness added another weight to Packi's aching head. She lifted her right hand to her forehead, and fresh pain shot through her shoulder and elbow. Adhesive tape yanked at the fragile skin on the back of her hand where an IV needle pricked a blue vein.

"Be still now." Marilyn patted Packi's wrist and settled it beneath a crisp sheet. "You'll be sore for a while. They couldn't find an open vein. Most were collapsed." She grimaced, remembering the clumsy, rushed insertion by the EMT. Marilyn had fought the urge to push him aside. Judging from the growing bruises, the ER nurse also searched for a new vein and failed several times. "Try to sleep. We'll be right here."

Packi read the concern on her teammates' faces. *Marilyn's a nurse*, she remembered. *Kay, too. Maybe I should worry about myself.* The thought darted through her mind like the shadow of a hawk. "Can't sleep. I'd rather talk." Compared to the night spent in the Skyview condo, she felt pretty good. Fluids flooded her veins and quenched her body's thirst. "I don't understand. Mark saved me."

"That's not what I saw," Beth said from the foot of the bed. The willow-green room seemed too small to hold her energy, her anger. Her pacing stopped beneath the soundless television suspended from the ceiling. Inches above her head Kevin Mitchell's image played on the screen, a microphone in his fist and Skyview Towers behind him.

"Please turn that off," Packi said.

Kay glanced up at the TV and snatched the remote hanging from the bedrail. Just as she found the off button, an unflattering picture of Mark Hebron flashed on the screen. The blood on his cheek had dried in a ragged, brown trickle.

The image captivated Packi until the screen flickered and snapped to black. "I can't believe Mark did this." She remembered the blood, but not how he was wounded. *Porcelain?* She didn't trust her memory. Details blurred. *Maybe the bad parts were nightmares. Or mirages. And the good parts, wishful thinking.* "They arrested him?" She directed the question to Marilyn. "Where did they take him?"

A miserable expression clouded Marilyn's thin, pale face. She shrugged and turned her gaze to the wall behind Packi's bed.

"The city cops took him," Kay said. "That deputy friend of yours said they searched the storage room where Mark lived. They found every news article and editorial ever written about the dead man, Danny Golden." She clenched her teeth. "They also found the Big Joe articles. And your picture. I don't know what's going on, but it doesn't look good."

Beth paced between the hospital bed and the dark window. She crossed her arms over her chest and stared out at the lights of Fort Myers. "Obsessed is what I'd say."

Packi's head fell back on her pillows. *Obsessed? Had to be him. I'm so naive.* "What about Jake?"

"He's mentally ill." Outrage awakened Marilyn's spirit. "They found him in the bushes behind the building and brought him here. He put up a terrible fight." Tears dampened her anger. "I'm going upstairs to see he gets a good advocate."

"I eavesdropped on the cops in the ER when they brought him in," Kay said. "Jake's his name? They say he is an accomplice to the guy who trapped you up there. He can't, or won't, talk. Mark insists Jake had no part in it. Looks bad for Mark." She sent a sympathetic glance toward Marilyn. "Sorry."

Suddenly too tired to be sociable, Packi closed her eyes. A swirling storm of gray thoughts dragged her toward sleep.

"Packi?" Marilyn whispered. "The medication is taking hold. You'll feel better tomorrow."

"I'll pick you up when they release you in the morning." Kay's voice seemed far away.

"Goodnight, Packi," said Beth.

Someone stroked her arm. She nodded to the familiar voices, but didn't see them leave.

33

Purple bruises on her hands and wrists had bloomed and spread since the night before. As Packi searched her body for other damage, she lifted her arm to the morning light. Her forearm's thin skin crinkled and puckered like used crepe paper. *When did that happen?* She poked at the rippled, baby-soft skin in fascination. "Geez." She had never been a vain person, but planned to ease into old age gradually, not overnight. Disgusted that dehydration had sped the aging process, she gulped water from the quart container the nurse had left her.

What does my face look like? Packi groaned. No longer tethered to IV tubes, she rolled from the bed and tucked the hospital gown closed behind her. The nurses had instructed her to call for assistance, but Packi preferred not to bother them. *I feel fine.* She limped toward the bathroom. *Ouch. Except for that pain in my ankle.*

Shocked by the woman in the mirror, Packi scrubbed at the tape residue on her cheeks and splashed her face with cold water, hoping to at least put on a healthy glow. *I don't even look human.* She raked her fingers through matted hair and tried to push new wrinkles back into her hairline.

"I tried that. Doesn't work." Kay's wide grin appeared in the mirror over Packi's shoulder. "I brought some help." She held up a familiar makeup bag. "I hope you don't mind. We broke into your house and rummaged around for your stuff."

"You're a lifesaver." She gave Kay a quick hug and looked for the rest of the tennis team.

"Just me," said Kay. "We have a match at Pelican Preserve this morning. Remember? I have a bye, and Grace took your spot on court three. They're all thinking about you, though, and send hugs and kisses."

Kay turned toward the room and pulled back the cotton curtain. "Marilyn drove with me. She's up on the sixth floor looking for Jake and worried he won't have anyone on his side." Additional lines creased her forehead. "She seems to be mad about something. You, maybe."

"Me? Really?" Packi slumped against the door jamb. "But why?"

"I don't know." Kay shrugged her shoulders. "On the way over she talked about Jake and Mark. She's worried, that's all. She doesn't want to be angry with you, but their trouble seemed to start with you defending Big Joe."

Kay dumped the contents of a tote bag onto the rumpled blankets and white sheets: a pair of shorts, a sleeveless blouse, a light jacket, sandals, a hairbrush. "And undies," she said. "I bet they let you out today."

"Thank you," Packi said, taking the practical cotton panties from Kay. "I get released when the paperwork is done. My organs are healthy. Tests came back good. No real injuries." She sat on the side chair with her underwear in her hands. Moments before she had felt the warmth of having a team, a group of friends. That sense of belonging began to evaporate. "I don't want Marilyn, or anyone, mad at me," she said, "but it must have been Jake who attacked me." She folded the panties into a neat, little square. "And apparently Mark was part of it." The thought crushed something inside her.

"Beth heard that Mark guy say it was all his fault." Kay patted Packi's shoulder. "He kept saying how sorry he was. The police have him in jail, so you don't have to worry anymore."

Packi appreciated Kay's effort to wrap the situation up for her, to put her at ease, but her mind remained unsettled. "Then why did he rescue me?"

"Well." Kay arched both eyebrows. "Beth and I think he wanted to scare you away from poking your nose into the real estate stuff and Danny Golden's murder. Mark probably killed the guy. *But* he changed his mind and came back to be the hero, so you wouldn't suspect him."

Packi sighed in sorrow. "I thought the same thing when he untied me." Ugly images sapped her energy. She didn't want to believe he could be so cruel, that she had been fooled. She tried to remember what persuaded her to trust him, but couldn't.

"Confusion is part of heat exhaustion." Kay regarded Packi as if she were a stray dog in the animal shelter. "You're safe now."

"I guess." Still too muzzy to think straight, Packi gathered up her clothes and shuffled into the bathroom. "I need a shower."

"By the way," Kay said before the door closed. "A message came through when I was at your house. Art Maddox is very concerned about you." She grinned as if about to drop a juicy, gossip bomb. "You know, he's not bad looking, in an accountant sort of way, and he seems smitten with you."

Packi rolled her eyes at Kay's teasing and closed the door.

"He's got hair," Kay called.

So, it's come to that. Hair. Packi glanced at the woman in the mirror who badly needed a visit to a salon. She liked the idea of smitten. Pleasant images broke through her grogginess. *I need a break, a good dinner, a walk in the woods. Why not say yes to a date?*

* * *

As the doors slid open, Packi loosened her death grip on the hospital volunteer's kind and patient hand. She fought the urge to catapult herself out of the elevator. Packi kept her seat as the woman pushed the wheelchair into the spacious, cool lobby. She dabbed sweat from her face and squinted to read the volunteer's name badge. "Thank you, Marie. Sorry I freaked out a little."

"Better now? You had me worried." Marie waved to the guard at the front doors and parked the wheelchair at the curb.

Packi gave the older woman a wan smile and shielded her eyes from the sun's glare to hide her embarrassment. "I should have taken the stairs."

"Can't. Hospital policy." Marie set the brakes and flipped up the footrests. "You did fine."

Eager to get away from the wheelchair and the helpless image of herself, Packi scanned the parking lot. "There's my ride." She pushed out of the chair immediately and tried to slip the woman a twenty, but the volunteer frowned and waved the tip away.

"Take care, sweetheart." Marie stood at the curb as Packi settled into Kay's Prius. She cracked a small smile and waved before returning to her transport duties.

Packi tossed her bag onto the floorboard and belted herself into the front seat "I came down in an elevator."

Kay arched her brows and grinned. "Proud of you, partner."

"Yeah. I did okay." Packi shuddered.

Marilyn reached over the seat from the back and patted Packi's shoulder.

"Hi, Marilyn. Thanks for coming. What did you find out about Jake?"

"They wouldn't let me see him or tell me anything about his condition." Irritation sharpened Marilyn's voice. "But I spotted the social worker assigned to his case and recognized her from the food pantry. She says he's getting proper medication." Her words lost momentum. "I guess the police can't arrest him until he understands what's happening."

Packi flipped down the visor and watched Marilyn in the mirror. Kay had guessed Marilyn blamed Packi for Mark and Jake's predicaments. *How can she think that?* Asking her straight out was the only way to clear the misunderstanding. "Marilyn?" Packi twisted in the seat to look her teammate in the eye. "I'm afraid you think I'm responsible for starting this mess. Do you?"

"Aw, Packi." Marilyn winced. "I'm sorry. I'm really struggling with this. I liked Mark, and Jake always seemed harmless, but with what the reporters are saying, I see I was wrong." She covered the misery in her eyes with her hand. "Of course it wasn't your fault. Please forgive me, if I gave that impression."

Kay glanced at Packi and winked. They drove without a word until they stopped for a light on Daniel's Parkway. A city bus, painted in tropical colors, caught Packi's eye. She watched a Latina in a waitress uniform get off the bus and wade through the weeds at the side of the road. The woman continued into the ditch where she picked up a bicycle hidden in the long grasses, brushed off the dust, and rolled it to the asphalt path at the side of the road.

"Look at that," Packi said as the Latina pedaled down a side street. "She knew the bike was there."

"Yeah," said Marilyn. "People do that so they don't have a long walk home. I've always wondered why the bikes aren't stolen, but it seems to work."

"Do you think that's what happened out at Hammock Preserve with that bike we found?" Packi asked Kay. "The one I thought might be connected to Danny Golden?"

"Maybe so," Kay said, adding a tsk. "That means the police hauled it out of there for evidence, and some poor guy looked for it after a hard day on the job. Yikes."

"I guess things aren't always what they seem." Packi pondered the bus full of people as the Prius accelerated with the traffic. *What else did I get wrong?*

* * *

Home never looked so good. The blue periwinkle Ron had planted along the brick walkway welcomed Packi back after her two-day absence. Royal palms overhead waved gracefully, shading her path. Sun glinted off clean windows.

"Feels like I've been gone for ages," she said.

Kay stepped to the side as Packi fitted her key into the front door. "Well, you've had a rough time." She and Marilyn followed Packi into the house. "I hope you don't mind. The team didn't know how else to help you, so they vacuumed and dusted."

Packi plopped the tote bag on the sofa and glanced around the room. She had always kept a neat, clean house, but now it looked fresh and new. The furniture shined. The chandelier sparkled. The kitchen counter was lined with trays of baked goods. *How am I going to repay everybody for this?* "This is overwhelming." She opened the refrigerator door and stared at the rows of casserole dishes.

"That's what we do," said Kay. "We see a problem and fix it with food. Never fails." She winked and lifted the cover from a tray of cupcakes. "Grace made these, I bet. Looks like carrot cake. Can I fix you a cup of tea, or are you ready for lunch? Helen's chicken soup is out of this world."

"Sounds good." The team's generosity and attention embarrassed Packi. Uncomfortable in her own kitchen, she retreated to a stool.

"You just sit," said Marilyn. "We'll heat something up."

34

Years ago Packi and Ron quit setting an alarm clock. Each morning in the gray predawn, the groundskeepers came out to tend the golf course. Headlights crisscrossed the fairways. Automatic sprinklers beeped. Machinery skimmed over the manicured greens. Her favorite was the woman who sat on her mower singing at the top of her lungs over the roar of the motor.

As the landscapers mowed, Packi struggled into waking by pinning down the day of the week and fixing her mind on the plan for the day. An ugly memory startled her. She slid an arm onto her pillow and slit open one eye. Purple bruises and a swollen wrist confirmed the nightmare of Skyview Towers. She shuddered and hid deeper within the blankets.

Think of something good, she told herself. She ran through her list of blessings which she kept tucked in the back of her mind: *I live in a tropical paradise. I have memories of happy years with Ron. I'm healthy and play tennis—well, maybe in a few days. And today I'll visit Big Joe.*

Packi stretched her back and shoulders and tested her wrists and ankles. Determined to put yesterday's nightmare behind her, she reviewed her morning regimen: yoga exercises, a simple breakfast, a cup of Earl Grey, the Gazette's crossword puzzle, and then the nature preserve. Fortified with positive thoughts, she rolled out of the blankets and swung her legs over the side of the bed. She dressed in her spandex outfit and positioned herself on the lanai, ready for her usual yoga routine. Her aching body thought otherwise. She gingerly moved through a few easy poses, but soon retreated to her kitchen.

Grace's carrot-raisin muffins beckoned her. She gave into temptation and settled with the goodie in front of the newspaper with a cup of tea. *Healthy eating starts tomorrow.* She sighed and flipped through the paper for the crossword puzzle. A headline caught her eye.

Kidnapped Woman Rescued from Abandoned High Rise. Kevin Mitchell's byline headed the article. She scanned the text. *Patricia Walsh, the woman who leads the campaign to save Lee County's largest alligator, was rescued by police...* The facts in black and white overwhelmed her. A picture accompanied the story. She identified the nature preserve in the background before she recognized herself. "Oh, my."

Dazed, Packi raised her empty teacup to her lips and put it down again. She stared at the newsprint until the telephone jangled.

"Packi? Did you see it?" Marilyn's soft voice sounded breathless, worried. "I hope you don't mind. I called that reporter. I thought the publicity would be good for Big Joe. He must have gotten more information from the police. Is it okay? Do you mind?"

"It's fine," Packi murmured. "It's fine." She beat back her embarrassment and began to see the benefits of having her name and picture splashed all over page two of the paper. "In fact, Marilyn, you're a genius."

"Really, Packi? I was so worried, but I didn't want to bother you with it yesterday. You don't like the spotlight, but you're okay? I just thought..."

"Hold on, Marilyn." Packi interrupted her teammate's onslaught of words. "Someone's at the door. I'll call you back." She hung up the phone and limped to the front door. *Now what?*

"Patricia Walsh?" The man wore an FTD shirt and carried a tall, paper-wrapped package.

"For me?" A flower delivery always sent a ripple of excitement through her. Ron had surprised her with roses or a spring bouquet once or twice a year. She opened the envelope first and almost expected to see his name on the card. Instead, it read: *Sorry to cancel our date. Let me make it up to you. Art.*

Packi sighed. She ripped apart the paper to reveal purple, yellow, white, and blue flowers. Beautiful, but the colorful arrangement puzzled her. According to Victorian tradition, each choice of bloom sends a message. Asters could mean dainty. Gloxinia means love at first sight. That made her laugh. The silliness amused her as she trimmed stems of purple hyacinth. *The florist must have helped him with that one.* In the language of flowers, hyacinths mean *please forgive me.*

She dismissed the Victorian florist's marketing gimmick and added water to the glass vase. Then she pondered a long-stemmed snapdragon. *Gracious lady or deception. Which did he mean?*

Art Maddox called an hour later.

"Thank you for the flowers," Packi said. "They're lovely." She tried not to think about the gloxinia's meaning, but warmed to the man's soft voice and gentlemanly manner.

"Are you well?" Art asked. "I was devastated to hear you were attacked at Skyview Towers. My deepest apologies. I didn't know you had gone in, but I should have been there to protect you."

"Thank you for your concern," Packi said, "but the doctors took good care of me at the hospital and my friends are looking after me here."

"What can I do to bring happiness back into your life? Dinner this evening? A concert at Barbara Mann Theater? Deep sea fishing?"

"Whoa," she said, laughing at his desperation. "This is too much, too fast, Art. Maybe in a week or two. Today I must prepare to meet the Lee County lawyer." His silence told her he had not kept abreast of her campaign on Big Joe's behalf. "The alligator. I still intend to persuade the county to let him live."

"Ah, of course," he said as if he mused upon the animal. "What a treat it would be to see this alligator of yours. He must be a real specimen."

His enthusiasm pleased Packi. She had planned to visit the slough after dinner as she and Ron used to. They had enjoyed watching flocks of egrets, herons, and other large birds fly in to roost for the night. *Do I want to share that with someone new?*

"Well, Mr. Maddox, I intended to visit Big Joe late this afternoon. Would you care to join me at the slough?"

"Wonderful," he said in his soft-spoken way. "Afterwards, I'll treat you to a lovely dinner."

"Let's not rush this," she said, though she planned to say yes the next time. "Let's meet at Hammock Preserve an hour before sunset so you can see the migrating birds."

Sorry, Ron. Guilt nagged at the edges of her consciousness as she hung up the phone. *You said you want me to be happy.* She hummed a golden oldie to drone out the trepidation that crept in alongside her aches and pains.

Stay busy, Packi thought. The abundance of food left by the tennis team needed to be wrapped and put in the freezer. She welcomed the task. As she divvied up the casseroles into serving-sized plastic bags, she ramped up her nerve to call Kristen Curtis. The red-haired lawyer, who represented Lee County in court, did not intimidate her. Kristen seemed sympathetic, but Packi feared she couldn't convince the young woman to take the case; that her argument wouldn't save Big Joe; that she'd hear bad news.

Packi's father had tried to instill assertiveness in her. He often used the old cliche, *Take the bull by the horns.* Fearlessness did not come naturally to her. Still, she cleaned up the kitchen debris and went in search of the lawyer's number.

Miss Curtis remembered Packi and her own promise to follow up on Big Joe's case. "I got your variance request put on the agenda for tomorrow's meeting," she said. "The Board of Commissioners will hear your side. You have a chance, if you can tell a compelling story."

"You mean, you want me to speak?" Packi was flabbergasted. She had hoped the young lawyer would be a fiery, energetic advocate for Big Joe.

"You did well in court last week, Mrs. Walsh," the young lawyer said. "Do that again to get the commissioners' attention. Alligators are routine. There are so many, the Department of Natural Resources' policy is to remove any over seven feet long. There's not much I can say to convince them otherwise."

"Remove?" Packi gripped the phone as if it was a weapon. "As in slaughter!"

"That's right, Mrs. Walsh. Use your anger to energize your argument," the lawyer said with a hint of humor in her voice. "I'll contact a few of the commissioners and try to get them on our side."

This girl is not the enemy, Packi reminded herself. "Thank you, Miss Curtis. I do appreciate your help."

"My pleasure, Mrs. Walsh. Meet me at the county building downtown, tomorrow at three o'clock."

Packi wrote the address and time on Ron's notepad in a shaky hand. She settled the phone into its base and drummed her fingers on the buff-colored handset.

Do the very thing that scares you, her father had preached.

She snatched up the phone again and began to dial. As she made the first call to Beth, she rummaged in the drawer for her address book and flipped to the letter A.

35

This was our place. Packi reminisced while she waited at the entrance to Hammock Preserve for Art Maddox. She knew well the natural rhythms of the slough. Its serenity eased her mind. Always had. She and Ron had often strolled along the boardwalk to watch the birds fly in for the night. The slough had given him peace in his last days. Or so she had thought.

From under the pavilion, Packi watched Art maneuver his Lincoln into a parking spot, slip a dollar into the pay station, and put the receipt face up on his dashboard. *His hair is thicker than most of the men at Paradise Palms,* she thought, *and he's tall.* She smiled in anticipation of walking arm in arm with a man again, out for a pleasant stroll in the preserve.

Art's long strides carried him over the gravel driveway to the pavilion. "Good evening, Packi. You look lovely." He made a little bow and offered his hand to help her from her seat. "I've been looking forward to visiting your slough all day."

She silently thanked him for not noticing her bruises, or at least not commenting on them. *Such a gentleman,* she thought. *I guess we could have gone to dinner, too. Next time.*

"Well," he said. "Let's go see this gator of yours that caused all the trouble."

Packi darted a sharp look at Art, but caught a slight twinkle in his eye and decided to tease him back. "Now if Big Joe likes you, he may show himself. Otherwise, you're out of luck." She gestured toward the boardwalk entrance. "This way."

"Is it all right? Where is everyone?" He glanced around the near empty parking lot. "Maybe it's too late."

"We have a half hour or so of daylight," she assured him.

"But I put two hour's worth in the parking meter."

She turned her face away and laughed for his benefit. *What can you expect from an accountant?* "Consider it a donation, Art, and deduct it from your taxes."

"Good idea. I'll save the receipt."

She threw an involuntary look of disbelief at him, but stopped the glare when she caught that twinkle again. His deadpan face broke in to a grin. "I'm kidding, Packi. We bean counters get a bad rap."

He has a charming smile, she thought and wondered why she was surprised. "Come on, I'll give you a quick, official tour. I've been a docent here for five years and know all the slough's secrets."

"I'll bet you do."

He ushered her ahead of him while she pointed out deciduous trees, hammocks, pig wallows, lichen, and other often overlooked points of interest.

On the pier at Gator Lake, Packi and Art leaned their elbows on the same railing Deputy Teig had leaned against while watching divers retrieve the body of Danny Golden. She pushed the images into the back of her mind. Instead, she marveled at an anhinga's snakelike neck cutting the surface of the water. A gentle vee followed in the bird's wake, rippling the mirrored reflection of trees on the far shore. The snake-bird dipped beneath the surface and disappeared. "Isn't this lovely?"

"Very picturesque," he said as if his mind wasn't really on the scenery. "What did you see out here? I mean, that day when they found Danny's body?"

The question jolted her.

"Oh," he said when he saw her reaction. "I'm sorry to bring back bad memories." Art straightened and crossed his arms. He stared at the pier at the other end of the pond where an old man in a straw hat watched the sunset. "It's just that I keep thinking there must be something I could have done to save him. I should have seen the signs."

"You still think it was a suicide?"

"No, I guess not, but they haven't proved anything, have they?"

"Not proved exactly." Packi sympathized with his regrets. She watched his impassive face and wondered how such a restrained man dealt with grief and sadness. She patted his forearm and hoped the peace of the slough healed him.

"If this were January," Packi said to break the silence, "a thousand birds would fly in here at this time of evening to roost for the night. Those trees across the pond would be dotted with white. It's a spectacular sight." She unzipped her fanny pack and offered her binoculars to him. "These aren't as powerful as my professional lenses, but you should be able to see a few egrets and anhingas."

"I'm just pleased to be here with you," he said, smiling down at her. He put the compact-sized binoculars to his eyes and scanned the pond, the reeds to both sides of the pier, and the boardwalk along the shore. "I don't see anything. I guess I'm not good at wildlife sightings."

Packi took the glasses from him and raised them to her own eyes to hide her disappointment. She had hoped his request to visit Big Joe indicated an enthusiasm for nature, something they could share. If this dating thing developed into a relationship, they'd need common interests.

"There's Big Joe." She pointed to the marshy area along the shore further along the boardwalk. "I see his nose just above the waterline at the edge of the fire flag."

"Ah, well, let's go see him."

"We really should head back to the parking lot," she said, noting that the man in the straw hat had already gone. "They lock the gate once the sun sets."

He glanced up at the sun which seemed to perch on the dark silhouette of the slash pines on the far shore. "We have time." He took Packi's elbow and propelled her further into the slough.

Packi let herself be guided along the boardwalk, but worried about Fran, the volunteer on duty, waiting to go home; waiting for them to return to the cars. *Or will she leave and figure security will be along eventually to lock up? I'll apologize to her the next time I see her.* Packi hurried her steps. "I'll introduce you to Big Joe real quick and then we should leave."

The walkway veered toward the marshy shore near where Packi had seen the alligator. She quieted her steps and motioned for Art to do the same. "There he is." She put the binoculars to her eyes. Fifty feet from the raised boardwalk, the fourteen-foot gator's ridged back showed above the waterline. His tail curled into a J-hook several feet behind him. The sight of the prehistoric reptile thrilled her every time she saw him.

"Isn't he impressive?" Packi glanced up at Art, unprepared for the harsh glare that greeted her.

"That beast should be shot and skinned." Maddox stared down at her, not at *the beast.*

"Skinned!" She matched his glare.

"Think about what that animal did to poor Danny. What a gruesome way to die!"

Maddox's ferocity raised Packi's hackles and put her in combat mode. "Blame the guy who threw Danny Golden in the pond," she said. "Blame the guy who hit him with a log or something! But don't blame Big Joe." She pounded her clenched fist on the railing. Her unnatural anger surprised and unsettled her. She clutched the wooden board to steady herself. *He has a right to his own idiotic opinion.*

Embarrassed by her outburst, she closed her eyes, searching for a calm image. She took a deep, cleansing breath.

The heavy, humid air filled her lungs and carried a scent. Something new in the preserve, not from the ferns or cypress, not from the duckweed below their feet. Something with a hint of spice, foreign to her slough. She lifted her chin and flared her nostrils. *Spice.* She opened her eyes to find Maddox studying her.

"What else do you know, Mrs. Walsh?" His ferocity had been replaced with a thin smile, no, a smirk. Heat emanated from his cotton shirt sleeve like a branding iron hovering over her shoulder.

"Nothing," she murmured. She turned her face away from his scrutiny and stared straight ahead at the darkening water. *What's going on?* Her instinct told her to freeze, act cool, fly away. She dared to breathe again, just once. That spice... and the memory of turpentine. She knew then, and grappled with the knowledge. *They said Mark did it,* her logical mind argued. *Verify,* she commanded, beating back a quickening terror. Her gaze slid to his hands, so close to her own white knuckles clamped to the railing. Certain that those long, thin fingers had once held her head in a vice-like grip, she glanced down the long, empty boardwalk.

Don't panic. Act normal. She kept her face neutral, frozen in a placid expression. *Just walk away.* But her shoes weighed her down as if glued to the wooden planks.

"Packi, what's on your mind?" His voice had changed. Cruelty underscored each word.

She flinched remembering the muffled words telling her the penthouse would be her tomb.

If I look at him, he'll know I know. Get out of here. "Nothing," she said. "Except I was thinking it's the wrong season for the big flocks." Packi raised her arm to point across the slough, but her finger trembled and wouldn't zero in on the vacant nesting sites. *Not even the herons will witness my murder.* She curled her finger back and lowered her fist to her side.

In a burst of speed, she whipped around and ran. Three steps into her sprint a hand gripped her neck and lifted her off her feet. "Not this time, Mrs. Walsh."

She thrashed and kicked. Her shrill, unnatural cry sent birds into the sky, shrieking and beating their wings. Wild to be free, she turned on him and raked his face with her fingernails, catching his left eye. Maddox snarled and lost his grip.

Packi fell on all fours and scrambled to her feet in a low crouch, bent to run. He lunged at her from above. Like a bear pouncing on a dead moose, his weight fell upon her shoulders and forced her down. She crumpled beneath the overwhelming pressure.

Maddox flipped Packi on her back as she beat at him with flying fists and brought her knees up to kick at his crotch. He shoved her down, banging her head against the boardwalk sending vibrations down the length of the wooden boards. Her screams ended when his fingers dug into her jugular vein and his thumb wrenched her jaw up and back toward her shoulder.

Duct tape, turpentine, pain. Memories sparked warnings in her brain. *Pepper spray.* Ron had insisted she carry a canister. It was in her fanny pack. Her attacker's grip tightened. She clawed at his unyielding fingers.

Maddox loomed over her with saliva dripping from his mouth. His injured eye bled. His gargoyle expression held no human warmth as he choked the breath from her body. "Unless you want to be gator bait, Mrs. Walsh, you'll tell me what you know," he hissed as he applied steady, calculated pressure to her airway. "What did Vern Baker tell you?" He let up the pressure and expected answers. "Was someone sent to kill me? Are you spying for them?"

She gulped in air and groped for her fanny pack.

He shook her like a bobble-headed doll. "Tell me!"

"I don't..."

As his thumb closed her windpipe, her blind and fumbling fingers found the canister.

"What did that bitch find in my files?" He punctuated each word with a shake as if he intended to jar facts stuck in the recesses of her mind. "I'll throttle her, too!"

Packi's face bulged with internal pressure. *What do you want from me?* She begged for her life with her eyes until her struggle turned feeble. Her brain malfunctioned. *One chance,* she thought as Maddox's form blurred into a mere shadow. She squeezed her eyes shut and forced her fingers to obey. The pepper spray hissed upward.

"Stupid..." Maddox yelled and knocked the canister from her fist. In that instant of distraction, Packi jerked to the side and dragged in a deep gasp of air. With sickening clarity, she heard the splash of her last line of defense hit the water. Ron's gift hadn't helped her.

Maddox shoved her shoulders back onto the walkway with such force that her eyes popped open. With teeth bared, he snarled like a hyena. *He's insane.* She could not bear the intensity of his savage eyes, but fixated instead on the oily, yellow pepper spray which stained his forehead and dripped into his eyebrows.

Useless stuff. Broken ideas bounced in her brain as he shook her. *What did I... Out of date? ...do wrong?* Images blurred. *Ron.* The pummeling dragged shadows across her mind. Determined to hold on to a shred of consciousness, she tethered her thoughts to the tall cypress behind her attacker, to billowing clouds, to Ron waiting.

Suddenly, the battering stopped. Maddox lurched back, clutching at his eyes. "It's burning! I'm blind!"

His high-pitched screams jerked Packi out of her lethargy. Shocked by the reprieve, she rolled over, gulped in air, and hauled herself by her elbows from beneath the man. A few inches into her escape, he put a vice grip on her ankle and flipped her on her back. Her vertebrae counted out each wooden board as he wrenched her toward him.

On his knees, Maddox hurled insults at her as he swiped the yellow oils from his forehead onto his clean white sleeve. "Get me water!" He glared at her from one eye like a wild Cyclops and gouged at the other with his fingers.

"You're on your own," she hissed. Packi grabbed hold of a post and kicked at him with her free leg. Her sturdy walking shoe met soft, unresistant flesh. With a guttural moan, he doubled over and clutched his belly with one hand and rubbed at his eye with the other. Before he could regain himself, Packi decided to take her chances with the alligators rather than endure another beating. She dove under the guard rail and splashed into the slough.

Packi flailed in the water, desperate to get out of the reach of Maddox and trying to remember how to swim. She choked and sputtered as tannin-brown water filled her nose and mouth. Panicked and disoriented, she fought the water until she reached the shadow under the boardwalk. She clung to the support post and looked up through the spaced boards for Maddox and out toward deeper water for Big Joe. Neither were in sight, but she heard Maddox's cursing and yelling for water.

Safe for now. Taking a deep breath, she calmed herself. Soft, cool mud pressed against her knees. Duck weed, disturbed by her plunge, still swirled on the water's surface or clung to her chest. *Idiot.* She stood up in the thigh-high water, but quickly stooped again to remain hidden beneath the boardwalk. Scanning the slough for snakes and alligators, she crept further away from the man above her.

Spiderwebs clung to posts and boards inches overhead. Brown anoles scurried for their lives. Progress was slow in her crouched position in the slippery muck. She stopped behind the third support post for a bit of protection and to assess her situation. The man's footsteps thudded heavily above. His reflection on the water paced back and forth as he screamed in anger. *With any luck, he thinks I've drowned.*

Maddox stopped his pacing and leaned over the railing. Packi held her breath to prevent ripples in the water from giving away her position. An anguished growl escaped the man. She wondered if his eyes still burned and if he'd see her if she climbed onto the boardwalk and made a run for it. *Or can I sneak beneath the boardwalk past him?*

A great splash startled Packi and cut short her questions. She ducked down with only her nose and eyes above the surface. Maddox thrashed around to right himself and then bent over with his face in the water. He dunked his head again and again. He gurgled and moaned, tested his sight, and threw more water into his eyes.

Packi watched in stupefaction. *Get out of here.* Goaded by logic, she grabbed a hold of the deck above, but the slough seemed to suck her back in. Muck weighted her shoes. Vegetation clung to her. Her body hung like a wet bag of sand from her thin arms. Time weighed on her. *He's coming!* She swung one sodden shoe out of the water and found a foothold on a crossbeam. Splinters dug into her skin as her fingers lost their grip. She plunged beneath the water.

Packi got her feet beneath her, pushed, and surged upward. She broke the surface and swept back her hair, coughing up water. Through blurred vision, she spotted the still figure of a man fifteen feet away. Her vision cleared. Maddox leered at her from his one good eye. His second had swollen shut.

She calculated her next move. *He's blocking the shallows. Impossible boardwalk above. Deep water to the right.* They faced each other like gunfighters, intent, staring, deadly serious. A sneer curled his lip. He began to wade toward her.

"Big Joe," she said.

The sneer fell from his ashen face as his gaze followed her point to the prehistoric spine poking above the water's surface in amongst the reeds a stone's throw away. The gator growled.

Maddox shrieked and made a panicked attempt to climb onto the boardwalk. He fell back repeatedly. Packi withdrew to the shadow of a support post and stilled herself while the man drew the great alligator's attention. As the beast approached, Big Joe expanded his body and lifted himself high in the water, appearing more massive than Packi had ever seen him.

Maddox saw Big Joe's expression of dominance, too, and lost another attempt to climb. He screamed in fright and thrashed through the water to a fallen log. He hoisted himself onto the fern-laden cypress log and scrambled along its length on all fours. From two feet above the water, Maddox stared down into Big Joe's gaping, pink mouth. The gator clapped his jaws shut with a loud snap before settling back into the water, leaving only his eyes and snout visible.

A head-slap, Packi thought. *He's just marking his territory. A bluff.* Still, her own fright sent tiny ripples through the water toward the gator. She prayed Big Joe would dismiss her as inedible.

Maddox howled. "Get him out of here. Do something!" He crawled higher on the log and took refuge in the hollowed-out stump causing a turtle to tip into the water.

Big Joe cruised around the sprawling cypress stump. The tree's long trunk inclined from beneath the water to the stump, making a convenient ramp for the reptile. Big Joe dragged his heavy body onto the log's end. He huffed, growled, and snapped his jaws. The man cowering in the fractured stump shrieked in panic. "Do something!"

While the alligator menaced Maddox, Packi moved slowly and deliberately away from them to shallow water and to a reachable section of boardwalk. She found a foothold and hoisted herself onto the wooden platform. Once she crawled over the railing and out of Big Joe's reach, she gasped in relief and glanced back at the scene fifteen feet out in the slough. The gator had settled into one of the last patches of sunlight and closed his eyes.

"Don't move," Packi said, hushing the man with her outstretched hands. "I'll go for help." Her natural inclination to save a fellow human won out over her loathing of him.

Maddox glared at her, narrowed his eyes, and surveyed the sleeping alligator. He swung his leg over the splintered edge of the stump to enter the water. Packi jumped back, recoiling at the thought of him cornering her again.

"Stay there!" she screamed, pointing at the man as she gave the order.

Big Joe opened his lazy eyes, snapped his jaws, and growled his annoyance. He slid backwards into the water causing the log to bounce and vibrate. Maddox snatched his foot from the water and crouched again in the hollow stump. Joe's snout and eyes appeared above the surface alongside the fallen tree.

"Now who's gator bait?"

He gave her a murderous look. "Get somebody out here to kill that thing!"

Hate left a bitter stain on her tongue, so Packi turned away. As she ran, she prayed Big Joe would keep Maddox pinned down. Water-logged shoes made running difficult. Tears blurred her sight, but she jogged along the walkway until Maddox's curses faded behind her.

She finally neared the pier, the last place she had felt at peace. The sun had fallen behind the tree line. Herons, egrets, and anhingas dotted the pines and live oaks, roosting for the night. The natural order, the routine, overwhelmed her. She leaned against the railing and sobbed.

After a few seconds of self-indulgence, Packi lifted her face to the evening sky and asked for strength. *Keep going.* She drew tranquil air into her lungs, felt it radiate through her chest, her arms, her mind. She also felt vibrations beneath her feet. Heavy steps shook the boardwalk. *He's coming!*

Packi darted a look over her shoulder and sprinted in panic toward the preserve entrance. *Too far away. Too far. He'll catch me.* Her legs protested the heaviness of her sodden shoes. Her lungs screamed for air. Her ears heard her name.

She jolted to a stop and heard it again. "Packi!" She searched the slough for the direction, the familiar voice. Through a blur of tears, she saw the tennis team emerge from around a bend in the boardwalk. Shocked, Packi's will to stand upright left her. She fell to her knees, crumpled into a ball, and cried.

Beth, Kay, and Marilyn swarmed over her, touching, stroking, lifting. "For God's sake, Packi, what happened to you?" The nurses assessed her body, questioned, comforted.

"I'm okay," she whispered, but most of all she wanted to sleep, to be in her bed, safe, dry, and warm. Instead, she tried to stand. "He's back there. Big Joe might..." She told them then in clipped words about Maddox, about the alligator.

"Let the gator have him," said Beth, urging her to rest.

"No!" Packi protested. "They'd kill Big Joe for sure. Please, we have to save him."

Kay and Marilyn helped her to her feet. "Your deputy friend called looking for you," Kay said, still inspecting her body for injuries. "Mark's alibi checked out, so he'll be released soon."

"Good. Good," Packi murmured. *Maybe he'll be okay.* Guilt had weighed on her for her part in getting Mark arrested. *Maybe he'll forgive me.* Packi sighed and pulled her attention back to her teammates. They each carried a golf club.

"We came armed." Beth brandished a nine-iron and scowled out over the slough. "When Kay told Teig about your date with Maddox, he got concerned and that scared us, so here we are. That son of a bitch." She glanced back at the group. "Maddox, I mean." She pulled out a business card and her phone. "He's off-duty, but I'll tell him to get out here." She looked up from the screen. "Teig, I mean."

Her feisty team captain's anger and the promise of reinforcement bolstered Packi. "And Jake?" She straightened herself out and took a tentative step back toward Gator Lake. "He's innocent, too."

"I know," Marilyn said. "They admitted him to another hospital, but they won't be able to keep him against his will." She stroked Packi's arm where yesterday's bruises had turned an ugly yellow. "You've had enough. Come back to the parking lot with me. We'll wait for the deputy."

Packi hesitated and looked back toward the darkening slough. "No. Go wait for him, Marilyn, please." She took the putter from her teammate's hands. "I have more questions for Maddox."

"Me, too." Kay took Packi's elbow, giving her more support than necessary. "Come on, partner." She pointed her golf club down the boardwalk. "Let's see that pasty-faced, bean counting freak take on the three of us."

Fear percolated around Packi's heart. *What if Maddox got away? What if he ambushes us? What if Joe...* She couldn't finish that thought. Instead, she concentrated on the energy flowing from Kay's grip on her arm and from Beth's combative confidence. Buoyed by their presence, she quashed her fears and hastened toward Gator Lake.

Beth pocketed her phone and ran ahead. "If the gator has him cornered, we'd better hurry," she yelled over her shoulder. "Where is he?"

"Just follow the boardwalk," Packi called as she and Kay picked up their pace. "You'll hear him before you see him."

* * *

Big Joe kept his vigil. Art Maddox still crouched in the tree stump, clinging to its ragged edges and staring at the reptile floating between him and safety. The alligator huffed and growled.

Beth taunted her ex-employer from the boardwalk. "Not such a big man now, are you? Beating up on a woman. What a coward!"

"Beth, please! Hit it with that club," Maddox pleaded. "Throw a rock at it."

"Not until you answer some questions." Packi arrived at Beth's side and leaned over the railing to take advantage of her tormentor's predicament. "How could you leave me in that condo to die?"

"I'm sorry, Packi."

She cut him off. "Don't you dare call me that, you miserable pig!" Her rage boiled over, fueled by pent up fear and pain. Instinct told her to fly at him and wring his neck.

"Ask your questions." Kay lay calming fingers on her partner's forearm. "You can beat on him later."

Packi stilled her shaking hands, took a long cleansing breath, and eyed the pathetic man in the old stump. "Did you check for a water moccasin nest in there with you, Art?"

Maddox's face went beyond ashen. He jumped to his feet and danced a jig in a tight circle as if stomping his feet would ward off the fangs of angry vipers. "Get me out of here!" he screeched. "Packi. Mrs. Walsh, please!"

She almost regretted her wicked harassment of the man. "It was you, wasn't it? Say it. You tied me up and gagged me. You left me for dead. Why?"

"Yes. Yes. It was me." He watched his feet, stomped, and circled around again. "You knew about Danny, about the payments. I wasn't going to leave you there. Honest."

Beth shook her fist at him. "Liar!"

"Wait, Beth." Packi held up her hand to stop her team captain's rant. "Why did you kill Danny Golden?" she shouted.

Maddox stopped his dance. "I had to, don't you see? He wanted to sell everything, declare bankruptcy." He stammered and held out his hands like a beggar. "*I* set up the consortium. *I* made promises."

Big Joe yawned, exposing rows of jagged teeth, and then clapped his jaws shut.

The man spilled out his words faster, as if the reptile was his interrogator. "They'd come after me if I didn't pay. One of us had to be sacrificed. We had insurance. That money will save the business, and my life, and my reputation." He raised his eyes and pleaded to the women on the wooden deck. "Get me out of here."

"I'll get you out of there, you sorry piece of shit." Deputy Teig spoke from out of the dusk, fifteen feet back along the boardwalk. "Excuse my French, ladies." He hauled his body over the railing and dropped into the slough, more agile than expected for a man of his size. He waded toward the stump with wetness wicking up his *World's Best Dad* T-shirt. His holstered gun was well above the waterline.

"Billy!" Packi pointed to warn him of the alligator, but the spot where Big Joe had lain in wait was empty. He had darted away with the swish of his tail, leaving only a gentle ripple in his wake. Maddox saw the reptile's disappearance, too, and jumped in the water before Teig reached the stump.

"Don't let him get away," Kay yelled, clutching her golf club.

Maddox's white shirt was easy to track in the gloom. The women ran to station themselves along the railing as the man thrashed below through water clogged with ferns. He ducked beneath the walkway.

"I see him." Beth rushed across the boardwalk. "This side!"

Waterlogged jeans slowed the deputy's slog through the thigh-high water, yet he made steady progress as Maddox flailed about and tripped over cypress knees.

"Big Joe!" Packi shouted. She spied the shadow of his scaled body under the water ten feet in front of Maddox. He was headed directly at the reptile.

The alligator surfaced, opened his cotton-pink mouth, and snapped his jaws. Maddox's scream pierced the quiet preserve and chased flocks of egrets from their roosts. The man's knees buckled as he fainted, but Teig's beefy hand horse collared him and held his face above water.

"Go!" Deputy slapped the water and shooed away the alligator as the women looked on in shock. Big Joe darted away in an instant. A vee-shaped wake trailed behind him as he headed for open water.

"How did you do that?" Kay asked in awe.

Teig sniffed. "Nothin' but big lizards. If you ain't the size of a dog or possum, you got nothin' to worry about."

"What about Danny Golden?" Beth asked.

"Already dead," said Teig. "That's different." He grasped Maddox under the arms and roughly patted his cheek to revive him. Maddox coughed and sputtered before yelping like a wounded beagle. He swam through the air, grappling for the boardwalk.

Teig shook the prisoner's collar. "Hold still before I let that gator have you."

"No!" The man stiffened and then went limp. "Okay, okay," he pleaded. "Get me out of here."

"Arthur Maddox," the deputy said. "You're under arrest for the murder of Danny Golden, attempted murder of Mizz Walsh, assault, kidnapping, endangering wildlife, and anything else I can think of. Now, get up there."

Teig recited Miranda rights as he shoved Maddox from behind to help him clamber up the post. The three women dragged him over the railing, dug in their nails, and forced him facedown on the boardwalk. He didn't resist. Packi stabbed her knee into his back while Kay held his face to the wooden slats with a tight grip on his head.

Packi eyed the pathetic man pinned beneath her. His thin dress shirt clung to his skinny back. Duckweed littered his shoulders like green dandruff. Black dye dribbled from his hairline. The thought of almost believing his cloying, romantic advances brought vomit into her throat.

Kay glanced at her partner's pallid face, clenched her teeth, and leaned harder against the man's skull.

"Take it easy on my prisoner, ladies." Teig passed a set of handcuffs through the railing. Beth released the captive's legs and followed the deputy's instructions on how to secure the man's wrists. She took great delight in yanking Maddox's arms to the small of his back while Teig fought to get himself out of the slough and haul his body over the railing.

The women held fast to the prisoner in grim determination until Deputy Teig stood over them, dripping wet. "I'll take it from here, ladies."

The slough went to full darkness as the deputy marched his prisoner along the walkway by feel, rather than sight. The tennis team followed along chattering about the capture, the gator, and the confession. Beth took off her jacket and wrapped it around Packi's shivering shoulders.

"Thank you, Beth. I must look like a drowned rat."

"Yeah, you do," teased Kay, bumping against Packi, "but we love you anyway." The three women synchronized their steps and huddled closer to share their body heat.

Halfway back to the parking lot, the women spotted lights bouncing among the cypress and palms. Heavy footsteps tromped along the boardwalk. "Lee County Sheriff's Department," a brusque voice announced from behind blinding flashlights.

"Prisoner here," Teig called, hustling Maddox ahead of him. He handed the man over to uniformed deputies and gave his fellow cops a quick account of the charges as they paraded to the parking lot.

Packi followed behind and felt a sudden sorrow for Art Maddox. Disheveled and beaten, he bore no resemblance to the accountant who sat behind the mahogany desk at Suncoast Realty, nor to the ghoul who had trussed her up at the Skyview Towers. She turned away as they thrust him into the backseat of a cruiser. In the flashing red and blue strobe light, she spotted Marilyn standing in the shadow of the information kiosk.

"Packi, you're soaking wet!" Marilyn dug into her tote bag for a small tennis towel and motioned for her to dry her hair. "I was so worried." Her fingers worked their way up and down the buttons on her blouse. "I heard screaming."

"It was all him. Art Maddox." Packi put her arms around the shaken woman. "He confessed to killing Danny Golden."

"He confirmed it wasn't Mark?" Marilyn sank onto a bench.

"No, not Mark." Joy leapt inside her. *Not Mark!* She motioned for Kay and Beth to sit with Marilyn. The thought needed time to filter through her mind, changing everything. She blotted her hair as she moved away from the parking lot's halogen lights.

Thirty feet away from the chaotic world, darkness reigned. Night creatures stirred, and a barred owl hooted. Low in the eastern sky, Virgo and Leo revealed themselves in spite of a crescent moon hanging in their midst. Cypress and slash pines cast hulking shadows. Insects and frogs sang in chorus. The slumbering preserve's magic lifted a burden from Packi's shoulders. With sudden clarity, her path became obvious, her future more exciting. She sent a note of thanks skyward and returned to civilization with her mind at ease.

"Billy," she said after finding him among his fellow officers and tugging at his elbow.

He puffed out his cheeks and looked down his shirt sleeve at her. "Yes, Mizz Walsh?"

Packi recognized the warmth beneath his rigid, cop facade and grinned up at him. "I believe I owe you a Bundt cake."

"No, Mizz Walsh. No, you don't."

The sharp tone pushed her back a step. She glanced up at him just as a blue strobe light caught the frown between his brows. The next rotation of light showed regret possibly, or sadness. "I'm trying to diet," he said. "How 'bout bringing me an apple?"

"A diet? That's wonderful, Billy." As if he were the Doughboy, she pressed her fingertip into the mound of his belly, inches below the stretched and water-stained words, *World's Best Dad*. "I'm so proud of you." The faded lettering reminded her of her phone call to his home. "Your son," she said. "Does your boy like chocolate cupcakes?"

The deputy excused the offending fingertip and rubbed his jaw to hide his amusement. "Yes, Mizz Walsh. Mikey loves chocolate."

36

The coconut palms and slash pines on the far side of the golf course glowed in the first sun rays to reach over the horizon. An artist's light, Packi thought. A groundskeeper's mower glided over the manicured seventh green like a speedy snail, leaving a trail in the heavy carpet of dew.

From the shade of her home's lanai, Packi watched the landscaper's morning ritual and went through her own routine. She worked through a series of yoga stretches. Her balance seemed off, her joints painful. Yet, she refused to dwell on the injuries she'd sustained in the last few days and settled her mind on the sound of water trickling into the pool. *Thank you for this new day, for this tropical paradise, for my life.* She breathed away bodily pain and eased into Warrior pose. The doorbell broke into her meditation.

Packi trotted into the house toward the front door and grabbed a light jacket to throw over her spandex yoga outfit. She peeked through the slats of the plantation shutters. *Oh, no.* She combed her fingers through her hair and wished for a bit of make-up.

"Good morning, Mizz Walsh."

Packi tugged her jacket closed across her chest and peered up at the silhouette filling her doorway. "Billy. What's wrong?" She waved him inside." Come in. Come in."

"Nothin's wrong," Teig said as he stepped across the threshold. "This is a wellness check."

Oh, good. No emergency to start my day. She thought about Beth, Kay, and the rest of the team and wondered who would request a wellness check. "Someone was worried about me?"

His leather utility belt creaked as he shifted from one boot to the other. "Just me." One side of his mouth grinned. "And that fellow I arrested at the high-rise condo. How you getting along, Mizz Walsh?"

"Mark?" Heat rose to her cheeks. "I'm fine, Billy. I was just outside exercising. You spoke to Mark? They let him out of jail?"

"Afraid not. They got him on trespassing." Teig tugged up his belt. "I went to visit him. Guess I roughed him up some back at the condo, but he didn't hold it against me. All he wanted to know about was you."

"Really?" She turned away to hide her unsettled emotions and led him into the kitchen where she inspected the goodies left by her teammates. "I'd offer you some of these, but fruit is what you need, Billy. You've been eating too many sweets." His bulk made her kitchen feel too small. "Go sit on the patio. I'll be right there with a nice cup of tea."

"Tea is good," he said, but didn't move. He watched her fuss over the steaming teapot. "The ladies said Mark Hebron scared you. You care about the guy?"

"I don't..." She sifted through her feelings and surprised herself. "I guess I do care about him." The tea infuser shook a little as she immersed it in the hot water. "But he did scare me once when he lost his temper. He blamed Danny Golden for ruining his life."

"So, you don't want to see him again."

"No." She jerked a bit, sloshing tea into the saucer as she offered it to the deputy. "I think I *would* like to see him, Billy. His anger wasn't directed at me. He wanted retaliation against the men who cheated him. I think Mark agrees with what my Ron used to say, *Success is the best revenge.* Look how hard Mark works."

Teig humphed in response. He held the teacup like an injured bird and frowned at the infuser coloring the hot water. "I went to high school with the president of Gulf Coast Bank. Football team. They own Skyview Towers now and might need a maintenance man."

"You mean they might give Mark a job? In Skyview?" Packi reached to remove the dainty tea cup from the big man's paw and poured the tea into Ron's favorite oversized mug. "That's exciting. And they won't press charges because he lived in that room?"

"I'll try, Mizz Walsh." He blew on the tea before taking a drink. "I shouldn't have roughed him up."

"You were saving me, Billy." Packi resisted the urge to put a cupcake in front of him. She slid a bowl of fruit across the counter instead. "Thank you for finding me," she said, "and for getting Mark out of trouble."

"No promises, Mizz Walsh." Teig hefted himself off the rattan stool, yanked up his belt, and headed for the door.

"Deputy Teig?" Packi's need to know outweighed her efforts to put the nightmares of the last several days behind her. "What about that man?" She imagined bugs crawling beneath her skin. "Maddox?"

Billy Teig crossed his arms over his neatly ironed uniform shirt. "I guess you have a right to know." He hesitated, as if going against a long-held belief that citizens, especially little old women, shouldn't be trusted with police business. "After his confession at the slough, the investigation team had no problem making him talk. He insists he never meant to hurt you. Or Danny Golden, for that matter. It was all an accident." The deputy continued his walk through the living room with Packi trotting behind.

"What about the cigarette pack I found in the weeds," she asked, "and the bicycle? Any of that help?"

"The bike turned out to be nothin', but the cigarette pack had Danny Golden's fingerprints on it, putting him on that side of the lake before his death." Teig scowled down at her. "Course your fingerprints contaminated that evidence."

"Oh, I'm sorry. I didn't know. I…"

"I'm teasing, Mizz Walsh."

His large hand rested for a moment on her shoulder. She felt its warmth, its power, and its kindness, but didn't let on.

"The footprints you pointed out matched Danny Golden's shoes and a pair Detective Leland found in Art Maddox's closet. He says he and Golden often scouted out vacant property for investment."

"Let me guess," said Packi. "That night, he spiked Danny's drink with an extra dose of oxycodone and drove him out to the slough to look at a great deal on land. Maybe Maddox hustled him out. Remember the glasses and wallet left on the mantelpiece?"

Teig huffed, but begrudged a nod. "The detectives agree with that. And the trail of footprints led right to the lake and mud on the shore where they found signs of a fallen body and a log with flecks of blood. Bits of the same type of wood were embedded in the deceased's head wound."

Sadness overtook Packi. Her suspicions were correct, and she may have helped solve the crime, but that didn't erase the sorrow over the life lost and other lives ruined. She put up a hand to stop the deputy's description. "Thank you, Billy."

"So you've had enough of police investigations?" He cocked on eyebrow and tightened his lips. But he didn't delight in her discomfort; didn't contend that he had been right, that civilians get in the way.

"Never again," Packi said. Suddenly, she brightened. "Wait right there, Billy." She jogged into the kitchen while he waited at her front door. In less than a minute, Packi returned with a bag of cookies and cupcakes. "Give them to your son and his friends. Now don't you eat any. These are for Mikey."

Deputy Teig's cheek twitched as he stared at the bag. His nostrils flared when he caught the scent of chocolate.

"You can do it, Billy. You have willpower." Packi took his hand and curled his fingers over the top of the bag. "Thank you for checking on me."

Without saying goodbye, Teig stepped into the sunshine and assumed the police demeanor, complete with mirrored sunglasses. The big man stopped beneath the royal palm as if he'd forgotten something. He glanced back and pulled the glasses down his nose to reveal his startling blue eyes. He winked. "You're a real pistol, Mizz Walsh."

37

Later that morning, Packi waited at her front door. Even in the air conditioning, her cotton blouse and rayon skirt clung to her. She folded the suit jacket over her arm, planning to slip it on when she got to the county building. *How can anyone wear so many clothes in this climate?* She wet a tissue on the tip of her tongue and wiped away a fingerprint on the door jamb, assuring herself that she'd done all she could to prepare to face the commissioners.

Through the etched glass, she spotted movement on the street. She rested her hand on the door handle until the car pulled into her driveway. Kay was right on time. Packi locked the door behind her and rushed down the walkway.

"Do you mind if we stop by the clubhouse?" Packi threw her purse onto the floorboard and slid into the seat. "I'm anxious to see if anyone shows up."

"Good morning to you, too," Kay teased as she cleared the area at Packi's feet and threw her umbrella into the back. "Don't worry. Grace says she's got things under control. You look nice, a bit harried, but nice."

"I'm sorry. Good morning and thanks." Packi brushed damp hair off her forehead and tilted the AC vent toward her face. "I hope this heat doesn't keep anyone away." She tightened the seat belt across her hips and welcomed the snug security. They drove in silence past landscapers trimming palm trees and golfers strolling across the seventh green. The tropical scenes were at odds with the turmoil in her mind.

Kay turned in at the clubhouse and threaded through cars and people bustling about. "I told you they'd be here."

At the far end of the parking lot, Packi spotted familiar faces from the tennis teams and the book club, and a few she didn't know. "This is amazing. It looks like they're getting ready for a parade."

"Almost," said Kay as she pulled abreast of a line of cars.

"Good luck, Packi!" Beth stood up from a crouched position to wave, then went back to taping a neon green poster to the door of her convertible. *Save Big Joe* was written in thick black marker.

Other tennis team members milled around Grace's open SUV reaching for banners and signs. "Don't you worry, Packi." Grace grinned like a leprechaun. "I got enough stuff packed back here for a real bash. They'll get the message." Balloons bobbed in the rear seat, threatening to escape through the open door. Grace bustled from car to car to pass out printed maps and directions before each vehicle pulled away from the curb. Mary, Valerie, and even Helen waved as if they were off to a party. "Good luck, Packi!"

"I'll see you there," Marilyn said as she took several rolls of green streamers from the box on the curb and dumped them into her front seat. "I volunteered to help Amanda Simpson get her students organized. They happen to be going on a field trip to see how our county government works." She laughed lightly, as if pleased to be in on a conspiracy, and pinned a 'Save Big Joe' badge on her blouse.

The parking lot emptied as the tennis team took their energy and enthusiasm toward downtown Fort Myers. Packi was glad to miss some of the hubbub. With just Kay in the car, she relaxed and planned her presentation to the Board of Commissioners—if they'd give her the chance to speak at all.

"You're kind of quiet," Kay said as she steered the Prius out of Paradise Palms. "Nervous?"

Packi grimaced. "I'm afraid I'll let everyone down." She smoothed possible wrinkles from her navy blue skirt and then dropped her hands into her lap. "Do I look okay? What should I say to them?"

"You look fine," Kay said, but her glance drifted to the bruises on her passenger's arms and neck. Packi noticed the look and pulled her collar closed. Kay shifted her attention back to the traffic zooming past them on Daniels Parkway. "Hey, oldsters like us bruise easily. No one will think anything of it." She drummed her fingers on the steering wheel as an inspiration hit her. "Or maybe bruises make you a more sympathetic witness." She grinned at Packi. "Right?"

"I guess." Packi massaged her temples, hoping to ward off a threatening headache. "Dave Stanford said he'd try to be there, but he might be stuck at the courthouse on another case. I'm supposed to tell my story."

"I have faith in you, partner," Kay said, "and you'll have a few cheerleaders outside to back you up."

"Thanks, Kay." Packi decided to trust her teammate's driving and closed her eyes to envision a calm, serene place. The click of the turn signal brought her back to reality. Kay made a left-hand turn onto Edwards Street and maneuvered the car down the quiet street with the Caloosahatchee on the right and a row of high-rise buildings on the left. The sight of Skyview Towers replaced Packi's peaceful thoughts with terrifying images. She leaned forward to peer through the windshield to the upper floors of the glass behemoth. Sunlight speared through the windows above like an oven on broil. Her throat begged for water and her wrists began to ache.

"Are you okay?" Kay glanced at her passenger and then at the buildings. "I'm sorry we came this way. I forgot. We should have come north on Cleveland Avenue. I am so sorry."

Kay's startled expression shook Packi out of her momentary nightmare. "Hey, watch out for that motorcycle." Kay braked, and Packi stiff-armed the dashboard and then calmed herself as the bike roared away. "I'm okay," she said with a sigh, "but the memory of that night just kind of rushed at me when I recognized the building. Time for me to get over it."

Kay flashed a quick smile, but then set her jaw and yanked down the sun visor as if she wanted to hurt someone. "Where to now, partner?"

"Drive up a few blocks and turn left at the end of the street. We'll find a parking garage."

The Prius threaded through the business section of downtown Fort Myers. Brick pavers hummed beneath the tires. They passed trendy restaurants, an antique theater, boutiques, stout buildings dating from the eighteen hundreds, and a row of glass office towers. Kay stopped at an intersection and stared down the block to her right. "I think we found the right place."

Commotion crowded the narrow street. As if waiting for a rock star, people lined the sidewalks waving green streamers and homemade posters. Streamers adorned hats, light posts, cars, bicycles, and tree branches. Children skipped about with balloons in primary colors tied to their wrists. More than a few balloons escaped into the sky.

Packi blanched. "Oh...my...goodness."

"The team really came through." Kay nudged her passenger's shoulder. "This will get the commissioners' attention."

Packi sank into the seat under the weight of her responsibility. *Take me home.* "This is too much. What if the board says no? What if they kill Big Joe no matter what I say? It's policy."

"Think positive, Packi," Kay admonished. "Don't let down now." She inched the car toward the parking lot around the corner from the festivities.

"I'm trying." Packi sighed. "There. Pull in there. Parking's free in this lot."

The women parked the Prius in a gated lot and headed for the county building, hoping to slip through the crowd without any fuss. Packi ducked into the shadow of a banyan tree as the WFMK TV van passed by with Kevin Mitchell at the wheel. He bumped up onto the sidewalk and rushed to set up his camera equipment. Several school buses parked in front of the county building's expansive, cement courtyard. More signs appeared. Innocent bystanders stopped to watch the commotion and were offered green streamers by Miss Simpson's students. The children chanted, "Save Big Joe," and danced to their own music along the sidewalk and around benches. The adults in the crowd caught their enthusiasm.

Packi stood inside the double doors on the side of the county building and watched Kay disappear into the crowd. *You're on your own, lady.* The interior of the building tried to intimidate her with its long, tiled hallway, cubicles, and office doors. Her footsteps sounded hollow as she passed walls with faded, tattered announcements.

"May I help you?" An older, bleached-blonde with hoop earrings and a tangerine blouse called from behind an enclosed cubicle. Behind her were desks piled with stacks of papers and books. File cabinets were the cheeriest part of the decor. The woman pointed her toward the public meeting room around the corner. "They already started, honey. Sit in the back."

Packi cracked open the antique oak doors and peered inside. Eight officials sat at a raised dais behind brass name plates. A uniformed Robert E. Lee presided over the county's governance from his frame on the wall behind the commissioners. A sparse audience of lethargic men and women sat in rows of connected chairs. None looked her way, except Dave Stanford.

The lawyer gestured to draw her inside. She gingerly closed the door and sidled past tripod legs as a cameraman recorded the meeting. She chose an empty row still in the shadow of the balcony and slid into a padded chair to listen to the commissioners drone on through their business. Treasurer's report, permits, variances. The man at the center of the dais dominated the proceedings and did most of the talking.

Once or twice the chairman frowned at the noise from the hubbub outside, but pushed through the business before the commission. After fifteen minutes, he squinted in amused surprise at the paper in front of him. "I see we have a new issue on the agenda." He adjusted his bifocals and looked down his bulbous nose. "Miss Curtis?"

The red-haired county lawyer stood up in the front row with a Manila folder grasped in both hands. She lifted her chin. "Commissioner Krueger, Mrs. Patricia Walsh is in the audience." Krista Curtis pointed.

Packi felt skewered by the attention, but straightened her back, stood, and murmured a greeting to the officials.

The young woman returned Packi's weak smile. "She asks that our standard policy of removing nuisance alligators be reconsidered in the case of the animal at Hammock Preserve."

Krueger must have eaten a disagreeable breakfast. His scowl grew as he shook his head. "Word of the recent death in the slough is out, and people are afraid of that alligator. Rightfully so."

Packi's hopes deflated as Miss Curtis faded under the commissioner's withering glare and his recitation of the nuisance-animal ordinance.

"Wait!" Packi rushed toward the conference table, but banged into a desk. She righted the furniture and ignored frowns from the officials. "Big Joe's not a nuisance," she insisted. "He did *not* kill that man." She brandished the autopsy report at the board. "The police have the real murderer in custody."

"Sorry, Mrs. Walsh, we have our policies." The chairman looked down the row of board members, letting them know what their judgment would be. Several doodled on their copies of the agenda. One woman dropped her pen and bent to retrieve it. None of them glanced Packi's way.

Packi looked to Dave Stanford for help. Emotionless, he nodded once. She glared at the lawyer, irritated and disappointed that he had caved under the commissioner's bluster. Packi turned her hopes to Miss Curtis who gave her a slight shrug, abdicating her support.

Exasperated, Packi pointed at the board members. "Shouldn't you do what the people want?" Her voice had risen to argument level, not familiar territory. With the crumbled papers in her hand, she pointed out the window. "They love Big Joe. Why not save one old alligator?" She fought back tears that always came with anger. "He's unique! A wonder of nature, and he never hurt anyone."

"I will not allow outbursts in this meeting, Mrs. Walsh," the commissioner admonished, barely controlling his own anger and banging his gavel. "This is not how we conduct our business…"

The low growl of engines, getting louder and louder, interrupted his lecture. Pictures on the wall clattered in their frames.

Commissioner Krueger squinted at Packi as if to assess whether she was responsible for the disruption. He pushed his chair back to the window and adjusted the shutters. "They'd better have a permit." The remainder of his threat was drowned out as the roar from the street rose to deafening levels.

Packi joined Miss Curtis at a side window, peeking through the slats. Fifty or more motorcycles rolled past the county building, revving their engines, and blocking both lanes of traffic. Banners flew in the wind and every biker wore a green streamer tied around his or her arm.

One rider broke from the middle of the pack and pulled his Harley in front of the building's main doors. Packi focused on the beard, chains, and black leather vest covered in embroidered patches. *Flanigan.* A young boy in a blue helmet straddled the seat in back, wearing his own leather vest and green streamer.

Packi wiggled her fingers through the slats of the plantation shutters and waved. The biker revved the Harley's engine in another roar as if to say, *I'm here.* Flanigan folded his muscular arms across his vest. A green streamer strained against his tattooed bicep as he settled back in his seat. His son raised both his skinny, little arms overhead as if in triumph.

Commissioner Krueger and the board members watched the bikers thunder past and go around the block again. At the end of the conference table, the older woman in the gray tweed suit covered her ears. Her opinion of the high decibel level was clear on her face. As the board member shrank from the overwhelming noise, Miss Curtis bent close to the woman's ear. The young lawyer punctuated her remarks with her hand and her frizzy red hair bobbed as she motioned several times to the noise outside the building. Still wincing as if she suffered a migraine headache, the older woman rose to stand behind the commissioner and shouted into his ear. Packi picked out the words *public relations* and *election.*

The commissioner jerked away from the window to glower at the woman. She crossed her arms over her ample chest and cocked one pencil-thin eyebrow as if to dare a retort

"Fine." Krueger spun his chair back to the table and thumped his fist on its surface. "Let's get this over with." He scowled at Packi and Dave Stanford. "Give me the paperwork."

The lawyer responded to the commissioner's aggression with a slight inclination of his balding head. He withdrew a paper from a Manila folder, and slid a legal-sized document across the aged-oak dais. The commissioner made a show of clicking the end of his pen and scrawled his signature across the bottom line. He shoved the paper at the secretary in disgust. "You have your variance, but I command that a 'No Swimming' sign be posted at that pond—today!"

Five minutes later, Packi had Big Joe's reprieve, notarized and recorded, clutched to her chest. She stood in the lobby outside the meeting room, but hesitated to go outside. From behind a plate glass window, she watched in awe the carnival-like chaos in the courtyard and street. She glanced at Dave Stanford for guidance.

"Go ahead," he said. "This is your show."

The scarecrow of a man held open the first set of doors. She regretted that she had mistaken his gentle ways for weakness and saw wisdom behind pale blue eyes. Now in on the secret to his strength, she almost winked at him. "Thank you, Mr. Stanford."

She sucked air into her lungs to pump up her confidence, and pushed against the heavy double doors. A murmur went through the crowd as she emerged from the building. For an instant, the crowd held a collective breath, until she raised the document above her head. She caught sight of the tennis team and shouted, "We did it!"

A cheer went up, traveling down the narrow street and around the block. Kids jumped up and down. People clapped and pumped their fists in the air. On the edge of the crowd, she spotted a familiar bicycle with a balloon floating above the handle bars. Mark Hebron raised his hand in a tentative wave. Her heart swelled in relief and something else. A slight crook of her finger brought him bounding up the steps to her side. Beth, Grace, and Marilyn gathered around, ready to celebrate.

From the curb, Flanigan lifted his chin to her in a subtle salute. He patted his son's knee and gunned the Harley's engine. He wheeled the big machine around and joined the parade of motorcycles. The roar of fifty engines echoed off a canyon of buildings as the bikers funneled into pairs and rode out of sight.

"How the heck did you do that?" Kay yelled into her ear as she watched the spectacle.

"I don't know." Packi shrugged. "Good things just happen, I guess." She slipped her fingers into Mark's calloused, carpenter hand and squeezed.

END

ABOUT THE AUTHOR

Jeanne Meeks belongs to Mystery Writers of America, Sisters in Crime, Gulf Coast Writers' Association, and two critique groups. She loves to attend the annual Love is Murder convention in Chicago where she speaks on various topics, learns the finer points of forensics, and hangs out with mystery authors who like nothing better than studying blood splatter and learning new ways to kill off their characters. When not writing, she backpacks, kayaks, volunteers with the local historical society, and plays tennis or golf. Married in 1969, she lives with her husband on Florida's gulf coast and in a suburb of Chicago.

In the 1990s Jeanne was committed to poetry, belonged to Poets and Other Writers, and gave poetry performances as part of that group. Her work appeared in several anthologies. She also self-published a book of poetry, *My Sister's Quilt*. She regularly writes human-interest articles for *Schoolhouse Life* news magazine.

After twenty-eight years in business, Ms. Meeks and her husband sold their security surveillance company in 2005. She had been recognized by the Illinois governor as the Small-Business Person of the Year. She was also the Tax Collector for New Lenox Township, the President of the Chamber of Commerce, on the board of a local bank, and on Silver Cross Hospital's Community Trustee Board. Now writing is her job.

Life is good.

RIM To RIM - Death in the Grand Canyon

Backcountry Mystery series. Book 1

A novice backpacker becomes prey for a murderer on the rim to rim trail. Can a backpacking trip across the Grand Canyon rebuild Amy Warren's self confidence or will the trek break her and leave her clinging by her fingernails to the edge of the abyss?

The awesome Grand Canyon scenery is marred when Amy and Sarah find a mangled body in a ravine. The women, who each hike for their own reasons, must face the physical hardships of the five-day trek *plus* stay alive as an eerie danger stalks them.

* * *

"Empowering Women, Dispensing Adventure. Ladies take note: Jeanne Meeks has created a first novel that puts her up in the company of fine adventure/mystery writers..."

-- Grady Harp, Los Angeles reviewer

"Couldn't put it down. You owe me a night's sleep."

--Kathy Eversman, Rhinelander, WI

Rim To Rim was nominated for a Lovey Award - Best First Novel at the 2014 Love Is Murder writers convention in Chicago. It is available in e-book and print from Amazon, Barnes and Noble, from the author, and from other retail outlets.

To sing along with *The Ballad of Rim to Rim* (lyrics by Jeanne Meeks, vocals by Mary Beth Hafner, and keyboard, bass, and guitar by Mike Evon) visit my website at www.jeannemeeks.com

Wolf Pack - Mystery on Isle Royale
Backcountry Mystery series, Book 2

Can a backpacking trip to an island famous for its wolves mend the relationship between Amy and her grown daughter? Will blackmail and betrayal bring them together—or bury them on Isle Royale?

Emboldened by her adventures in the Grand Canyon, Amy Warren again laces up her hiking boots. She ferries with her daughter, Meagan, to Isle Royal National Park. When volunteer ranger Sarah Rochon is accused by a co-worker of assault and theft, Amy is torn between spending precious time with Meagan and clearing her best friend's name. When Amy rescues Remington, a pampered Havanese show dog, from the frigid waters of Lake Superior, he becomes her champion. Together they sniff out clues to the evil that threatens the natural tranquility of the magical island.

* * *

Her fresh voice and captivating story will have you reading well into the night.
- Lydia T. Ponczak, Author of *Reenee on the Run*

I loved the book! Can't wait for your next one!
- Mary Baker, Illinois

Wolf Pack was nominated for a Lovey Award - Best Amateur Sleuth Novel at the 2015 Love Is Murder writers' convention in Chicago. It is available in e-book and print from Amazon, from the author, and from other retail outlets.

Dear Reader,

I hope you've enjoyed meeting the tennis team as much as I enjoyed writing about them. May I ask a favor? Will you help spread the word about these stories? Your opinions will help another reader decide to open the cover and visit Big Joe's pond and Paradise Palms.

I'd appreciate your feedback in any of these ways:
* Leave a comment on Amazon or Barnes & Noble,
* Write a review for Goodreads.com,
* Pin a picture of yourself with the book on Pinterest,
* Post your opinion on Facebook and Twitter
* Request that your library carry my books
* Or simply mention my novels to your friends.

Do you belong to a book discussion club, civic group, scout troop, or women's club? I'd be more than happy to visit your group to discuss my novels or speak about my publishing experiences or hiking adventures. Contact me and let's talk.

Website -   www.jeannemeeks.com

Facebook - www.facebook.com/JeanneMeeksAuthor

Pinterest - http://pinterest.com/jeannemeeks

e-mail   - ChartHousePress@aol.com

If you wish to receive notice of new writing adventures, appearance, and updates, send me an e-mail, and I'll put you on my Favorite Reader list. I'd love to hear from you. Thanks so much for reading.

Jeanne

22891692R00158

Made in the USA
Middletown, DE
12 August 2015